80p

Readers who know me as JOSEPHINE COX often ask why I write under two names.

Both the JOSEPHINE COX and JANE BRINDLE stories are drawn from the tapestry of life. They are about ordinary people with dreams and aspirations. People with loves and fears and longings of one kind or another. They are stories of pleasures and regrets, of deceit and friendship. Stories of ordinary and extra-ordinary people, of a kind that might live down your street; people you have known for ever, or you've only just met; people you think you know, then realise you don't know at all. People who fill your lives so com-pletely you would not know how to live without them.

Relationships. Emotions. Situations that bring out the best and the worst in all of us. This is what I write about in both the JOSEPHINE COX and JANE BRINDLE stories. So why the different names, you ask.

Since time began, there are things far deeper than first imagined. Wicked, dangerous things, to create evil and mayhem in any one of us . . . the dark side. These are the sinister stories. As a child, and for reasons I can't say here, I suppressed many frightening feelings. These have now surfaced in the JANE BRINDLE books.

Many JOSEPHINE COX readers enjoy the JANE BRINDLE books. Yet because there may be others who don't wish to delve into that darker side, I was obliged to keep the JOSEPHINE/JANE BRINDLE my mother's name.

D1471782

The Hiding Game

Jane Brindle

HEADLINE
FEATURE

First published in 1998
by HEADLINE BOOK PUBLISHING

First published in paperback in 1999
by HEADLINE BOOK PUBLISHING

A HEADLINE FEATURE paperback

10 9 8 7 6 5 4 3 2 1

ISBN 0 7472 5571 7

Typeset by Avon Dataset Ltd, Bidford-on-Avon, Warks

Printed and bound in Great Britain by
Mackays of Chatham plc, Chatham, Kent

HEADLINE BOOK PUBLISHING
A division of Hodder Headline PLC
338 Euston Road
London NW1 3BH

www.headline.co.uk.
www.hodderheadline.com

'Whom God would destroy He first sends mad'
Sophocles, *Antigone*

PART ONE

August 1980

Out of the Darkness . . .

CHAPTER ONE

'I'm cold.' Inexplicably afraid, the boy shivered. 'I want to go home.'

Mike glanced up at the sky. Only a minute ago the sun was blazing down. Suddenly, the clouds were gathering; the air strangely chilled. There was a sense of danger all around. 'It's getting dark.' He looked at his watch; it was just gone three. 'Must be a storm on the way. Come on, son, we'd best pack up and make our way home.'

'I'll just give the ducks these leftovers.' It was a shame to waste them and the birds seemed so hungry.

Mike nodded. 'Sure. But don't be too long about it.'

While the boy gathered the stale sandwiches, Mike packed the picnic basket, his thoughts going back over the past few days. Lately, he had been so on edge, there were times when it put a strain on his relationship with Kerry.

The picnic had been a great idea. Kerry was right, as always. He and his son needed some time to themselves. They needed time to get to know each other. Ever since Jack had been born, Mike had devoted himself to building a successful

3

business so he could provide for his family. It meant sacrifices. It meant working every minute God sent and, worse than that, it meant neglecting the ones he loved most. He had not realised the cost. He had not seen how it was taking over his life and swallowing everything in its wake. Now, Jack was five years old, and he hardly knew the boy.

He looked at his son and pride filled his chest. Jack had a look of him, especially the eyes, brown and serious; right now they were gazing out across the pond, watching the ducks scurrying for the bread. Ruffling his hair, Mike reminded him, 'Time to go, son.'

Scrambling up, Jack looked scared. 'Why is it so dark?'

Strapping the picnic bag over his shoulder, Mike led him by the hand. 'It's just a storm. Don't worry.' He didn't want to frighten him. But it was a strange sky, darker now, pressing down. Such cold, eerie silence. It was like nothing he had ever experienced.

As they approached the car, he heard someone call his name. 'Mike! Mike Peterson!'

Swinging round, he saw a woman and for a moment she was just another stranger. Then, as she ran up to him, he couldn't believe his eyes. '*Rosie!* Rosie Sharman, after all these years.'

Still slim and attractive, the years had been kind to Rosie; her long auburn hair shone, and her skin was like that of a child. But then she couldn't be very old; when he last saw her she wasn't much more than a child. Seeing her now, the memories flooded back – along with the guilt.

Dropping the picnic bag he grabbed her as she ran into his arms. She felt soft and warm against him. 'How long has it been?' he asked, reluctantly releasing her.

'Fifteen years,' she reminded him with a grin. 'And you don't look a day older than you did then.'

'Liar!' Flattered, he laughed out loud. 'I'm thirty-eight and look ninety.' Pressure of work aged a man before his time.

Rosie quietly observed him. 'Rubbish,' she said. 'You're as handsome as ever,' and in a move that startled him she kissed him soundly on the mouth. 'I recognised you straightaway,' she said. 'The turn of your head . . . the way you walk. I knew it was you.' Her thoughts flew back over the years. As if she could ever forget! In their young, carefree days, there was a time when Mike Peterson had been her whole life.

'You look well, Rosie.' Over the years he had often wondered about her. Did she still think of him? Did she cherish the wonderful times they'd had together? Did she have a new man? Married? Children? Was she a career woman? It was always at night when he thought about her. Always after he and Kerry had made love. 'It's great to see you.' She still had that uncanny way of making him feel good. 'But what are you doing here?' he asked. 'Do you live around these parts?' Life was a funny thing, he thought; after they had parted all those years ago, he was sure he would never see her again.

Avoiding his question, she brought her attention to Jack who was shifting impatiently from one foot to the other. 'Is this your son?' Her voice was soft, her green eyes smiling on him. 'Of course,' she answered her own question. 'Anyone can see he's your son.' She introduced herself. 'I'm Rosie. What's your name?'

'Jack.'

'Hello, Jack.' She held out her hand and laughed when he hesitated. 'I'm told I can be a bit overwhelming but I promise I don't bite.'

Allowing her to shake his hand, Jack remained silent.

For a long moment she smiled into Mike's eyes, started to say something, and then, with a proud gesture, swung away. 'This is *my* son.' Half turning, she urged a boy to come forward. 'Luke, come and meet an old friend.'

Mike had not noticed the boy standing behind her. Rosie had a son! It didn't seem right somehow.

'Hi, Luke.' Mike guessed he was about fifteen. He was tall and good-looking, with brown hair and eyes of a paler shade than his mother's.

The skies began to rumble. 'I reckon we're in for a drenching,' Mike said. 'That's why we packed up – just as we were enjoying our picnic.

Isn't that right, Jack?' Smiling down on the boy, he drew him closer. Where was Rosie's husband? he wondered.

Rosie read his mind. 'If you're curious about my other half, he's not here.' She gave no explanation.

'So you *are* married then?'

Leaning forward, she said softly, 'You didn't think I could love you for ever, did you? Life has to go on, Mike.'

Mortified that she should have misunderstood, Mike actually blushed. 'I didn't mean . . . I was curious, that's all.'

A mischievous smile put him at ease. 'Look, Mike. Seeing as your picnic was spoiled, why don't we all go for a drink and a bite to eat? Luke and I are in no hurry to get back.'

He was tempted, but before agreeing he turned to Jack. 'What do you think, son? Are you hungry?'

A hesitant nod was all Mike needed. 'OK. Everyone into the car.'

As they loaded up, Rosie turned to glance at him, and the years seemed to roll away. With the memories came a sense of nervousness and, for a fleeting moment, Mike wondered if he was doing the right thing.

Just a few minutes away, the inn was a welcome sanctuary. The moment Mike drew into the forecourt, the heavens opened. Making a run for it, the four of them burst in through the door, shaking the rain from their clothes and laughing.

Before directing them to the family room, the landlord took their order. 'One coffee, a pint of lager . . . two lemonades, and four chicken salad sandwiches.'

'Don't forget the crisps,' Rosie reminded him, 'and plenty of mayonnaise on my sandwich.' Rosie was partial to mayonnaise.

'I'll be as quick as I can with the sandwiches,' the landlord said, 'but what with the rain and everything, there's been a rush on.' He wasn't complaining though. The more people, the bigger the orders, and the bigger the orders, the more profit. 'Sit yourselves down. I'll have your drinks here in no time at all.'

Settling at a table by the window, Mike glanced out. 'Good God! Look at that!' The rain was lashing down, the wind so violent it was bending the trees almost to the ground. 'It's as well we came here, Jack,' he said, 'or we might have been blown off the road.' On the other hand, it might not be wise to linger here too long. The lanes were narrow and might soon be impassable.

The drinks arrived. Jack's attention was on a young couple nearby. 'Look at that,' he exclaimed. 'What's that game?'

'It's called table football,' Rosie's son explained. 'When they've finished, I'll show you how to play if you like.' When Jack seemed excited at the prospect, Luke grinned from ear to ear. 'I'll give you a head start,' he promised. 'We'll play best out of three.'

Rosie laughed. 'You against the boy? That's not fair. Besides, he probably won't even be able to reach the table.'

Jack was indignant. 'Yes I will!'

'If not, I'm sure the landlord will find him a box to stand on.' Luke had it all worked out.

Jack was sold on the idea. 'Can I, Daddy? Please.'

'What about your sandwiches? They'll be here any minute.' He wasn't sure whether he wanted to be left alone with Rosie.

'I'm not hungry now.' Jack's appetite seemed to have disappeared.

'Might as well say yes,' Rosie laughed, 'or we'll get no peace.' Unlike Mike, she yearned for the two of them to be left alone. She and Mike had unfinished business. *He* may have forgotten, she thought bitterly, but she hadn't.

Mike relented. 'One game then, and only if that young couple finish their game before your sandwiches arrive.'

Rosie regarded the couple. 'Poor little buggers,' she commented wryly. 'By the looks of them, I'd say they were on the run.'

Mike was intrigued. 'What makes you say that?'

'Come on, Mike. You've only got to look at them. The girl is what? Fifteen, sixteen? She's about the age I was when we first met.' She let that sink in before going on, 'The boy isn't much older, and the pair of them are filthy.' Pointing to two grubby rucksacks leaning against the table leg, she muttered, 'Travelling light. And they're thin as rakes. I shouldn't be surprised if they haven't eaten for days.'

Mike gestured to the tray of sandwiches and drinks close by. 'Looks to me like they're not short of money.'

'They're probably sleeping rough at night and begging on the streets during the day.' She laughed. 'Some of these beggars are better off than any of us.'

'What d'you reckon they're running from?'

Rosie shrugged. 'Who knows? Bad parents? Violent background? They could have been abused in some way. They might even have been brought up by the authorities, and now they've been turned out to make their own way in life.'

'If you ask me, they're just enjoying themselves. I can't see they're any thinner or scruffier than other kids of that age.' He didn't share her obsession with the couple.

Rosie was adamant. 'No, Mike. They're running from something, or somebody. All the signs are there. And look how they keep glancing towards the door – look at the eyes, how haunted they are.' She shook her head decisively. 'No, if you ask me, there isn't a soul in the world who gives a monkey's where they are, or what happens to them.'

'How can you be so sure?'

Meeting his gaze, she said quietly, 'Trust me, Mike. I know about these things.'

The young couple finished their game and left the table hand in hand. The two boys rushed across the room, and Mike resigned himself to a lengthy stay. Raising his glass, he laughed nervously. 'Well, here's to you, Rosie.'

Rosie looked across at Mike's son. 'You've got a good kid there, Mike.'

Taking a gulp of his drink, Mike was quiet for a moment, before answering, 'Yeah, he's a good kid. Trouble is, I'm not a good father.'

'I don't believe that.'

'I have a daughter too. Susie's three years old. She's a good kid also but I'm so busy working, I hardly see them.'

'What about your wife?' She had to know everything.

'Kerry?' A smile crossed his features. 'She's the best thing that ever happened to me – apart from the kids of course.' Not realising how his comment had shocked and hurt her, he looked to where Jack was scrambling on to a small crate. 'Look at that. By hook or by crook, eh?'

Laughing, Rosie made another toast. 'Here's to being young and foolish.'

'And not giving a sod!'

Clinking glasses, Rosie regarded him thoughtfully. 'We were young and foolish once,' she said carefully, 'and you didn't give a sod, either.'

Embarrassed, he looked away, pretending to concentrate on what the boys were doing, but he could feel her eyes burning on his face. Suddenly, he felt threatened.

Swigging back the last of her drink, Rosie said sweetly, 'I wouldn't mind a rum and coke.'

He stared at her. 'I thought you didn't drink spirits.' After all these years, he hadn't forgotten.

'Times change.' Her smile betrayed how pleased she was that he had remembered.

Unsettled, he swung out of his chair. 'Rum and coke it is then. Keep an eye on Jack for me, will you?' When she nodded, he hurried away; thinking the sooner he got out of here the better.

'The old magic is still there,' he muttered. 'She's still a looker . . . and she still sets me trembling. But don't flatter yourself, Mike old son. A lot of water's gone under the bridge since you and Rosie rolled in the hay.' His expression became grim. 'Put it behind you,' he told himself sternly. 'For *all* your sakes.'

Chasing from one end of the bar to the other, the landlord was at his wits' end. 'I'll be with you in a minute,' he told Mike. 'It's like bedlam in here!' In his hurry to be rid of one customer he spilled a pint of beer over him. 'Sorry, mate,' he said, and got a mouthful of abuse for his trouble.

Looking over his shoulder, Mike saw that Rosie had gone to supervise the boys' game. For a long moment he watched, wondering about her, trying to guess how she had come to be here, in this area, so far away from where they had grown up – and so close to where he had chosen to settle down.

Feeling the need for a breath of fresh air, and realising he might not get served for some time yet, Mike went outside.

The wind seemed to be settling and the sun was once again trying to struggle through. He walked along the side of the inn and down towards the gardens at the back.

At first he couldn't quite make out what the sounds were. Gruff, breathless sounds, almost like those of an animal in distress. Concerned, he looked about. The sounds were coming from the spinney. Quickly, he made his way there, peering between the trees as he went.

The sounds got louder – behind him now. He swung round, and there, only yards away, he saw them. Spreadeagled in the undergrowth, the young couple were blissfully unaware that he could see them.

Outstretched on the ground, her hair matted with leaves and debris, the girl's long legs were tightly wrapped round the young man's thighs, her arms about his body, keeping him there, trapping him to her. The young man, body low and head high, thrust in and out of her with brutal force.

The sounds Mike had heard were cries of pleasure, and pain. Being so close and seeing them together like this, his own heart beat faster.

'Jesus!' Into his mind came an image of himself and Rosie. It was almost more than he could bear.

Much as he wanted to tear himself away, his curiosity kept him rooted to the spot. He watched them clawing at each other, and recalled how it was when you were that young. He wondered why Kerry had never given herself in the same way Rosie had; why she always seemed to hold back at the crucial point. Now, shamelessly watching these kids, he felt the need for that kind of love again.

Filled with regrets, he hurried away and returned to a quieter bar. He remembered how it had been between himself and Rosie. She was like that girl out there in the shrubbery, exciting and demanding, insatiable. But not his Kerry. She was different.

But he wouldn't blame her for that. No two women were the same, thank God. Kerry was a lady, while Rosie had been a wild thing. He had been wild too, as he recalled. But that was when they were young and rebellious. Now, he was a family man, older and wiser. He had other things to occupy his mind – bills to pay, responsibilities that came with growing up. He had a beautiful wife and two adorable children. When he and Kerry made love it was always good, and he wouldn't change her for the world.

He told himself all these things, and still could not rid himself of a nagging feeling that he was missing out.

He made his way back to the table, where Rosie and the boys, who'd finished with the table football, were waiting. 'I was beginning to think you'd run out on me,' she said, her bright eyes twinkling. 'We've eaten most of the sandwiches.'

'The weather seems to have changed for the better,' Mike said. 'Jack and I should be making our way home.' He offered to give her and Luke a lift back and was greatly relieved when she declined.

'No need, thanks all the same,' she said. 'But I would like to see you again. We've had so little time to talk.'

Mike was wary. 'I don't have much free time,' he said. 'But if ever I do, you'll find me and Jack picnicking down by the river.' He wanted to say he thought it better if they never saw each other again, but some sixth sense warned him to humour her. So, against his better judgement, he unwisely encouraged her.

She smiled at him. 'I'll look forward to that.'

Jack was ready to leave. 'I don't like that game,' he said sulkily. 'It's no good.'

Luke grinned. 'That's because I beat you every time.'

Luke's triumphant smirk turned to a scowl when Rosie remarked, 'Jack seems to have got the hang of it now, so don't count on winning next time.' Glancing at Mike, she murmured, 'You won't forget me, will you? When you have that moment of free time?'

Smiling, he made no reply. Somehow he thought it wiser. Not because of her, but because of the overwhelming feelings rising inside himself. Feelings of want . . . lust. Feelings that had lain dormant all this time – until she had appeared. It was disturbing.

Outside, she kissed him. 'Remember how it was between us?' she whispered. 'Shame it had to end.' Her fingers wandered to his thigh, tenderly touching him. Sending shivers down his spine.

He drew away. 'It was good seeing you, and if we don't meet again, take care of yourself.'

They went their separate ways; Rosie and her son headed back towards the river, while Mike and Jack walked towards the car.

'Will we see them again?' Jack wanted to know.

Opening the car door, Mike ushered him inside. 'I don't think so, son.' Rosie was dangerous. She got inside him like no other woman ever could.

They had gone only a short way when the rain started again. 'Is the storm coming back, Daddy?' Jack was nervous.

Mike peered through the rain-spattered window. 'Let's hope not.' Switching on the windscreen wipers, he settled back in his seat. 'I think the worst is over.' Instinctively, his hand went to his mouth. Rosie's kiss still burned his lips. 'We'll soon be home, son. Just sit tight.'

The journey was a nightmare. The rain defied

the wipers and blurred his vision. 'I'll have to pull over for a while,' he told Jack. 'I know this lane like the back of my hand but I can't see a damned thing now.' Sighing, he leaned against the steering wheel, his mind ticking over, wondering what to do for the best. 'But don't you worry,' he assured the frightened boy. 'We'll be all right.' All the same, he had a feeling the worst was yet to come.

Just as he feared, the storm came back with a vengeance. Howling wind rocked the car and dark clouds turned day into night. Rain fell in torrents, battering the car and pummelling the ground until the grass verges became slithering mud banks.

When the car began sliding towards the ditch, Mike knew it was time to get out of there.

He scrambled out of the car and dragged Jack after him. 'Hold on tight, son,' he told him. 'We'll have to go back.' Reasoning that the inn would be the safest place, he headed back down the lane, battling against the wind and carrying Jack in his arms. 'Don't be frightened!' He had to shout to be heard. 'We'll be all right, don't worry!'

If the lines were not down, he intended calling Kerry from the inn. He didn't want her to worry. And Rosie, he thought, was she all right? Did she and Luke get home before the storm returned?

Cursing himself for bringing Rosie to mind, he hugged Jack close to him, wrapping his arms tighter about the small, shivering frame. 'We can't be too far away.' But, to tell the truth, he had lost all sense of direction and had no idea which way he was headed.

Jack's voice invaded his thoughts. 'Daddy! Look!' Holding on to his father, the boy pointed towards the field.

At first, Mike couldn't see anything, then, peering through the blinding rain, he saw the shadowy figures. It was the young couple. 'Hey!' Relieved when he realised his sense of direction had not deserted him altogether, he yelled again, 'Hey, you two!' The wind carried his voice away.

They didn't hear him. Instead they kept going, hand in hand across the field and up towards the top of the hill. 'You'd do best to stick to the road!' he yelled out again, but still they appeared not to have heard. 'I hope they know what they're doing,' he muttered.

The wind was buffeting so fiercely he could hardly keep a foothold; branches were cracking from the trees and falling all around them. Then, with a suddenness that sent him stumbling forwards, the wind fell and the rain eased off. He could breathe again. 'Thank God!' But where were they? Nothing around them seemed familiar.

Something was very wrong.

After the noise and confusion, the silence was awesome. The air was unbelievably cloying; Mike felt as if he was choking. 'What the hell's going on?' He was no coward but now, caught up in this strange experience, he was afraid.

Jack sensed it. 'Daddy, what's happening?'

'I think it's over,' he murmured, but deep down he knew it wasn't.

He looked up to see the clouds clearing to reveal wide, amazing skies of brilliant blue. From some way behind, a solitary sheet of lightning daggered to the ground, splitting a tree wide open, where only minutes before he had trodden.

Following on the heels of that one came a second, nearer strike. The impact shook them both, making Mike cry out. 'Jesus!' The ripple of air became a terrifying force, throwing them to the ground. And, as they fell, with debris crashing all around, Mike wondered if it was the end of the world.

Trapped beneath the branches of a tree, Jack was sobbing, his arms reaching out to his father. 'Hold on, son!' Pitting his strength against the weight of the tree and the strange force of the air, Mike managed to grab the boy's arms before he himself was pinned by the legs. 'I'll get you out, son,' he promised but, without help, he knew it would be no easy thing.

Suddenly he felt the undercurrent sucking at his body, tugging at Jack, pulling him out of his grasp. Terrified, the boy stared up at him, his small fingers groping to hold on. Again, the eerie silence descended, striking new horror into Mike's heart; with all his strength, he clutched at Jack's wrists, his scream shattering the silence, 'Don't let go!

For God's sake . . . don't let go!' Something bad was happening, and they were right in the eye of it.

The undercurrent grew stronger: loose branches, enormous in size, were tossed about like matchsticks, spinning through the air as if some huge hand had snatched them up and sent them at unbelievable speed across the field, towards the young couple . . . into the soft, shivering light.

Mike felt weightless, helpless in the face of what was happening, but still he would not let go of Jack, not even if his arms were torn from their sockets.

While the wind screamed and the heavens shifted, Mike quietly prayed. He could feel himself losing the fight; the mighty tree which held them was beginning to lift, freeing them – to what?

Dear God above, he was losing Jack . . . '*Noooo . . .*' His cry stretched through the air. He tightened his grip, holding on, even while the two of them were dragged out, skin and sinew torn as their helpless bodies scraped along the rough bark; shoes and socks were stripped away, clothing and hope shredded as they were drawn, inch by inch, from their sanctuary.

Suddenly, a terrible coldness enveloped them, and the quietness after such fury fell about them like a blessing. With the weight of the tree lifted from them, Mike found he could move. But his limbs were numb and stiff, wet with his own blood and Jack's. Jack was lying face up, his stricken eyes staring out towards the field.

Mike followed his gaze.

He could see the young couple standing hand in hand, unsure, hesitating. Then they began to run, first one way, then another. It was as if an invisible wall held them trapped.

The air was bitter-cold now, deathly quiet with a strange kind of beauty. Mike knew instinctively it was life-threatening. The power that had destroyed was still there, quieter now, beneath the surface, sharing the very air he breathed,

'Daddy, I'm frightened.' White-faced and trembling, Jack clung on.

Mike kept his eyes on the couple, who were still in his sights. Hopelessly disorientated, they continued to run about, confused and frightened. 'Make your way back here!' Mike called out, but his voice was thin and empty, almost as though he didn't exist.

In that moment of incredible calm, he saw the youths driven apart; arms outstretched and calling to each other, they were carried away. Terrified, yet strangely intrigued, Mike watched as they were raised above the earth, spinning, gently at first, and then so fast he could not make them out at all. But he heard their screams; awful, shocking screams that made him tremble.

Like a great moving canvas, the sky seemed to roll back and take them into itself. One minute they were there, and then they were gone.

Mike had seen it with his own eyes but he couldn't believe it. The sky had swallowed them up!

Silent and disbelieving, Mike and Jack held on to each other, fearing that if they were seen to move, they, too, would be sucked into oblivion.

Some hours later, mercifully unconscious, they were found. 'God Almighty, they're lucky to be alive!' Hacking them free, the firemen stood back for the medical team to do its job.

As they were lifted into the waiting ambulance, somebody remarked, 'The poor devils look as if they've been through hell and back.'

Only Mike and Jack knew the truth of that.

CHAPTER TWO

Seated on the steps of the camper van, Rosie lifted her gaze towards the seafront. From the high vantage point, she could just make out the shape of West Bay harbour as a ring of lights and, further down, the many colourful boats bobbing on the water. 'It's lovely here,' she sighed. 'I think I could settle here.'

Lying in his bunk, Luke heard her sigh and turned his head. For a long moment, he stared at his mother, thinking how beautiful she was, with the moonlight playing on her long auburn hair and those pretty green eyes that could light the world with a smile. But they weren't smiling now. Instead they were sad and faraway. He hated it when she was like that.

'Why are we here?' His intrusive voice startled her. Clambering off his bunk, he pushed past her down the steps. 'I never wanted to come here,' he complained. 'Neither did Eddie. It was *you*. Eddie brought you here, and now you don't want to go. I heard what you said just now, about settling here.'

'It's not polite to eavesdrop.'

Incensed, he stood before her, legs astride,

deliberately blocking her view of the harbour. 'It was to see *him*, wasn't it? You made Eddie bring you here just so you could see that Peterson bloke.'

Rosie didn't look up. 'He's an old friend.'

'Hmh! An old lover, you mean.'

'All right, an old lover.'

'I thought you said it was all a long time ago.'

'That's right.'

'So why did you want to see him?'

'None of your business.'

'What if I was to tell Eddie?'

'Tell him if that's what you want,' she said with false bravado. Eddie had a vicious temper.

'Why is Peterson so important?'

Looking up, Rosie took stock of her son. Tall and gangly, he bore little resemblance to Mike, except for the unkempt brown hair that no comb could tame. But in many ways he reminded her of Mike – when he smiled, that swinging, easy way he walked. He had the same square chin too. Oh, yes, he was his father's son, in more ways than one. But she didn't want to tell him, not yet. The time wasn't right.

'What makes you think he's important?'

Answering one question with another was a coward's way but she had no choice.

Luke shrugged impatiently. 'If he isn't, why can't we leave?'

'We will.'

'When?'

'When I'm good and ready.' She had things to do here. Important things that had waited too long.

'Eddie doesn't want to stay either.'

'He can go when he likes. And so can you!' Angry, she tossed her head, eyes blazing up at him. 'You've two strong arms and you can find work at the drop of a hat, so you've no need of me.' No sooner were the words out than she regretted them. 'I'm sorry, son.' Opening her arms, she invited him to sit beside her. 'It's the Irish temper.' Laughing, she hugged him close. 'Sometimes my tongue runs away with my head.'

Distressed, he sat on the step beside her. 'I know I can earn a wage and I could manage if I had to. But you wouldn't really want me to go away, would you?'

'You know I wouldn't.' She gave him a stern glance. 'But I do love it here and I'm not ready to go yet.'

'OK, Mum.' Everything was all right again. He had stepped over the mark and meant never to do it again.

'So you'll stop going on about me leaving – for a while anyway?'

'I won't say another word, honest.'

She flicked his hair back from his forehead, the way she used to when he was a child. 'I'm sorry, Luke. I shouldn't have snapped at you like that. Only I don't want you nagging me.' Just then her gaze fell on a lone figure making its way towards them. In a low, sorry voice she added, 'I get enough aggravation from *him*!'

Luke's mood darkened. 'I'm going for a walk,' he said, and before she could reply, he was gone, making his way down the other path, away from the approaching man, towards the open fields.

'Don't go too far!' she called after him. 'You never know who's lurking about.'

'Leave him alone. The boy's old enough to take care of himself,' growled Eddie Johnson. He and Rosie had been partners for some years now, sometimes loving, sometimes hating. Lately, their relationship was strained to the point of breaking. He didn't want to lose her but Rosie did not care one way or the other.

Springing up, she stood on the lower step so he would not tower above her. 'You've been drinking again.' She eyed him with contempt.

'Been celebrating.' A squarely built man, with fair hair and close-set dark eyes, he had a high opinion of himself. 'The harbourmaster's taken me on as lookout.'

'Then he's a fool.'

'Don't be so bloody daft, woman. I'll not be drinking on the job.'

'Only before and after, eh?'

He laughed, rocking on his feet. 'You cheeky bugger!' He caught her to him. 'I'm feeling randy.'

'Are you now?' Laughing in his face, she taunted, 'The state you're in, I shouldn't think you could make him stand up long enough.'

'Long enough to satisfy you.'

Disgusted, she pushed him away. 'I don't think so. But I'm sure you could find yourself a whore to satisfy.'

As she turned to enter the camper van, he slid his hands over her thighs, gripping her so tightly she couldn't move. 'You're looking really lovely tonight, Rosie.' He swung her round. 'Why would I want a whore when I've got you?'

Angered, she slapped his face and he retaliated by crushing her to him. 'I came back half an hour since to tell you my good news, and you were nowhere to be seen.' Frowning, he added, 'These past weeks that seems to be happening a lot – I come back and you're not here. I don't like it, Rosie. Where were you tonight, for instance?'

'I went for a walk.'

'I missed you.' He kissed the back of her neck. 'I *always* miss you.'

'I'm tired, Eddie.' Again, she tried to pull away. But it was no use.

'I waited for you but you were gone a long time.'

'I walked across the fields, all the way into town.'

'Do you miss *me* when I'm away?'

'You know I do.' He had a mean, ruthless streak; she thought it best not to antagonise him.

'I got worried,' he murmured, 'thought you might be seeing another man.' Raising his face, he gave a long sigh. 'If you ever did that to me, Rosie, *I'd have to kill him.*'

Rosie knew he was capable of such a thing. 'I'm not seeing anybody.' When you hunt with beasts, she thought, you have to be just as cunning. And she was. 'I've always been faithful to you, Eddie.' Not in her *heart* though. In her heart and mind, she had always loved Mike, always dreamed of getting back with him. Now, because of what had happened, it would take that much longer. But she could wait. She had waited a lifetime already. All the same, knowing that Mike had fathered two children by another woman made her boil inside. Jealousy was an ugly, dangerous thing.

'Don't fight me.' Pushing her down on to the steps, Eddie kissed her, a long, brutal kiss that bruised her lips. 'Let's do it here.' Red-faced and excited, he tore at her clothes.

Rosie did not resist, though shame coloured her face. 'Not out here,' she chided. 'Luke could come back at any minute.'

'So what?'

'We should go inside.'

Unzipping his trousers, he held her there. 'I can't wait,' he groaned. 'You've really got me going now. And *you* want it as much as I do, I can tell.' Raising her skirt, he took her right there, across the camper steps.

It was quick and frenzied, and he was right, Rosie had wanted it too. Seeing Mike again, and knowing he was out of her reach for a while, had left her on edge. Eddie was small consolation, but it wasn't Eddie she was making love to; it was Mike – Mike who was invading her body, Mike whose arms held her tight; *Mike* whom she meant to have, by fair means or foul.

Luke heard them from some distance away and he knew from past experience that they were having sex. It was never love; it never could be. Eddie was a beast who had to satisfy his lust, and Rosie was just Rosie, indomitable and exuberant. She believed life was for living, and Eddie had to be tolerated.

Ever since that other man had come into their lives some time ago, Rosie had been different, quieter somehow, and oddly distant. Sadder too, and that wasn't like her. There was something about Mike Peterson that bothered Luke. His mother had a secret, and she kept it close. But he would find out. He had his ways.

Dismayed and thoughtful, he stood by the great oak tree and watched them for a while. His mother was spreadeagled on the steps, legs apart and feet touching the ground. Thrusting in and out on top of her, Eddie held her arms above her head, pressing the backs of her small hands into the rim of the camper van door. He cried out in bliss when Rosie arched into him.

Unable to watch any longer, Luke turned away, and as he did so, he heard Eddie give a long, shuddering sigh. At the same time Rosie uttered a name, the name Luke had on his mind at that very moment: *'Mike!'* In a moment of ecstasy, the name sprang from her lips, and Luke knew she would be punished.

'Bitch!' yelled Eddie. He dragged her up the steps and into the camper van. 'You lying bitch!' Digging his fingers into her flesh, he drew her up to face him. 'So it's Mike, is it? And where is he, this Mike?'

Fearful for her life, Rosie stammered, 'I don't know what you're talking about.'

'Liar!' He flung her across the camper van and then pulled her up again by the hair. He pressed his face close to hers, his voice grating. 'You'd better talk or I swear to God I'll do for the pair of you.'

Wiping the blood from her nose, Rosie was defiant. 'I don't know anybody called Mike.'

Another hard slap made her buckle at the knees. 'I mean it, Rosie. If I can't have you, nobody else will. I'll see to that.'

She didn't answer. Instead she turned her eyes upwards to look at his face, ugly and distorted with fury. In that moment she knew him better than she ever imagined. 'If I can't have you, nobody else will,' he had warned. *That was how she felt about Mike.*

Again he grabbed her, raising her to him by sliding her up against the wall. 'You've been seeing him, haven't you? All this time! And again tonight when I couldn't find you – you were with him, weren't you?'

Hating him, Rosie stayed silent.

A vicious slap across the mouth brought a fresh spurt of blood. Rosie raised her head as if about to answer, then spat in his face. Incensed, he held her away from him, bunched his fist and brought it crashing down against her temple. With a cry she slumped to the floor and he raised his foot to kick her.

'Leave her alone!' Luke burst through the door and without any thought for his own safety launched himself at Eddie. There was a vicious scuffle and for a time it seemed as if the boy's anger was more than a match for the man's strength. But after a few minutes, Luke was hurt and bleeding, and Eddie was triumphant.

Taking the boy by the scruff of his neck, Eddie asked softly, 'Tell me where I can find him or I swear I'll tie you both up and set fire to the place.'

'You wouldn't!'

Laughing, he shook his head. 'If you think that, you don't know me.'

Realising he was crazy enough to carry out his threat, Luke wondered if he should tell. Why should *he* care about Mike Peterson anyway? Nothing was the same any more. His mother was even talking about settling here, when their plans had always been to travel, to be free, see as much of the world as they could. He didn't know she had been scouring the country for *him*. Mike Peterson was all she cared about now, so why not let Eddie finish him off? The idea was tempting.

'Well? I'm waiting!'

It was on the tip of his tongue to tell Eddie that Mike Peterson was now in a mental hospital, and had been since the night they had first met him. But then he thought of his mother and how she would feel, knowing he had betrayed her, and changed his mind. 'His name is Mike Peterson,' he answered sullenly. 'And it's no good asking me any more, because I don't know.'

Eddie's answer was to smash his fist into Luke's face. 'Maybe that will loosen your tongue.'

'You can hit me again if you like, but I still won't know any more than I've told you.' He remembered his mother's courage and could not be less than she was.

Taken aback, Eddie hesitated. He had known Luke since he was a small boy, and knew him well enough to recognise that he might be telling the truth. 'Mike Peterson, you say?'

Luke nodded. 'That's all she's ever told me.'

Hard-faced, Eddie nodded. 'I'll find the bastard,' he rasped, 'and when I do, he won't be a threat any more.' With murder in mind he stamped out of the camper van.

Luke tended his mother. After a splash of cold water and a few minutes to recover, she managed to sit up in his arms. 'Where is he?'

Luke remained silent.

'Luke! What did you tell him?' Tugging at his sleeve, she made him face her. 'Please, Luke. I need to know.'

Looking down at her cut and bruised face, Luke felt ashamed. 'I didn't tell him where he was if that's what you're worried about.' Anger betrayed itself in his voice. 'I nearly did though.'

'So what *did* you tell him?' Wincing with pain, she drew herself up to sit in the chair, her eyes pleading with him to tell her the truth.

'His name, that's all. He's gone to find him.' The enormity of it all suddenly dawned on him. 'He won't kill him, will he?' Murder! A thing like that would touch them all.

Rosie leaned forward to rest her hands on his shoulders, her eyes wide with fear. 'You know what he's like. We have to stop him.'

Luke looked at her defiantly. 'Why should I stop him?'

'What do you mean?'

'Ever since that day when we met Mike Peterson at the river, you've changed. You always seem to be miles away . . . thinking about him. You take off and don't tell anybody where you go.' His voice stiffened. 'I followed you . . . the other night, when you thought I was nowhere about.'

'You had no right.'

'I know where you go.' His voice shook. 'I know what you do.'

'I have nothing to be ashamed of.'

Luke shrugged her off. 'Sitting outside a mental hospital like some sort of vulture, watching his wife come and go. I saw you creeping round the building, peering through windows, trying to catch a glimpse of him.'

'That's enough, Luke. I don't want to hear any more.'

'If you ask me, it should be *you* in there because you're as mad as he is.'

Rosie smiled. 'I'm in love, that's all. I've always loved him.'

Luke leaped up, his face warped with anger. 'You don't understand, do you? He's not yours to love!'

'Oh, but he is.'

There was a pause then, as these two looked at each other, a wealth of love between them; a love confused by all that Rosie knew, and Luke could only imagine.

'You'll find out one day,' Rosie said, 'so you might as well know now.' Pausing, she took a deep, invigorating breath. 'You have to understand . . . how it was . . .' Rosie's courage almost deserted her, but she had always known the moment for truth would come.

'What are you trying to say, Mum?' Like a prisoner waiting to be executed, Luke wanted it over.

'Mike Peterson is your father.'

For a long, agonising moment, he stared at her, eyes wide with disbelief. He saw the truth on her face but could not accept it. 'He can't be my father. You told me he was dead!'

'I lied to protect you.'

Grey with shock, Luke turned on his heel and ran into the night. Behind him, he could hear his mother's frantic cry, 'Eddie wants to kill your father. You've got to stop him!'

Painfully, Rosie pulled herself out of the chair and staggered to the water bowl where she sponged her face and neck, and wiped away the blood. 'Got to find him.' Mumbling to herself, she buttoned her blouse. Catching sight of her dishevelled self in the mirror, she was deeply shocked. 'I can't let him hurt Mike.' Without Mike she was nothing.

A moment later, she left the camper van and disappeared into the darkness.

The quickest way from West Bay to Bridport was on foot.

After leaving the camper van, Eddie had followed the ancient route through the spinney, across the meadow, and along the narrow footpath that ran alongside the river. The only light was the soft haze of moonlight above, and even that was muted by the tall trees.

Filled with murderous thoughts, he pressed on towards Bridport where he would find the nearest pub and begin his search. He suspected Rosie and Peterson must have been meeting in Bridport, and that was where he would find him, he was sure. Bridport was a small place; everybody knew everybody else. Someone was certain to know Mike Peterson.

He grinned. 'He needs to be taught a lesson . . . they *both* do. Nobody takes my woman.'

He leapt the stile and clambered over the gate – but his feet never touched the ground.

Stealing up behind him, the figure was stealthy, silent as the night and indistinguishable from the trees all around. Quick, agile fingers curled round a chunk of branch and, raising it high, brought it crashing down on Eddie's skull with a nauseating crunch. The terrified scream of a night creature sent the animals scurrying for cover and from somewhere in the distance came the sound of voices.

Satisfied, the figure went softly away.

In the ensuing silence, the broken body settled. Caught by its feet it hung upside down from the top rung of the gate, its eyes wide open, staring after the furtive figure.

There was no backward glance. The escape was swift and sly, and soon, save for those accusing eyes, it was as if nothing had happened.

CHAPTER THREE

'What do you mean?' Kerry's mother stopped what she was doing and turned to face her daughter. '*Who* was watching you?' Since Mike had been in hospital, Julie was over-protective of her daughter and grandchildren. If she had her way they would all move away from this area, and Mike could hunt high and low but he would never find them – not if she had her way, he wouldn't.

'That woman. She was there again tonight.' Unsettled by the incident, Kerry threw her bag on to the kitchen table, took off her jacket and sat down. 'I've seen her a few times,' she said, draping the jacket over her lap. 'She's always in the shadows, but I know it's her. She's there when I go in, and she's there when I come out.' Grimacing, she shivered. 'She's beginning to give me the creeps.'

Wiping her hands on the dishcloth, Julie leaned against the sink, her anxious gaze fixed on her daughter. 'What makes you think she's watching *you*? She could be waiting for anybody. Maybe she gave a friend a lift and has to take them back home.'

Kerry shook her head. 'No. She was watching me. I just know it.'

'What does she look like?'

Shrugging her shoulders, Kerry loosely described her. 'Early to middle thirties, attractive, thick auburn hair.' Anticipating her mother's next question, she went on, 'When I saw her there tonight, I deliberately drove past to see her in my headlights.' The whisper of a smile creased her mouth. 'She didn't like that. She tried to slink away but it was too late.'

'If you're right, and I'm not saying you are—'

'Mother, I am not imagining things.'

'OK. Assuming you're right, why would she be interested in you?'

'I've no idea. But if she's there again, I shall ask her.'

'Don't make a fool of yourself, Kerry. I know what a temper you've got, and if that poor woman is there for some perfectly normal reason, you'll frighten her half to death.'

Angered by her mother's casual attitude, Kerry snapped, 'I don't want to talk about it any more.' Grabbing her jacket, she strode across the kitchen and out into the hallway where she hung the jacket in the closet. A moment later she returned.

Pouring herself a glass of sherry, she asked, 'Do you want one?' Holding a second glass, she waited for her mother to answer.

Julie shook her head, then changed her mind. 'Why not?' She watched Kerry pour her drink.

'If you're so convinced about this woman watching you, don't you think the police might be interested?'

Thrusting the glass into her mother's hand, Kerry frowned. 'I've already said, I don't want to talk about it any more.' Sinking into the seat opposite, she gave a huge sigh and took a generous gulp from her glass. 'Instead of being so concerned about that wretched bloody woman, you might ask how Mike is.'

'Is he any different from the last time you saw him?' The question was dismissive, prompting a burst of anger from Kerry.

'You couldn't care less, could you?'

Julie regretted betraying her feelings, but then Kerry had known for some time how she felt about Mike. 'I'm sorry,' she said, 'but I do worry about you and the children. I can't help that.'

Leaning back in her seat, Kerry closed her eyes. 'I know,' she said heavily. 'I worry too. But we're all he's got. Somebody has to believe in him.'

'Do you mind if I ask you something . . . personal?'

'Yes, I do mind.' She took another gulp of her drink. 'But I expect you'll ask anyway.'

And, true to form, she did. 'Do you still love him?'

Opening her eyes, Kerry stared at her mother for a moment. 'I'm not sure any more,' she admitted softly. 'I've thought about it a lot these past few weeks, and it doesn't help. I loved him before but now, after all that's happened, I don't know how I feel.' Sitting up, she let her gaze fall to the floor. 'I never know where I am with him any more. Sometimes he's like the old Mike, happy and teasing, cracking jokes and making me laugh. And then, other times, he hardly talks. He seems miles away, and when I ask him if he's all right, he goes on about that night, and the storm, and how that couple vanished into thin air.'

'What does the doctor say about it?'

'I haven't told him.'

'Why not?'

'Because it's like talking to a machine. He analyses every word I utter. He makes me feel as if I'm being interrogated.'

'I'm sure he's only trying to help.'

'I dare say, but it's Mike who's the patient, not me. Besides, I don't think I should report everything Mike confides in me, however bizarre it seems. If they think he's still convinced those young people just vanished, they'll never let him out. I can't do that to him.'

'I don't suppose you'd be telling them anything they don't already know. They must realise he's not fully recovered, otherwise they would have let him out before now. He's in the best place.'

'Just lately you're full of wise, snide comments. Mike's in "the best place"? What's that supposed to mean?' The question was fired with resentment, and the moment it was out of her mouth

Kerry regretted it. She regretted a great deal these days – Mike's breakdown, his business folding, the effort and energy it had taken to create her own small catering business, although it was doing better than she had hoped and the money was enough to keep their heads above water. But the price was a heavy one. She regretted all the lost opportunities to be with the children, and now, with her mother doing all she could to help, she couldn't even sound gracious or grateful. Lately it seemed as if the whole world had climbed on to her shoulders, and the burden was breaking both her back and her spirit. She was living on her nerves, up one minute, down the next. This whole thing with Mike, and all that had happened since, was really getting to her.

Peeved, Julie snapped back, 'I mean exactly what I said. Mike is a sick man. His mind was badly affected by what happened on that night, and it's no use you pretending otherwise.'

'Leave it, Mother. Please.'

Unrepentant, Julie persisted. 'He's not the only one who's suffering. I've heard you in the small hours pacing up and down, and lately I've noticed you're drinking too much for your own good.'

'I don't want to hear any more!'

'Well, you're going to, my girl!' There were times when Julie was too outspoken, but when she had a bee in her bonnet, there was no reasoning with her. 'You're falling apart before my eyes and I'm worried sick. Since Mike's car hire firm went broke, you've worked like a dog to build up a catering business, and it's beginning to pay real dividends. But if you carry on like this, you'll see it go the same way as Mike's business.' Sighing, she lowered her voice to a softer, kinder tone. 'Oh, Kerry, I know how hard this all is. I really do want to help, and I do my best, but nothing seems to please you any more. You're hard on me, and you're even harder on yourself. I haven't seen you smile in weeks.'

Kerry defended herself. 'I know you do your best, and I'm really grateful, but you should understand, there are some things I don't want to talk about. Besides, as long as I take care of the kids and protect them from what's happened, isn't that all that matters?'

'You've set yourself an impossible task if you think you can protect the children altogether. Look how Jack came home from school the other day, upset and crying because some bully of a boy teased him about his crazy daddy.'

'Jack can look after himself.'

'He shouldn't have to look after himself. It might help if Mike would just accept what the doctors have told him, that the injury to his head caused him to hallucinate.'

'He can't because, like you said, he's a sick man.'

'But Jack was with him. And you don't hear him claiming to have seen two people disappear into the sky.'

42

Kerry felt exhausted. 'I don't know what to think any more,' she groaned. 'I'm just so afraid I'll go under.' Tears rolled down her face. 'Oh, Mum, what am I supposed to do?'

As she quickly crossed the kitchen to comfort her daughter, Julie caught sight of Jack standing by the door; confused and tearful, he was clutching his ragged teddy bear close to his chest. 'Jack, why aren't you in bed?'

At once, Kerry was out of her chair and rushing towards him. Throwing her arms round his shoulders, she hid her tears and smiled. 'Did you have a bad dream, sweetheart?' These days hardly a night went by when he didn't wake up in a sweat.

Unresponsive to his mother's embrace, Jack peered over her shoulder to stare accusingly at his grandmother. It was a long, uncomfortable moment before he spoke and when he did it was in a quiet, damning voice. 'I heard you arguing. You woke me up.'

'Sorry, sweetheart, we didn't mean to.' Beneath his gaze, Julie felt uncomfortable. Sometimes, like now, he had an unnerving habit of looking at her as if he could see right through to her soul.

Unaware of the tension between these two, Kerry swept him into her arms. 'Come on, big boy, let's get you back to your bed.'

Julie stared after them as they left the room and wondered what had been going on in Jack's

mind when he stared at her like that. 'He hates
me,' she murmured, then dismissed the idea as
ludicrous. 'Why should he hate me when all I've
ever done is to be here for him . . . for *all* of
them?' She shook her head. '*I'm* beginning to
imagine things now. If I'm not careful, they'll
have me locked up alongside his father.' The
thought was sobering, and with it came a burst of
hatred. 'It's his father he should hate. He's the
one who's torn this family apart.'

Kerry came quietly into the room. 'Talking to
yourself,' she smiled. 'That's a bad sign.'

Startled, Julie looked up, hoping she had not
been overheard. 'Is he all right?'

'He'll be fine.'

'Was it a bad dream?'

'He wouldn't say. But he's calm enough now.'

'And Susie?'

Kerry laughed. 'Sleeping like an innocent.'

'That's good.' Julie yawned. 'I shall be off to
bed myself soon. It's been a tiring day, what with
one thing and another.' Glancing at her daughter,
she saw the shadows beneath her pretty eyes. 'It
wouldn't hurt you to get an early night too.'

'Small chance of that. I've got the account
books to do, and on top of that I need to change
the schedule of deliveries. Since I started supply-
ing the cafés, orders are flooding in. I've had to
take on another driver. He starts tomorrow, and I
haven't even planned his route.' She began
rummaging about in a drawer. 'Honest to God,

there's hardly time to breathe any more.'

'Is there anything I can do?' Julie had been about to make her way to the lounge to curl up and watch half an hour's television before going to bed, but Kerry seemed to be getting frantic. 'If you tell me what you're looking for, I might be able to help.' Kerry had turned out every item from the drawer and piled it on the worktop.

'It's not here! I could have sworn I put the folder in here. I thought it would be safe until I got round to working on it.'

'What folder?'

Kerry stuffed the papers back in the drawer. 'Damn and bugger it! Where could I have put it?'

'Try the desk drawer in the sitting room. You probably put it in there when you hung your jacket up.'

'Of course!' Rushing past her mother, Kerry went into the sitting room where she flung open the drawers one after the other, all to no avail. 'Where the devil is it?' she muttered. 'I *know* I brought it home.'

'Then it must be here.' Julie curled up in the big armchair and switched on the television. The news was just about to start. She settled down, not really caring whether Kerry found the folder or not. This was her time of day, and she liked to watch the news.

'For Christ's sake, switch that bloody thing off, can't you?' said Kerry, still trying to think what she had done with her precious folder.

Julie sat up. 'Ssh! Listen. Somebody's been murdered, and it's not all that far from here.'

Alarmed, Kerry swung round, her whole attention now on the TV newsreader: 'In the early hours of this morning, two fishermen discovered the body of a man. He was found on an isolated track leading from West Bay to Bridport. According to police reports, he had been dead for two days. As yet he has not been identified. The police have mounted a murder investigation.'

'My God!' Julie's voice cut across the newsreader's. 'Two days ago? *You* walked that track on Sunday, didn't you?'

White-faced, Kerry shook her head. 'I only went as far as the church, then I turned round and came back.'

'All the same, I think you should tell the police. They'll want to know if you saw anything.'

Nervous, Kerry snapped back, 'If I'd seen anything, don't you think I would have reported it?'

Before Julie could question her further, Kerry rushed out of the room and down the hall. 'I must have left the folder at the office,' she called. 'I won't be long. Listen out for Jack, will you, Mum?' A moment later she was out of the house and away in the car.

Julie switched off the television. 'What's got into her? I only said she might have seen something.'

Shrugging, she put it out of her mind and

returned to the kitchen, where she switched on the radio and tucked into a yoghurt.

Clutching his teddy bear, Jack sat by the upstairs window and watched his mother's car drive away. Long after she had gone, he remained there, quite still, his gaze intent on the road, his thoughts on that particular night when he and his daddy had seen awful things.

After a while he turned away from the window, walked softly across the room and out through the door. On tiptoe he went along the landing and into the bathroom. Here he sat on the edge of the bath, turned the taps full on, and swung round to dangle his legs in the water, all the while holding tight to his beloved teddy bear.

When the water was ankle high, he turned off the taps and softly addressed the bear, an endearing smile on his face as he looked into those innocent brown eyes. 'Did you hear what they were saying?' he whispered intimately. 'They're always talking about the storm but they don't know *anything*. It was just me and Daddy . . . and those other people, who played the game.' His eyes filled with tears. 'Nobody else knows what happened because nobody else saw. *But we saw!*'

Leaning over, he dipped a finger in the water. 'It's nice and warm now,' he murmured. 'Time for your bath.'

Taking the teddy by the neck, he lowered him

into the water, first the nose, then the face, and now the whole head. 'I *hate* Grandma! She argues all the time. Sometimes she says things that make me angry. She says Daddy's crazy. She thinks the people were not swallowed up by the sky. *But they were!*' Glancing furtively at the door, he began to tremble. 'The sky just ate them up!' Tears flowed down his face. 'You remember, I told you. But I mustn't tell them. And *you* mustn't tell them either. That's why I have to drown you in the water, so you won't be able to tell.'

Squeezing the bear's neck between his fingers, his voice broke into a sob. 'I don't want to hurt you but I'm scared they'll lock me up too. Daddy shouldn't have told them. He should have pretended, like I did. But *I* won't tell them. I'll never tell anybody.' Raising his foot, he placed it squarely in the centre of the bear's back and pressed down, flattening the bear until it splayed out on the bottom of the bath. 'I wish I hadn't told you now, but they kept on at me and I was frightened. Please don't be angry. I'm sorry. I'm really sorry.'

Gently he raised his foot. Staring into the water, he gazed at his teddy, watching mesmerised as it swung over to stare at him. As the ripples settled, the boy imagined the bear was opening his mouth to speak. With a cry of alarm he ran out of the room and fled along the landing.

Inside his room, he clambered into bed and lay there, hardly daring to breathe. He needed his daddy but anger suppressed the need. *Daddy shouldn't have told them!* If he hadn't told, they would not have shut him away, Grandma wouldn't be living here, and he wouldn't be frightened all the time. It was all his daddy's fault.

He hated his daddy.

After parking her car, Kerry glanced nervously about. 'She didn't like it here after dark. Quickly she made her way to the front door of the building which was situated in one of Bridport's back streets.

After Mike was admitted to the psychiatric unit, Kerry did her best to keep his business going but it had foundered and she had had to think again. It was her mother who had suggested she should use her natural talents and set up a catering firm. Kerry took up the suggestion and never looked back; she now employed four people and owned two delivery vans; she had a growing list of satisfied customers and quotations out on six new projects. 'Kerry Catering' was not a huge organisation by anyone's standard, but it paid the bills and was expanding all the time.

She unlocked the door and entered. A cold shiver ran through her. Even in the height of summer the old stone building struck chilly, but Kerry didn't complain because it was ideal for the preparation and storage of fresh food.

Switching on the light by the door, she crossed

the floor and climbed the steps to the upper level. She went into her office and straight to her desk, and there, much to her relief, lay the missing folder. Closing her eyes, she clutched it to her chest and sighed aloud, 'Thank God for that!'

'Oh, it's you!' said a voice behind her.

Alarmed, Kerry swung round. 'Steve!' she cried. 'What are you doing here? I thought you'd be home ages ago.'

Steve Palmer's lanky frame was clothed in a boiler suit and his fair hair was covered in dust. Holding up a wrench, he explained, 'Jason came back with a slow puncture in his front tyre. Considering the busy delivery schedule for tomorrow, I thought I'd better change it before leaving.' Glancing at the folder in her hands, he asked, 'Is that what you came back for? I thought you were an intruder.'

Relaxed now, she laid the folder on the desk. 'I thought I took it home with me. It's got all my calculations in it for the month ahead, and now that we've taken on another van and driver, I need to reschedule the routes. Apart from all that, there are the figures for this new hotel contract. I've been working on them all day and meant to work on them tonight at home.'

He stepped closer. 'You'll work yourself into the ground if you're not careful.'

'Somebody has to do it.'

He came closer still: she could see the steely glint in his dark blue eyes. 'Not right this minute though.' He gave her a slow, inviting smile that melted her resolve.

Taking off her jacket, she laid it across the desk. Then came her panties and shoes, which she left on the floor. 'That's as much as you're getting,' she warned. 'It's too bloody cold in here to strip off.'

He smiled. 'You came back to see *me*, didn't you?'

'Don't flatter yourself, Steve Palmer.' Crawling her fingers up the front of his overalls, she drew him close to pluck at the buttons. Sliding her hands up to his shoulders, she pushed the overalls back and let them drop to the floor. 'I didn't even know you were here,' she confessed. 'But since you are, I'm lonely enough to be grateful.'

Purposely, he spread her jacket out, then bent her backwards over the desk. 'You're cold,' he whispered, nuzzling her neck.

'Warm me up then.' Opening wide her legs, she gripped his hand and guided it up under her skirt and on to her thighs, shivering with delight when his sensitive fingers found her innermost parts.

Weak for the want of him, she groped inside his trousers, making him groan with bitter-sweet agony. Taking hold of his bulging organ, she drew it out and for a time played with it until he could stand it no longer. With the urgency of a man toyed with for too long, he pushed forward and thrust himself inside her with a force that momentarily lifted her from the desk and into his arms.

Fired by the same wanton passion, she raised her legs and wrapped them tightly round his thighs, capturing him to her.

CHAPTER FOUR

Alone in that quiet meadow, Rosie might have been the only person in the whole world.

Like a fairy from a tale, she sat cross-legged beneath the cherry tree. The breeze lifted her long auburn hair and the early morning skies drew her quiet, thoughtful gaze. In the beckoning light she was incredibly beautiful.

Her quiet sobs disturbed the air. 'It's all going wrong,' she wept. 'It was never meant to be this way.'

For a time, she lingered in that lovely, peaceful place, her mind going over all that had happened, and she knew what had to be done. 'We must leave before daybreak.' They couldn't stay, not now.

Like a child she scrambled up and ran, barefoot, to the brook. Wading through the chilly water, she came to the opposite bank where the camper van was hidden in the spinney.

Luke was sitting on the steps, waiting for her. 'Where have you been?' His face was dark with anger. 'I've been everywhere looking for you.'

Standing before him, hands on hips, she looked him in the eye. 'You're not my keeper,' she told him in a cutting voice. 'Eddie thought he was but now he's dead, and I'm free of all that.' She regretted the manner of his passing but it was no more than he deserved.

Luke remained defiant. 'How can you be so sure it was Eddie?'

She let her gaze fall to the ground. 'I just know.'

He smiled slyly. 'I see.'

'We'll have to leave.'

'What about the police?' Lowering his voice, he glanced towards the lane. 'They're bound to come looking for us.'

Rosie smiled knowingly. 'They can look but they'll never find us.'

'A hiding game, eh?'

A rush of pleasure filled her face. 'You remember?'

'It was always my favourite game.'

'You mustn't worry about them finding us.'

'Where will we go?'

'Anywhere . . . everywhere.' Softly laughing, she embraced the countryside with a wide, extravagant gesture. 'We'll be as elusive as the fox.'

He laughed with her. 'You're mad!'

'Maybe,' she answered warily. 'Sometimes.'

As daylight began to flood the skies, they started their journey.

But Rosie made a detour and halted the camper van outside the hospital.

'Why are you stopping here?' Luke was on edge. 'We'll be seen. If the police start asking questions, people are bound to remember us.'

Ignoring his protests, Rosie switched off the engine and opened the door. 'I'll only be a minute.'

Silently running along the pavement, she went towards the bench where she had spent many hours watching and waiting; seeing Mike's wife come and go, wishing it could have been her.

When she sat down, the film of dew on the metal struck cold through her skirt, making her gasp. Sliding the flat of her hands beneath her buttocks, she sat forward, gently rocking, her gaze going longingly to the rows of windows in the building opposite her.

Imagining him inside, she gave a long, agonised sigh. He was in there and she was out here, separated by a wall, bricks and mortar, that was all. And yet there was a vast world between them. 'I'm here, Mike,' she whispered. 'I'm right outside . . . still loving you, just as I've always done.'

Her eyes were drawn to a far room on the ground floor. The light went on, and from where she sat she could see shadowy figures moving about.

Her curiosity aroused, she got up from the seat and made her way to the other side of the road. As she ran across the lawns, she felt the dew-wet blades of grass tickling her legs, and before she reached the lighted window, the dampness had soaked through her sandals and settled beneath her toes.

Uncomfortable, she took off her sandals and silently slunk up to the wall, her small, soft fingers gripping the windowsill as she raised herself up high to peer in. What she saw sent her pulses racing.

Tousle-haired and wearing only pyjama bottoms, Mike sat on the edge of his bed; he wasn't doing anything in particular, just sitting there, tiredly ruffling his hair and gazing at the door, as if expecting someone. When the door opened to admit a nurse, he smiled and said something which Rosie could not hear.

The nurse was carrying an oval tray containing a small brown bottle, a clear drinking glass, and a tall jug filled with what looked like water. Fresh-faced and confident, she struck envy in Rosie's heart.

Wagging a chastising finger at Mike, the nurse went straight to the bedside table where she set down the tray. She picked up the bottle, poured a measure of the liquid into the glass and gave it to Mike. He seemed reluctant to take it. Then she picked up the small brown bottle and shook out a number of tablets into a short, plastic phial. Turning to Mike, she took hold of his hand and tipped the tablets into it. After protesting with a grimace, he raised the tablets to his mouth.

The nurse remained by his side until he had swallowed the last one. That done, she exchanged his old water jug for the fresh one, and seemed to order him into bed.

To Rosie, the nurse appeared to be taking quite a time to tuck him in beneath the sheets. Mike said something to her, and she laughed, and when he settled down to sleep, she stood over him for a time, just gazing at his face, almost like a mother watching over a child; until at long last he drifted into a deep, comfortable slumber.

And then, to Rosie's astonishment, she did a strange thing. Leaning over him, the nurse stroked his forehead, tenderly running her fingers through his hair, smiling the whole time.

After a while her fingers moved to his chest, digging into the thick hair that grew there, lingering, wanting. Her hand moved down, towards the lower part of his body, her small, strong fingers slithering deeper, beneath his pyjama bottoms . . . touching him below, her face uplifted in rapture as she enjoyed his nakedness.

From her place at the window, Rosie watched, first mesmerised and disbelieving, then wide-eyed and enraged. She was about to bang her fists on the window when the nurse caught sight of her. Filled with horror, Rosie backed away. She saw the nurse run across the room and return with a man in a white coat. When the two of them approached the window, Rosie fled.

A few moments later the main doors were flung open and the same white-coated orderly appeared. He looked up and down, but made no attempt to search for her.

The nurse joined him, and another, more senior figure. 'What's happening, Nurse Henshaw?' she asked, and was told there had been intruders. Obviously with the intention of calling the police, she went smartly back inside. Nurse Henshaw dutifully followed.

The orderly remained a moment longer, staring about but seeing no one. 'Bloody tramps!' he muttered before he, too, went back inside. What did he care if there was a peeper? Besides, he didn't get paid for chasing loonies.

Rosie ran across the road to the camper van and Luke. She gripped him by the arms, her eyes wild with pain. 'Your father is in there. I've just seen him.'

Luke pulled away. 'So what?'

'Don't you feel *anything* for him?'

'No!' His face curled with contempt. 'When I was a kid, you told me lies. I used to cry, wishing with all my heart that he wasn't dead. Now, I wish to God he *was* dead!'

Shaken by the vehemence of his outburst, it was a moment before she spoke. 'We'd best get away from here. You drive, son,' she told him quietly. 'I need to think.'

The face of that nurse was etched on her mind. So, too, was the way she had smiled at Mike, pawed him when he was asleep. What else might the devil have done if she hadn't realised someone was watching? Rosie only hoped the fright of being observed would make that nurse think twice before she did anything like that again.

Rosie turned to look back at the building. 'I have to go now, Mike,' she murmured, 'but you mustn't worry because I'll never be far away.' She smiled. 'I'll be back before you know it,' she whispered. 'I promise.'

Suddenly, the smile fell away and her whole body stiffened. 'And, if you remember, my darling, I never break a promise.'

The detective inspector paced the office floor, his voice clipped and authoritative as he addressed the sergeant. 'It's been two weeks, for God's sake! Are you telling me there are still no leads?' Swinging round, he bent to press his face close to the other man. 'Have we found the murder weapon yet?'

'No, sir. We carried out a fingertip search of the area and left no stone unturned in a five-mile radius.'

'Then extend the search area.'

'Will do.'

'Witnesses?'

'None as far as we can tell. We've questioned everyone who uses that track to walk the dog, or anyone who might have been fishing there at that particular time. We've carried out door-to-door questioning, but there's nothing. Some old biddy reported a couple of kids supposedly kissing and cuddling on the riverbank that night, but it didn't pan out.' Shrugging, he confessed, 'I'm afraid we keep coming up against brick walls.'

'What about the gypsy?'

'It's as if she's vanished from the face of the earth.'

'Don't be so bloody stupid! She's out there somewhere, her and the lad. I want them found. Do you hear me? *I want them found!*'

'Yes, sir.' Sergeant Madison wished the old sod wouldn't yell like that. When he yelled, his eyeballs stood out like hatpins; worse than that, the long piece of hair that he combed over his bald patch became dislodged. If it wasn't so repulsive, it might be comical.

All the same, he decided to risk his life. 'To tell you the truth, sir, I don't think they had anything to do with it.'

'Oh? And how did you come to that conclusion?'

'Think about it, sir.' Growing confident, Madison sat up straight. 'If they did kill him, why leave him hanging there? They must have known it wouldn't be long before he was found, and once we discovered who he was, we'd be making a beeline for them.' The harbourmaster had identified Eddie Johnson from the photograph they had circulated, which was just as well, thought Madison, or they'd be up against an even

bigger brick wall and there was no telling what
that would do to the inspector's blood pressure.

'Go on, Sergeant. Don't stop now.'

'Well, it doesn't make sense, does it, sir? If they
were both in on it, why didn't they drag him off
somewhere and bury him? Why didn't they take
him with them, out of the area? Better still, if
they meant to kill him, why didn't they do it in
the van? I mean, Eddie Johnson was living with
them. They must have had ample opportunity to
do away with him quietly. So why wait until he's
climbing a gate, then bash him over the head.
I mean, it's a bit messy, don't you think? A bit
unnecessary?'

'My, my. You really have given it some thought,
haven't you?'

Pleased as punch, Madison allowed himself a
smug little smile – which was soon wiped off
when an iron fist came down on the desk with
such impact that the floor shook beneath him.

'If that's all you've got to offer, it's no wonder
we're no nearer finding the culprit. As to your
theories, let's see.' The inspector feigned a look of
concentration. 'For a start, they might not *both*
be involved. As to why he was struck while
climbing the gate, whoever did it could have
killed him in a fit of anger, in the middle of a
violent argument maybe. And if it was just one of
them involved, that could also explain why the
body was left hanging there. Johnson was a big
man, don't forget.'

'I see what you're getting at,' said Madison. 'You think one of them killed him but didn't want the other to know.'

'It's possible. *Anything's* possible when I'm surrounded by idiots.' He stormed across the room and flung open the door. 'Shift your arse before I do something I might regret. Get everybody together in the outer office. It's time I shook the buggers up!'

Madison scurried off, softly muttering to himself, 'Yell and scream all you like, but I still think we're barking up the wrong tree.' He had been giving it a great deal of thought and two things stood out in his mind. Where was Eddie Johnson going when he was brutally killed? And why was he carrying a vicious blade in his pocket? It was almost as though *he* was the one with murder in his heart.

He had mentioned this but his theory was dismissed by those in higher authority. 'He was a traveller, wasn't he? And they have a nasty habit of carrying knives, don't they?'

The gypsy woman and her son were the prime suspects but Madison felt in his bones that there was more to Eddie Johnson's murder than any of them realised.

Rounding up the crew, he ignored their sighs and groans.

There was something else he couldn't get out of his mind, and that was the look on Johnson's face when he was found; the way he was hanging there, like a rag doll, his head caved in, eyes wide open. He had seen his murderer; it was there in those awful, stricken eyes.

If only he could speak!

PART TWO

1983

Nightmares Are Real

CHAPTER FIVE

'No! Leave me alone!' The boy was hell bent on causing chaos.

'For God's sake, Jack, what's the matter with you?' Kerry was close to breaking point. 'Eat your breakfast, *now*!'

While he sulkily toyed with his food, Kerry was taken aside by her mother, Julie. 'Why don't you relax?' Knowing what a monster Jack could be, she was sympathetic. 'You're like a bear with a sore head.'

'Don't interfere.'

'What's wrong?'

'Nothing I can't handle.'

'You would tell me if I wasn't needed here, wouldn't you?' Julie said. 'I wouldn't want to stay where I'm not wanted.'

'Of course you're needed.' Her mother had been here almost a week, ever since they had heard that Mike was being considered for release. 'I've come to help,' she said, and, much as Kerry loved her, there were times when she could happily murder her! She had stayed for months after Mike entered the psychiatric unit.

'I could take the children home with me for a

few days if it would help?' Julie offered. She was no fool. She knew that her daughter was seeing another man but she had wisely made no mention of it. Besides, she was secretly thrilled. If Kerry decided to leave Mike and take the children with her, she would be only too delighted.

For a long moment it seemed as if Kerry was actually considering her offer but then she smiled and touched her mother's hand with a hint of fondness. 'It's kind of you to offer but it's best they stay here.' Julie lived some fifty miles away, too far to be convenient.

Julie understood. 'You'll cope. You always do.'

'It's been three years, Mum. I've made a new life . . . built a business.' Her voice faltered. 'It will never be the same again, will it?'

Julie never minced words. 'Whatever happens between you and Mike, I know you'll do what's best for you and the children.'

'You're hoping I'll desert him, aren't you?'

'Why do you say that?' She could sound offended even when guilty.

'I know you don't like him. You've never liked him.'

Julie was silent.

Kerry crossed to the window where she stood, arms folded, her sorry gaze reaching out to the garden beyond. They had been so happy here, but it seemed so long ago it was hard to remember the way it was.

These days, she was angry all the time. Angry

because Mike was away; angry because he was most likely coming home. Her business was bound to be a source of irritation to him, especially since his own business had folded. He had not said as much but he probably blamed her for not saving it. God knows, she had tried her best, but hiring out trucks and cars was not something she had taken to. On top of that, she had had to contend with Jack withdrawing into himself and giving her cause for concern. Then there was her mother, helping and hindering, and her own nightmares, about Mike, and the business, and the way forward.

The work and worry had left her tormented. She was slow to forgive and quick to anger. Most of all, she was angry with herself, for being weak and taking a lover. But that was Mike's fault, not hers!

These past few days had been too much. After the doctor had spoken to her, she had been constantly on edge, her emotions in turmoil. But today of all days she needed to stay calm and collected because Mike might be coming home. It was bound to change their lives and she had a great deal to think about.

Her mother wasn't helping. In fact, if anything she was making matters worse, criticising Mike at every opportunity. But then those two had never got on; right from the first she had taken against him and no matter how hard he had tried, she had put him down at every turn. Life was difficult when two people you loved were at each other's throat.

Wouldn't it be wonderful if, once he was home, her mother grew to accept him? A wry smile touched her mouth. Somehow she doubted things would change so easily.

The very fact that she was entertaining these disloyal thoughts only added to Kerry's burden of guilt.

Her affair with Steve Palmer was a source of joy to her, but now she didn't know what to do. If Mike did come home, she knew she ought to finish with Steve and devote herself to Mike, for the children's sake, if not her own. But the thought of giving up Steve filled her with dismay. She hadn't said anything to him yet. What was the point until she knew definitely that Mike was coming home?

The children sensed her turmoil, especially Jack who had loved his father with all his being and now would not even talk about him. Jack had always denied seeing anything untoward that night and when Mike had urged him to corroborate his story, Jack had seemed terrified.

For one brief, insane moment, when Mike was so convinced he had seen that young couple disappear into the sky, Kerry had wondered if it was really true; after all, Mike was the most normal, practical man she had ever known. What if it had happened? Just as he described?

She had dismissed the thought. It was

impossible. How could such a thing have happened? Mike was sick, that was what they said and she had to believe it, but it was hard. Before that night he was a normal, sensible bloke, running a successful business, providing for his family, juggling deals and working long, back-breaking hours. Maybe she and the children had expected too much from him. The stress must have been taking its toll and she had not even realised.

Their love had always been their strength. But now she wondered whether it would be enough to carry them through the difficult times ahead. If she couldn't cope without flying off the handle just thinking about Mike's return home, how would she cope when he was here? In this house? In her bed . . . *touching her*, in that intimate way she had loved?

Right now, she didn't even want to think about it. She had more than enough to occupy her mind; mundane, aggravating things such as Jack's bad temper, not to mention her mother who turned up when you least wanted her and stayed until you could pull out every hair on your head. It had been hard enough to get her to go home when Mike was first taken into the psychiatric unit. Maybe this time, with Mike coming home, she would withdraw gracefully.

Kerry deliberately turned her mind to more immediate things. She went into the hallway where she got together the children's coats. Her mother followed.

'You look so tired, Kerry,' she said. 'I'm worried about you.'

'I am tired,' Kerry admitted. 'If I wasn't saddled with so many responsibilities, I'd pack my bags and bugger off for good.' Julie looked at her in such a way that Kerry felt obliged to reassure her. 'I would never leave Mike and the kids, you know that.'

'He doesn't deserve you. Any other woman would have been long gone by now.'

'I don't think so.'

'What about your boyfriend?'

Astonished, Kerry stared at her. 'What boyfriend?'

'I might be naïve but I'm not stupid. I've known for some time that you've been seeing someone, and don't think I disapprove because actually I'm delighted.' Leaning forward, she asked, 'Someone from work, is it?'

Kerry shook her head. 'I swear, you're an old witch!'

Julie laughed. 'Not so much of the "old"! I pride myself on looking younger than my years.' At fifty-five, she was smart and attractive with vivid green eyes and a mop of fair hair.

'Whether I have a boyfriend or not is none of your business.'

'I'm worried about you, that's all.'

'It's not me you're worried about. It's Mike, isn't it?'

'I don't know what you mean.'

Lowering her voice so the children wouldn't hear, Kerry said, 'You don't want to see me and Mike back together. You're frightened he might murder us all in our beds, isn't that right?'

'Don't be silly.' But Kerry was right, she *was* frightened. She thought Mike was capable of anything. Even murder.

Movement behind her made Kerry turn. Jack was standing in the kitchen doorway. How long had he been listening? He smiled knowingly at her and Kerry felt oddly unnerved. It was as if he was trying to tell her something – or keep it from her.

While Kerry saw to the children, Julie began clearing the breakfast dishes. 'By the time you get back from the school, I'll have the house shining like a new pin,' she promised.

While she worked, she thought about Jack. He troubled her. There were things here, bad things, which she suspected would touch them all.

At eight years old, Jack was small for his age. He had the same serious brown eyes and dark hair as his mother. He hardly ever smiled, at least not since Mike had been shut away. Once a happy, loving child, he was now sullen and difficult, with a cunning ability to twist any situation to his own ends. Susie, on the other hand, seemed unaffected by all that had happened. Slight of build, with baby blue eyes and long fair hair, she had always been her daddy's little angel.

'Come on, you two.' Kerry ushered the

children across the kitchen. 'A kiss for Granny, then we'd best be off.'

'I can take the children to school if you like.' Having got on Kerry's wrong side, Julie was keen to make amends.

'You don't drive, remember?'

'Lucy Roper told me the bus goes right to the school door.'

'Thanks all the same, but we've got time enough.' Giving Susie a gentle shove she told her, 'Hurry, sweetheart. Granny's waiting for a kiss.'

Wrapping two tiny arms round Julie's neck, the girl hugged and kissed her, ''Bye, 'bye.' Her bright smile was like a summer's day.

''Bye, 'bye, Susie. You be a good girl now.'

While Kerry helped Susie on with her jacket, Jack moved forward to kiss his grandmother.

As always, he was reluctant, and Julie gave him a way out. 'It's all right if you think you're too grown-up to kiss your gran.'

'I don't mind. Besides, Mummy said I have to.'

Julie laughed. 'We'd best do as she says then, hadn't we?'

Reaching up, he wound his arms round her neck and drew her down, pressing his thin lips to hers. Then, in a move that took her by surprise, he opened his mouth and sank his teeth deep into her lower lip.

Recoiling in pain, she covered her face, staring down through her fingers with wide, shocked eyes.

'Jack! Get a move on!' Kerry called.

At the kitchen door he turned, his avaricious eyes following the trickle of blood as it ran through her fingers. 'I'm sorry, Gran.' His smile was cruel, his voice marbled with joy. 'Now I don't suppose you'll ever want to kiss me again.'

After the door was softly closed on her, Julie stood for a moment, trying to come to terms with what he had done to her. All kinds of things ran through her mind, but only one came back time and again.

There was evil in him.

CHAPTER SIX

His screams of terror brought the nurse running.

'Ssh! It's all right.' Wrapping her arms round his trembling frame, she raised him to the pillow. 'It was just a dream.' Her voice soothed his shattered senses. 'A bad dream, that's all.'

More vivid than the horrors that stalked his sleep were the fears that haunted his waking hours. 'You won't tell them, will you?' he pleaded. 'Not today. Please!'

Regarding him fondly, she reminded him, 'I'm obliged to report everything.'

'There's no need to tell them.' Inside, he was panicking, his every nerve-ending crawling. The sweat ran down his face and body but he knew if he lost control now, he would lose his chance of getting out of here. 'You said yourself, it was just a dream.' His voice was remarkably calm.

She wanted to believe him. 'Tell me about the dream, Mike. Was it the same as before?'

He shook his head. 'No,' he lied. 'Not the same.'

'Are you sure?'

'That was all over, a long time ago.' The truth was, it had never ended, and never would. In his dream he saw them disappear as clearly as if it was happening all over again.

'Tell me about it.'

He paused to think. He had to be careful, stay one step ahead of them. 'It was . . . vague . . . kind of mixed up.'

'Why were you screaming?'

Casually shrugging his shoulders, he answered confidently, 'I'm not sure, but I know it had nothing to do with that night.'

'What then?' She was insistent.

'A game.' With his liberty at stake, the lies came easily. 'Me and the kids were playing this game . . . the ball was heading straight for Susie. I was afraid she might be hurt, and that's all I can remember.'

'I see.'

'Like you said, just a crazy dream.' Using a corner of the sheet, he wiped away the sweat.

For a while, she continued to observe him. 'It's only natural you should be concerned about your family,' she conceded. 'There's nothing sinister about that. Besides, I expect you've been worrying about today, what they might ask you.' She laughed softly, dry, warm breath escaping through her nose to bathe his face. 'It's not easy facing that lot but they're only trying to help. You know that, don't you, Mike?'

He nodded. 'But it doesn't make it any easier.' He had to be sure of her. 'Please, Alice, you won't tell them, will you?'

It took a moment for her to answer; a long,

agonising moment for Mike, but then she put his mind at rest. 'No. From the way you described it, the dream was harmless enough.' Eyeing him intently, she asked, 'You *are* telling me the truth, aren't you?'

Without hesitation, he answered, 'You know I am.' Thank God she couldn't read his mind.

Satisfied, she stood back, her soft blue eyes looking down on him, admiring. 'Is there anything you need?'

'No.' What he needed was to be alone; to get his head together before facing the inquisition. 'I'm really tired though.' His handsome face crinkled into an easy smile. 'If I'm to look my best for the interview, I'd best get my beauty sleep.'

Tucking the covers round him, she chuckled, 'I've never heard it called an interview before.'

'Interrogation then.' When he smiled into her eyes, he turned her heart over.

'Don't be silly. All they want to know is that you're able to cope.'

Unwisely, he let resentment get the better of him. 'I was *always* able to cope.'

She stared at him. 'It wouldn't do to lose your temper in there tomorrow.'

He didn't answer. Anger flooded through him. The bastards had kept him here long enough.

'See you in the morning then.'

'Alice?'

She turned. 'Yes?'

'Thank you.'

Her answer was a half-smile. But it told him what he needed to know. He could sleep easier – for now at least.

In the morning, as he was escorted to the outer office, Mike could hardly recall the dream. All he knew was that it took him back to a place he didn't want to go.

'Nurse Henshaw will be along directly.' Matron was in a hurry as always. 'No doubt she will take you straight in. Meanwhile, make yourself comfortable.'

With that she smartly departed, leaving the door wide open.

Across the hall, a leather-faced nurse glared at him. 'Old battleaxe!' he muttered under his breath. When she stared all the harder, he nodded and gave her his slow, easy smile, confusing her.

When she turned away, the smile slipped and he was flooded with resentment. Why leave the bloody door open? he thought. What the hell was he, a peep show?

He was tempted to close the door and shut her out, but that would be seen as a defiant act. For the moment, he could not afford such luxuries.

There was a second door to his right. He assumed it led into the other office where they were waiting to see him, and it made him nervous. He sat a while, then he began to pace, not anxiously but steadily, calmly. He didn't want to seem agitated. The room struck cold. Folding his arms over his chest, he shuddered. 'Please, God, let this be the day they say I'm fit to go home to my family.'

After the agonies he had put his wife and children through, there were moments when he wondered if they really wanted him back and he would torture himself with doubts. Why should they want him back? And if they did, was it out of loyalty, or love? Had they put it all behind them, or were they still afraid of the happenings that had brought him here? More importantly, could he and Kerry enjoy the same wonderful relationship as before? Ten years and two children; it had been so good. What now? Was it too late? Three lonely years. It was a long time to be apart.

The all too brief times when Kerry had come to visit him, was it because she *wanted* to see him? Or did she consider it her duty? 'Duty' was an ugly word. He didn't want that from her, from his sweet, lovely Kerry, with her dark, bobbed hair and mischievous brown eyes. He had loved her from the first moment he set eyes on her, and he loved her still, though maybe not in the same fiercely jealous way. But then he was that much older. They both were. Here he was, forty-one, and Kerry, what? Thirty-five?

Things changed, that was inevitable. Kerry was not the same, and neither was he. They had both been to hell and back, and now they had the chance to make a new beginning. He was determined to make it all up to her. The children too. He had missed what no father should ever miss; the 'formative years', isn't that what they called it? He smiled, a sad smile.

Sometimes, late at night or in the waking hours, he would wonder about that night, until he thought he might *really* go crazy. Then he would think of Kerry and Jack and Susie, and somehow, through all the nightmares and memories, he was able to hold on to reality.

He had always comforted himself with the knowledge that none of this was his fault. Kerry knew that, and understood. Susie and Jack were young and resilient. They would adjust. Children had a way of doing that. Look how they had coped since he was shut away.

But what about Jack? He had seen it all, and yet he had denied it – like Peter denying the Lord three times. At first he had hated the boy for letting him down, but after a while he had reasoned that maybe Jack didn't recall the exact way it was. Maybe he really didn't see what happened to that young couple. After all, he was only a boy; he was hurt and frightened. And yet it was Jack who had pointed out the young couple. It was Jack who had screamed with terror when he saw the sky open up and take them.

Mike let his gaze rove the room; so many times before he had been brought here filled with hope, only to have it dashed. 'Too early, Mr Peterson,' they said. 'We don't believe you're ready to leave just yet.'

Bastards! What did they know?

He stood in front of the window and anger flooded his senses; other feelings too, feelings that frightened him. The mood was fleeting, but while it lasted it was very powerful. It was always the same: a feeling of being watched – *manipulated*.

'Mr Peterson.'

He didn't hear. The feelings overwhelmed him; like a dark premonition.

Alice remained by the door, not certain whether she should disturb his last few quiet moments here. She recalled the night when he was brought to this place; a broken man, disorientated and terrified by the demons that haunted him. But that was three years ago. A lifetime in a place like this.

The mood passed. He sensed her there and was safe.

His voice was warm and calm as he asked, 'Is it time?' Keeping his back to her, he stared through the window. Out there was freedom. He could almost taste it.

'You have a few minutes yet,' she told him kindly. 'Are you ready to face them?'

He turned, half smiling, and nodded. 'I think so.'

'Not worried then?'

'Should I be?'

'No.'

'Then I'm not. Coffee would be nice,' he added. 'If you're making.'

She smiled. 'Why do you always say that?'

'What?'

'If you're making. You know I never drink the stuff.'

'I know.'

'I make a mean cup of tea though, and there's a new packet of chocolate biscuits in the cupboard. I think Nurse Jenkins must have brought them in. She won't begrudge us a couple, I'm sure.'

'No tea, thanks all the same. Coffee and biscuits.' He was smiling. Alice had been a good friend; though at times, like now, she could be a pain in the arse. He knew she had feelings for him, and the knowledge was a burden.

Sighing, she conceded. 'Strong and black, three sugars. Coming right up.' With that she thoughtfully closed the door and was gone, her narrow heels clattering as she hurried across the tiled hall floor. 'I'll miss you, Mike Peterson,' she mumbled. 'More than you can imagine.'

They had been nurse and patient, and friends, too. But, given half a chance, she would have been much more than that. The truth was, she had fallen for him the first day he was admitted. 'I should be glad for you,' she muttered. 'You have a loving family and you deserve a life outside these walls.'

All the same, her days would not be the same

without his warm, stirring smile to greet her.

Alice had made the coffee and was about to put the biscuits on the plate when in came Nurse Jenkins. 'That'll cost you, you thieving bugger!'

Sally Jenkins had been here for years; bright and cheerful, she had a round, pink face atop a pear-shaped body, and thick, capable hands the size of shovels. 'I wondered who'd been pinching my biscuits,' she teased. 'I could have sworn it was Matron.'

'You don't mind, do you?' Alice felt guilty.

'Don't talk so bloody daft!' All the same, Sally grabbed up the opened packet and rammed it into her pocket. 'You can buy the next lot.' Gesturing to the tray, she asked, 'Who's that for?'

'Mike Peterson. He's waiting to see Dr Carlton.'

'Do you think they'll let him loose?'

Alice shrugged. 'Who knows?'

Sally took a moment to study her colleague; she saw a pretty young thing, with long fair hair tied in the nape of her neck, and soft, blue eyes that could melt a man's heart. 'I expect you've had it off with him a few times, you randy bugger.'

Shocked, Alice rounded on her. 'What the devil are you talking about?'

Sally's smile said it all. 'I know how you feel about him.'

Alice blushed, turned away, then in a small voice confessed, 'I didn't know it showed.'

'Don't worry. Nobody else knows.'

'You won't say, will you?'

'What? And get you in hot water? What do you take me for?'

'In a way, I'll be sorry to see him go.' Alice's heart sank at the thought. 'But I could never begrudge him that.' Sighing, she admitted, 'Besides, he would never look twice at me, not with a gorgeous wife like he's got.'

Sally was born mischievous. 'So, you *didn't* have it off with him then?'

'What do you think?'

'Pity. Mind you, I would have been mad jealous. I might have enjoyed a bit of that myself. He's a real looker.'

Alice laughed. 'You're too fat!' she teased. 'You would have broken the bed between you.'

'You cheeky bugger! But you're right all the same.' She laughed out loud. 'Mind you, we could have rolled about the floor.'

'Well, he's going, so we've both missed our chance.' Needing to change the subject, she said, 'I'd better get this coffee to him before it goes cold,' and before Sally could question her further, she was away, eager to get back to Mike, wishing he would be made to stay here, and hating herself for wishing it.

'Here we are!' she said brightly as she entered the room.

Mike welcomed her with a smile. 'You've been gone so long, I thought you'd abandoned me.'

'Now, would I do a thing like that?' If he was to ask, she would spend the rest of her life with him. 'You cost me a packet of chocolate biscuits though.' Setting the tray on the table, she made a wry little grin. 'See what I do for you, Mike Peterson?'

He chuckled. 'Nurse Jenkins caught you at it, did she?' Taking a drink of the coffee he grimaced. 'God Almighty! It's stone cold. Are you trying to poison me, or what?'

Before she could answer, the door opened to admit an official-looking woman in a long white coat. Addressing Alice she told her, 'Nurse, you can bring Mr Peterson through now.'

CHAPTER SEVEN

Loath to go home, Kerry made her way to the office.

Steve was seated at her desk, dealing with the paperwork. 'I thought you weren't coming in today?' Getting up from the chair, he brushed past her to close the door. 'What happened to your "important business"?'

Kerry had not explained the reason for taking the day off. She was careful how she answered. 'It hasn't gone away,' she told him. 'I still have to deal with it.'

'Is there anything I can do to help?'

She shook her head. 'I've just dropped the kids off at school and I thought I'd pop in and make sure everything was all right here.' Glancing through the office window, she was pleased to see the two women hard at work. 'I'll nip down and have a word with them before I leave. I need to be sure they're on top with the orders. Good as they are, nobody's perfect. When the cat's away . . .'

'Kerry?'

'Please, Steve. No more questions.' Afraid she might weaken and tell him how it could be over between them, she thought it safer to say nothing at all.

He persisted. 'I know there's something troubling you.'

'Leave it, Steve.'

'Don't you trust me?'

'I wouldn't have left you in charge if I didn't.'

'Then believe me when I say I would like to help. And you have my word that *nobody* shirks when you're out of sight.'

Mortified, she knew he was right. 'I shouldn't have said that,' she apologised. 'I know how conscientious they are.'

'All the same, I'm glad you're here. I'm missing you already.' When he smiled, the dimple beneath his eye deepened. It was one of the things Kerry first noticed, that and the quiet, secretive way he looked at her.

'Ten minutes, then I have to go.'

'Pity.' Standing close, he looked her in the eye. 'I really would like to help, if only you'll let me.'

'You can't. Nobody can.' Her thoughts went to Mike. He was almost a stranger now. But for the children's sake she had to try, and maybe, just maybe, she and Mike could work things out.

With the tip of his thumb Steve wiped away a telltale tear from her cheek. 'Tell me.'

'No. It's something *I* have to deal with, and I will.' Averting her gaze, she rounded the desk and sat behind it, feigning interest in a batch of letters.

'Has it to do with us?' Leaning forward, he

spread his hands across the desk, staring down at her.

Disturbed by his persistence, she got up and went quickly to the door. 'I'll see you tomorrow.'

'Kerry, for God's sake, talk to me! *Has it to do with us*?' Coming up behind her, he grabbed her by the shoulders and shook her.

Swinging round, she flattened herself against the door, where she knew the women below could not see. 'All right,' she said, 'yes, it has to do with you and me.'

'I'm listening.'

'It's possible Mike could be coming home today.'

'Mike!' He looked at her aghast. He had convinced himself that Mike's breakdown was permanent.

'He goes before the panel today. They'll decide if he's well enough to come home.'

'And if he is coming home, what then? What about us?'

'I think you already know.'

He looked away. 'Is that what you want?'

'You know it isn't!' Clutching his arm, she pleaded, 'My feelings towards you haven't changed. It's you I love.'

'But you're *his* wife.'

'Don't make this any harder for me, Steve. Mike is almost a stranger to me now. I don't know how he thinks any more; I don't know how he feels about me, not really. I don't even know if

I love him the way I used to.'

'But you're prepared to give me up for him?' He could taste the bitterness on his tongue. 'Mike Peterson forfeited the right to you long ago.'

'Please, Steve, try and understand.' Kerry didn't blame him for feeling angry, but it was wrong. 'Mike is still my husband. Believe me, I'm not looking forward to starting all over again. But, for the sake of the kids, I have to try to make the marriage work.' She held him by the hand, remembering all that had passed between them. 'It's been wonderful, but now it's over. We have to accept that.'

'It's a pity he didn't die three years ago.'

Shocked, Kerry thrust him away. 'I don't want to listen to that kind of talk.' She turned to the door. 'I have to go.'

'It's *not* over.' Wrapping his fingers about her wrist, he made her turn back. 'We can't switch it off just like that, and you know it.'

'You're saying all the wrong things, Steve,' she answered him softly.

'True though, isn't it?'

Torn between loyalty to Mike and her love for Steve, she had no answer.

'Will we still work together, or would you rather end that too?'

Her heart sank. The days would be empty without him near. 'That depends on you, Steve.'

'I understand what you're saying but you needn't worry.'

'I'm glad.'

'You know I love you?'

'I know.'

'And if it all goes wrong, I'll still be here.'

Bowing her head, Kerry wished things could have been different. Now, when he took her in his arms and kissed her, she knew she would never love Mike in the same way.

A few moments later she left, regretting today, fearing tomorrow.

From the office window, Steve watched her go. Hard-faced and resolute, he twisted a paper-knife in his hands until it drew blood. 'You belong to me,' he murmured. 'I won't let him come between us.'

Slowly, he raised his arm, and with a swift flick of the wrist, threw the paperknife across the room. With a gentle thud it pierced the smiley face on the calendar. Steve thumped the desk triumphantly. 'Hah! It's good to know I haven't lost my touch.'

Striding across to retrieve the knife, he wiped his own blood from the blade. Once more he threw the paperknife, watching with satisfaction as it sliced through the eyes of the face on the calendar. 'Be warned, Mike Peterson,' he murmured. 'Kerry's mine. All mine!'

The phone rang as Kerry put her key in the door.

Julie took the call in the kitchen. 'Hold on,' she told the caller. 'It's my daughter you want.'

Kerry's heart was in her mouth. 'Is it the hospital?'

Julie nodded and handed her the receiver, then retired to a respectful distance where she slyly eavesdropped. Her face stiffened as she followed the conversation.

After a few brief moments, Kerry replaced the receiver. 'I suppose you heard all that.'

'When will he be home?' That was all Julie needed to know.

Going to the table, Kerry drew out a chair and sat down. 'Today, but first the doctor wants to see us both together.' She gave a croaky laugh. 'They probably want to give me the once over to make sure I'm able to cope.'

Julie made two mugs of strong coffee. 'And are you?' She placed the coffee on the table and sat down opposite Kerry.

'Of course,' Kerry confidently assured her.

'When do you want me to leave?'

It was on the tip of Kerry's tongue to ask her to leave the next day, but a deeper instinct made her pause. What if she found it hard going with Mike? What if he was much changed from the man she knew? How would she deal with it all, and what about Jack and Susie? How would they take to him?

'Leave it for a day or two, Mum,' she said. 'We'll see how it goes.'

'Whatever you say.' Secretly, Julie was relieved. She had never liked the idea of leaving her daughter and grandchildren alone with Mike. Whatever the doctors said, there was no doubt in her mind. Mike Peterson was hopelessly insane.

Kerry drove into the hospital car park. She made no move to get out of the car or to switch off the engine. Instead, she sat there, assailed by troublesome memories, her thoughtful gaze fixed on the sign above the entrance:

LANDSMEAD
INSTITUTE FOR THE TREATMENT OF
PSYCHIATRIC AND NEUROLOGICAL
DISORDERS

She had lost count of the times she had visited this place, and though she had walked beneath that sign on many occasions, she had never before noticed the exact wording there. Now, almost against her will, it seemed to imprint itself on her brain. *'Institute for the treatment of psychiatric and neurological disorders.'* What did it really mean? More importantly, how exactly did it apply to Mike? Could the doctors ever be sure that the treatment had worked?

Doubt flooded in, then guilt, and afterwards a determination that she and Mike would make it work. 'We *have* to make it work, for Jack and Susie.'

She switched off the engine, got out of the car and locked it, then with the quick, confident steps of a woman with a purpose made her way into the hospital.

As usual, the clerk greeted her with a glued-on smile. 'Nurse Henshaw asked if you would please make your way to the dayroom.' When Kerry thanked her, she answered, 'You must be delighted to be taking him home at long last.'

News travelled fast in this place, Kerry thought. 'Thank you,' she said, and hurried to the day-room.

Mike was standing by the window, hands thrust deep into his pockets and a faraway look on his face. Even when she closed the door he didn't turn to see who it was.

'Mike?' Crossing the room, she peeped round his shoulder to look into his face. 'Are you all right?'

When he turned, there was a look of fear in his eyes, but it soon melted when he saw who it was. 'Kerry! Oh, thank God, I thought you might not come.' Sliding one arm round her shoulders, he drew her close. 'I'm sorry, sweetheart. I've no idea why they should want to see you.'

Reaching up, she kissed him on the mouth, but it was a fleeting kiss, conveying only the fact that she was his wife and she was here to support him. 'It's only natural they would want to see us together. They have said you can go home today, haven't they?'

Drawing a deep breath of air, he let it out in a long, relaxed sigh. 'Yes, and isn't it wonderful?'

His gaze went to the window, to the world beyond. 'It's been a lifetime,' he murmured. 'I can't tell you how I feel at this minute.'

'I can imagine how you must feel.' But she couldn't. To be locked away from the outside world, to see your family only once a week and have your every move monitored – how could anyone imagine such a thing?

Shifting his gaze to her, he looked so hard into her eyes that she was unnerved. 'Please, sweetheart, don't patronise me,' he warned softly. '*I don't like it.*'

Shocked by the vehemence in his voice, she stiffened in his arms. 'I hope they don't keep us waiting long,' she said, pulling away. 'Hanging around always makes me nervous.'

His dark eyes appraised her. 'You look lovely, did I tell you that?'

Oddly embarrassed, she lowered her gaze.

He laughed, a soft, infectious laugh that told her he had not lost his sense of humour. 'Good God, Kerry! I don't think I've ever seen you blush before.' He placed his hands on her shoulders, his dark eyes looking into hers. 'I'd almost forgotten how beautiful you are.'

Her smile was delightfully girlish. 'I've *never* been beautiful.'

Placing a finger beneath her chin, he raised her face to his. 'You could have had any man you wanted, and you waited for me.' There was a pause when his dark eyes seemed to flash danger, then, in the softest voice, he asked, 'Tell me, has there been anyone else?'

Kerry skirted the issue. 'Are you suggesting I'm so desperate I couldn't go without a man for three years?' Her voice was flippant, her smile innocent, but inside she was in turmoil.

'Give me an answer, Kerry.' His grip on her tightened. 'The truth now.'

Thankfully, Kerry was saved by the arrival of Nurse Alice Henshaw. 'The doctor will see you both now,' she said in her best jolly manner. Her advice to Mike was, 'Don't let him frighten you. It's just routine stuff.'

Backing to the door, she allowed them to pass, Kerry first.

As Mike went by, Alice slid her hand in his, thrilled when he turned to give her a warm, intimate smile.

Ahead of them, Kerry was oblivious of their closeness.

Dr Carlton was a small, thin man with bright, wary eyes and a slight stoop to his shoulders. Straight-faced and serious, he beckoned them to the chairs set before his desk. 'Nurse Henshaw, I would like you to stay,' he said.

'Certainly, Doctor.' Closing the door, she stood like a sentry at the back of the room, her gaze on Mike, her love for him bared to the world.

Seating himself, Dr Carlton took out a folder, opened it and began perusing the contents. After a few moments he looked up. 'I won't take up too much of your time,' he said, smiling at Mike. 'I know how anxious you must be to see the back of us.'

Neither Mike nor Kerry commented. Instead they sat, rigid and uncertain, their eyes focused on his pale, narrow face.

'Right!' Leaning back in his chair he looked from one to the other, finally addressing Kerry. 'As we explained to your husband, the consultants are confident that he has made a good recovery and, as far as we are concerned, he is well enough to leave.'

'Does that mean he won't need any more treatment?' Kerry asked.

'We believe that won't be necessary. He has of course been weaned off the drugs over a matter of months, until now he seems not to need them. His own GP will be informed of his release and will want to see him from time to time, that's all.' He paused, seeming to think things through in his mind before continuing, 'As I have already said, in our opinion, your husband has made an excellent recovery, but as I'm sure you both understand, it is very important to avoid undue stress or worry of any kind.'

Mike pointed out that he had plans to restart his business.

'I understand. All I am saying is, don't rush things. See what your GP has to say and be guided by his advice.' Beyond that he would not be drawn. He stood up and shook them by the hand. 'There are forms to be filled out. Please go with Nurse Henshaw. She'll take good care of you.'

Throughout the consultation, Alice Henshaw had remained at the back of the room, her whole attention on Mike. There was only one emotion stronger than the longing she felt for him, and that was the hatred she felt for the doctor who was sending him out of her life.

Kerry and Mike followed Alice Henshaw down the corridor like two lost, trusting souls.

'We've already made an appointment for you with your GP,' she told Mike in the outer office.

'Is it really necessary?' Mike had seen enough doctors to last him a lifetime.

'Afraid so.'

Sitting there, watching nurse and patient together, Kerry felt like an outsider.

As if reading her mind, Mike took hold of Kerry's hand. 'You go out for a few minutes,' he suggested. 'There's no need for you to sit through all this.' He thought she looked pale and troubled. 'Go on, get a breath of fresh air.' Leaning forward he kissed her on the mouth. 'I'll be as quick as I can.'

When Kerry left, Mike's contented gaze followed her.

Neither of them saw the look of raw jealousy on Alice Henshaw's face.

* * *

Kerry made her way back to Dr Carlton's office, and then stood outside it for a moment or two, wondering why she was here. Surely he had told them all he could. What else could he tell her? Could he reassure her that Mike was as normal as anyone else? Could he convince her that their lives would be the same as before? Of course not!

She turned away.

'Mrs Peterson?' Dr Carlton had seen her shadowy figure through the glass-panelled door. 'Are you looking for me?' He seemed irritated. 'I thought we had covered everything.'

Embarrassed, Kerry was about to make her excuses and hurry away, but if she lost her chance now, she might regret it later. 'Can you spare me a few minutes?' It wasn't much to ask, she thought. After all, there were still a number of unanswered questions she couldn't ask in front of Mike. 'Mike is still with the nurse,' she explained. 'I just needed to see you on my own.'

'You had better come in.'

Once inside his office, with no one else to hear what she had to say, Kerry confided in him. 'I'm concerned that Mike may never be the same. My mother is convinced he'll always be unstable.'

This time his smile was genuine. 'I shouldn't be too concerned about that,' he chuckled. 'Mothers are known for being overprotective.' Tongue-in-cheek, he suggested, 'Unless of course she's a specialist in the field of neurological conditions?'

Laughing at the idea, Kerry shook her head. 'She has never got on with Mike. She seems to look for the worst in him.'

'That must be very difficult for you.'

'Not really. I don't let it get out of hand.'

'Very wise.'

Anxious in case Mike should come looking for her, she brought the subject back on line. 'I need to know. Is Mike completely cured?'

'Cured?' He sat back in his chair, regarding her with interest. 'Well, yes, I suppose you could say he's cured . . . to a certain extent.'

'What does that mean exactly?'

'I'll try and explain. Your husband had a severe mental breakdown. He suffered acute memory loss and anxiety. He experienced hallucinations that brought on sheer terror; these hallucinations were frighteningly real to him and, I have to admit, it was a long, hard battle before he could recognise the real from the unreal. You see, it's all in the mind, and none of us, not even those of us who have dedicated our lives to seeking the answers, can ever say we know enough about the mind to claim a cure.'

'So how will I know what to do? What to look out for?' Fear twisted her insides.

'All you can do is help him to live as normal a life as possible.' Settling deeper into his chair, he gave her hope. 'Mrs Peterson, your husband really has made a remarkable recovery.'

Afraid to ask yet knowing she must, she said

softly, 'Need I worry about leaving him alone with the children?'

'You're asking whether he might have violent tendencies?'

She shifted uncomfortably. 'I know it sounds a dreadful thing to ask, but however much I value Mike, I have to think of our two children.'

'Have you ever know him to be violent?'

'Never.'

'Apart from the need to forcibly restrain him when he was first admitted, I can assure you we have seen no evidence that he can be physically dangerous. And once he is home, you should be able to satisfy yourself on this particular matter.'

'Should I keep in touch?'

'If you're worried, yes.'

'Thank you, Doctor.' She rose from the chair. 'I'm sure he'll be fine.'

'So am I.' He led her to the door. 'Your husband is a very determined man, Mrs Peterson. He has suffered a very frightening ordeal and, I'm sure you understand, he will need a certain amount of understanding.'

'But he *is* well now, isn't he?'

He replied with a smile, 'Ready to face the outside world, shall we say. But no undue stress, remember. And try not to let your mother get under his skin.'

'Don't worry, Doctor.'

'Goodbye, Mrs Peterson.'

'Goodbye, and thank you.' No more hospital.

No more skirting her responsibilities.

She had gone halfway down the corridor when a sound from behind made her glance back.

A man, whom she assumed was a doctor, knocked on Dr Carlton's office door. 'Come in!' he called. Curious, she continued watching.

The man opened the door. 'I'd like a word, if I may, with regard to Mr Peterson.' The door closed and Kerry could hear no more.

Treading softly, she made her way back. Not daring to position herself outside the door in case he saw her there again, she pressed herself to the wall and listened. The voices were not very clear, making it difficult to follow the conversation.

Kerry leaned closer, concentrating hard. Dr Carlton's voice was firm and quiet. 'I'm sorry, Doctor . . . I have . . . your arguments before and . . . convinced . . . you are wrong. In my opinion, the man . . . sound of mind . . . keep him here . . . longer . . . harmful to his well-being.'

The other doctor sounded agitated. 'I recognise the fact that . . . senior to me, and . . . therefore abide . . . decisions. It does not . . . mean . . . that . . . must agree with them. Nor do I have . . . work . . . you. I . . . your manner . . . and overbearing . . .'

'Thank you, Doctor . . . your disapproval . . . noted.'

Sensing the conversation was over, Kerry hurried away to watch from a discreet distance.

The man who had gone into Dr Carlton's office

came rushing out, his face suffused with anger. A short distance from the office he stopped and thumped his fist into the palm of his other hand. 'Damn the man!' he muttered. 'Damn and bugger him!'

Intent on his own thoughts, he strode past Kerry, apparently oblivious of her presence.

Kerry found Mike and Nurse Henshaw laughing together. 'Oh!' The nurse seemed startled. 'We were just about to come and find you,' she said, glancing at Mike.

For just the briefest moment, as she looked into Alice Henshaw's pretty eyes, Kerry felt the awful pangs of jealousy. It was an odd, revealing experience, making her wonder if she loved Mike just as much as ever.

'We're finished here,' Mike told her. 'I'm all yours, my lovely.'

Glancing at his suitcase, boxes of books and other paraphernalia, Kerry expressed surprise. 'I had no idea you'd accumulated so much.'

'All good stuff,' he answered light-heartedly. 'Nurse Henshaw will vouch for that.' He glanced at Alice, who returned his easy smile. She might have smiled at Kerry, but Kerry was already on her way out of the door.

'I'll bring the car to the front entrance,' she called. 'It'll save us carrying that lot out to the car park.'

Parked some distance away, it took her a few minutes to locate her car. As she drove it to the front entrance, she thought of the angry conversation between those two men. 'It sounded as if the other doctor didn't agree with the patient being sent home,' she murmured. 'He mentioned Mike's name when he first went in, but how do I know they weren't talking about somebody else by the time I got there?' She was in a dilemma. She could go to the other doctor and ask him. But what if she was wrong? On the other hand, what if it really was Mike they were talking about and Dr Carlton had lied about him being 'ready to face the outside world'? A look of resentment hardened her features. *'I trusted you, Dr Carlton, and now I'm not so sure.'*

Mike and Nurse Henshaw were waiting at the entrance. He looked bright and eager, his eyes shining like they had not shone in a very long time. Maybe his ordeal is over, she thought, but if it doesn't work out the way I hope, mine may just be starting. 'Mike isn't the only one who went through hell,' she whispered harshly. 'What about me and the kids? Nobody cared about the agonies *we* went through. I only hope Dr Carlton wasn't foolish enough to release Mike before his time.'

Mike didn't talk much on the way home, except to say how much he loved Kerry, and how he could hardly believe he was going home at last. Kerry chatted about this and that, attempting to make him feel at ease. Occasionally she reached out and touched him, inwardly thrilled when he stroked her hair away to kiss the nape of her neck. They even laughed a little, remembering funny, ordinary little things that seemed so important now. Yet, in spite of all that, there was a kind of awkwardness between them, a sort of mistrust, which only time would heal. 'We have to learn all over again,' Mike murmured as they neared home.

Silently agreeing, Kerry thought how accurately he had expressed her own feelings.

The children were waiting at the door, having been collected from school early on Kerry's instructions. Julie stood behind them, her ever watchful eyes on Mike as he came lumbering up the garden path. They didn't speak. That would come later. For now, the children needed reassuring.

Having parked the car in front of the garage, Kerry stood back, allowing Mike his time with the kids.

Susie rushed towards him to be swept into his arms. 'You're so pretty,' he said, hugging her tight, and when she planted a kiss on his face, the tears rose to his eyes.

His gaze went to Jack. 'Hello, son.'

Jack stood small and upright, his eyes dark and sullen. He didn't speak, nor did he make a move. For a long, electric moment they stood, father and son facing each other, and the air was charged with emotion. But it was not emotion of a gentle kind. How could it be when they each knew what the other was thinking when their thoughts carried them back to a dark, stormy night where innocents were stolen, and all hell let loose.

Kerry stepped forward. 'Jack!' Fear sharpened her voice. 'Answer your daddy.'

With incredible calmness Jack stared her out and then turned to go indoors.

'Little bastard!' The blasphemy was uttered under Kerry's breath but not out of Mike's hearing.

'Leave him to me,' he said softly. 'It'll be all right.'

Julie had nothing to say but before she, too, went inside, the look on her face told Mike all he needed to know. 'She likes me even less now than she did before,' he said to Kerry.

'You'll just have to win her round,' Kerry answered brightly. 'She's staying with us for a while.'

'That's OK, sweetheart,' he said. 'I dare say you'll need all the help you can get. For now.' His last words warned Kerry that he would not expect Julie to stay one minute longer than necessary.

'Daddy.' Susie was six years old, going on twenty.

Keeping her in his arms, Mike closed the door. 'Yes, sweetheart?'

'Am I *really* pretty?'

Swinging her high in the air, he made her laugh. 'You're the prettiest, most delightful little creature I've ever seen,' he said, and won her heart for ever.

The remainder of the day was spent quietly talking.

Jack refused to come down from his room, while Susie would not be persuaded from her daddy's knee. Julie pottered about looking for things to do to keep her out of the way while Kerry and Mike talked about the practical problems that lay ahead. 'I need to think about work,' Mike told her. 'As you know, I'd like to get my old business off the ground again.'

They discussed the possibility at length, and also Kerry's need to maintain and expand her own business. 'I've been the breadwinner for too long now to go back to being a housewife,' Kerry admitted.

'I wouldn't expect that,' Mike said. 'I understand how hard it must have been for you, and I'm proud of what you've achieved.'

Kerry was taken aback. 'I imagined you'd want everything to be the way it was,' she confessed.

Mike looked at her and thought how lovely she was. 'No, I could never expect that. Everything has changed. You and I have to build on the old foundations, but it has to be a new life, a new direction, I know that.'

Gazing up into those dark, serious eyes, Kerry was lost in a swirl of emotions. She realised there might be a real chance for them after all.

Lurking in the kitchen, Julie heard what he said, and knew instinctively what Kerry was thinking. 'Kerry Peterson, you're all kinds of a fool!' she muttered. 'Let him get to you and, mark my words, you'll live to regret it!'

A short time later, Kerry searched her mother out. 'I suppose you heard all that.'

'Yes, and I think you're foolish to listen to him.'

'I'm no fool, Mother. I think I know what I'm doing.'

Kerry had her coat on and Julie asked her where she was going.

'I won't be long,' she answered. 'I think it would be a nice treat if we had fish and chips tonight.'

'Yes, I'd enjoy that.'

'Mike and Susie are asleep. Let them sleep, but tell Jack I've gone for fish and chips. It might draw the little sod out of his room.'

'He's a troubled soul.'

'No more than I am.'

'Did you see the look that passed between them?'

'Leave it be.'

'I will. *They* won't.'

'I won't be gone long, unless there's a queue. Put the kettle on and slice some bread and butter. Oh, and we'll have the chocolate gateau.' She laughed. 'We might as well push the boat out while we're at it.'

On her way out, she peeped into the lounge;

they were still fast asleep, Mike sprawled out on
the settee and Susie curled up in the curve of his
arm. 'There was a time when I would have done
anything for you,' she murmured, her gaze lingering on Mike's handsome face. 'But now I don't
know.'

Subdued, she left the house.

As always, Julie watched her go, surprised
when Kerry turned the car left at the bottom of
the road. 'That's funny,' she muttered. 'The fish
and chip shop is the other way.'

Shrugging her shoulders, she returned to the
kitchen where she filled the kettle and began to
cut the bread.

Dr Carlton was a weary man. Too many long
hours and a recent divorce had taken its toll, and
he never went home without taking a mountain
of work with him.

'Goodnight, Doctor.' Alice Henshaw was col-
lecting a folder from the reception desk.

'Goodnight.' He turned up the collar of his coat,
clutched the box of documents to his chest, and
went out into a grim, dark evening.

'Miserable bugger, isn't he?' commented Peggy
Earl. She ran the canteen when she wasn't
hanging about the reception desk gathering the
latest gossip. 'I don't think I've ever seen him
smile.'

'That's because he's got nothing to smile about,'
Alice explained. 'His wife took him for a small

fortune when they split, and he's never forgiven her.'

'Who are we talking about?' Having delivered an urgent message to Sister, Nurse Beatty was back to finish her shift behind the desk.

Cheeky as ever, Peggy answered, 'I was just saying how Dr Carlton never smiles, and Nurse Henshaw said it was because his wife took him for a fortune when they split up.'

'That's true, yes, and on top of that nobody likes him, do they?'

'I don't mind him.' Peggy looked for the best in everybody, 'Besides, he's the only one who likes my sausage rolls. Yesterday lunchtime he ate three, one after the other.'

Alice laughed out loud. '*That's* why he's not smiling, poor devil. He's probably crippled with indigestion.'

'He's certainly changed since he and his wife got divorced,' Nurse Beatty said. 'And then there's this latest thing.'

Alice was puzzled. 'What latest thing?'

'Well, there was that business last month when he gave out the wrong prescription and nearly killed a patient, and some time ago he blocked a proposed new wing for less serious patients – too much money, he argued, and he persuaded others to vote against it. That created even more bad feeling towards him.'

'Yes, I know about all that,' Alice said impatiently. 'I thought you meant something more recent.'

Nurse Beatty leaned forward. 'I did. It has to do with Mike Peterson. Apparently some of the other doctors think he was released too soon. There's already been an argument about it.'

The news shocked Alice. 'Why would Dr Carlton send him home if he wasn't ready? It doesn't make sense.'

'It's all to do with these budgets, isn't it?' Peggy chipped in. 'They're always looking to see how they can save money.'

Angered by what she had heard, Alice snapped at her, 'I think you should get back to your work instead of hanging around here listening to things that don't concern you.'

'Oh my, Dr Carlton isn't the only one who's got the grumps,' and with that Peggy flounced off.

Nurse Beatty was surprised by Alice's outburst. 'That was a bit harsh, wasn't it?'

Alice shrugged, then left without saying another word.

'Wonder what's upset *her*?' Dismissing the incident, Nurse Beatty resumed her duties. 'I'll be glad when the night shift arrive and I can get off home.'

Dr Carlton parked his car in the driveway of his home. Clambering out, his gaze was drawn to the large water fountain in the central garden. 'Damn!' he swore. 'Twice I've had the electrician out, and each time his back is turned, the damned thing fizzles out again!'

Opening the back door of the car he leant in to retrieve his briefcase and black bag. He thought he heard something behind him and looked round but could see nothing. He wasn't concerned. This was an isolated house, surrounded by woods and brooks and things that went bump in the night. He was used to it.

He took out his briefcase and bag, kicked the door shut and walked the few paces to the fountain. Placing his things on the ground, he stood for a time looking at the fountain, his face wreathed in pleasure. This rare, expensive piece of art gave him the greatest pleasure. Carved out of stone, with a pool beneath and a tall, elegant mermaid sitting astride a leaping dolphin, it was a magnificent sight.

'Can't trust anybody these days,' he grumbled, leaning over to see where the trouble might lie. 'Cost me an arm and a leg, this did, and still they can't seem to get the lights working as they should.'

He heard the sound again, like a creature moving about in the undergrowth close by. 'Foxes, I shouldn't wonder,' he mused. 'Hunting for some poor helpless creature.'

Rolling up his sleeves, he reached into the water and located the cable. He gave it a twiddle and the lights came on; a twinkling of soft rainbow colours shimmering against the water.

He stepped back to admire the effect, and then swore when they went off yet again. 'Damn and bugger it! Useless thing! I don't know why I ever let her talk me into buying it!' He gazed up at the face of the mermaid. 'You are beautiful though, and you never answer back.'

The sight of the mermaid's face went with him to the grave.

The intruder was on him before he realised. Incredibly strong fingers gripped him behind the neck, and one arm was pinned behind his back. He was thrust face down in the water, his free arm thrashing and flailing, but there was nothing to get hold of, only a fistful of water.

In his dying moments he found the strength to turn his head. Looking up through the sheet of water, his eyes searched out his attacker and widened with astonishment as he recognised the face leering over him. '*You . . .*' The water bubbled into his mouth and it was all over.

In the half-light, the murderer lingered, staring down at that pitiful face. The disturbed water rippled across the dead features, distorting them out of all recognition. But the shocked eyes remained wide open, glazed with disbelief.

The water became still, reflecting the dark, shadowy image of a murderer. But there was no one to see. No one to tell the tale.

The soft echo of laughter filled the air, and then the sound of footsteps leaving.

CHAPTER EIGHT

Luke was deep in the woods when Rosie found him. 'I've been looking everywhere for you.' Now she had found him, relief mellowed her anger. 'Do you realise it's three in the morning? Why didn't you tell me you'd be out until the early hours? I woke up and there was no sign of you anywhere. For all I knew you could have been lying in some ditch with your throat cut.'

Crouched low in the undergrowth, Luke looked at her; in the moonlight his face took on an eerie glow. 'Go home,' he told her. 'I'm not a child.'

'I wish to God you were!' she retaliated. 'I'd have some sort of control over you then.'

'I don't want you here.'

Disturbed by his manner, Rosie grew suspicious. In a quiet, clear voice she demanded, 'What are you up to?'

His low, sinister laugh echoed through the woods. 'I've been killing again.' He leaped up and swung his arm at her before she could move out of the way. When the warm, sticky blood spattered on her neck and face she stumbled back, her horrified stare fixed on the furry creatures swinging from his wrist, their bright, dead eyes staring at her in the moonlight.

'*Now* will you leave me alone?' Luke screamed.

Sickened by the stench of blood on her skin, Rosie turned and fled. With the moonlight already fading, darkness closed around her like a whispery black mantle. Blinded by panic, she crashed through the spinney at the mercy of overhanging branches which flicked and tore at her face and arms.

Through the trees, she could hear his laughter. 'He's gone mad!' she thought. 'This time he really has lost his senses.' Since he had learnt the truth about his father, Luke had changed from the son she knew and loved.

Sometimes she found it hard to cope. If only she had Mike to help her, things could be so different. One day though, one day, in the not too distant future, he would be at her side. She knew that, and it made each day worth the wait.

Behind her, low on the ground like a night predator, Luke worked feverishly. With his fingernails he dug into the soft earth, not satisfied until he had created a deep, round hole. Satisfied, he reached into the rotting trunk where he had stashed his secret and with a devious smile drew out the black leather bag, the sort a doctor might use.

He peeped into the bag to satisfy himself the contents were intact and then peered about to make sure he was not seen before thrusting the bag into the hole. Another cautious glance, then he scraped the earth back into the hole, covering it over with grass and rotting leaves.

Softly laughing, he grabbed up his prey and made his way home.

The camper van was parked some two miles away, through the spinney and over the long meadow. Beside the stream, it nestled, unobserved, beneath the boughs of a weeping willow tree.

Naked inside the van, Rosie was bent at the sink, washing and cursing. She scrubbed at her face until the skin grew red and raw. 'The bastard!' she muttered. 'The rotten little bastard!'

When at last she felt cleansed of the stain of blood, she towelled herself dry and covered her nakedness with a clean nightgown. She brushed her thick, wild auburn hair, twenty-one long, graceful strokes, the same as every night, and then laid down the brush and walked over to the tiny dresser.

Looking in the mirror, she saw a face that was bright with punishment; not so young, and not as pretty as she would have liked, but strong and attractive all the same. 'Will he still want you?' she asked the image. 'When the time comes, will he choose you above all others?'

Since the day she had been forced to leave him at the hospital not a moment, not a breath or a heartbeat had passed without Mike being in her thoughts. 'I should never have left you,' she said to her mirror image as if talking to another person. 'But they would have questioned us, and things might have got all mixed up, the way they do when police get involved. Especially where Luke is concerned.' Her face clouded. 'You see, Luke has been in trouble with the police before.'

Suddenly she smiled, and the smile was incredibly lovely. 'I did promise I'd come back,' she whispered, 'and I will. I'm much closer to you now.' Crossing her arms over her breast, she leaned towards the mirror. 'Can you sense my nearness?' she asked softly. 'Can you, Mike? Do you feel how much I love you?' As she spoke, the tears ran freely down her face.

Suddenly the door was flung open and Luke stood there. 'One for the butcher and one for the pot.' As he spoke he flung the two furry creatures on to the table; blood-stained and lifeless, they landed with a soft, stomach-churning thud, their heads only inches from Rosie's arm. There was a split second of absolute silence before her piercing scream brought him rushing across the room to clamp his hand over her mouth. 'For God's sake! What the hell's wrong with you?'

Fighting him off, Rosie yelled, 'Get them out of here!' Mesmerised, she could not look away from them – the dead, flat eyes staring up at her, reminding her of another time, another pair of eyes.

Looking into her face, Luke knew. 'Ah! The eyes, the way they stare at you. Remind you of

Eddie, do they?' Pushing her aside, he laughed cruelly. 'Now I understand.'

Slowly, Rosie backed away. Flattening herself against the side of the wardrobe, she pleaded with him, 'Take them away ... please, Luke ... take them away.'

The rabbits' heads hung over the edge of the table, crimson blood trickling over their faces and on to the floor. 'Women!' Disgusted by her reaction, Luke stamped his foot over the stain on the rug, snatched up the creatures and returned to the night.

Rosie made no move for a long time. She remained frozen, pressed against the wardrobe, her gaze fixed on the spot where Luke had stamped his foot; the stain was misshapen, like a child's attempt at painting.

Moving forward, she took up two sides of the rug and folded it in on itself. Carefully, she carried it to the door, which Luke had left open, and gingerly tipped the carpet down the steps and watched it roll across the ground. Coming to rest against the foot of the steps, it remained upside down, the stain out of sight, but not out of mind.

Much later, when the skies were lightening, she heard him return.

From her bunk she heard him unlock the door of the camper van. She waited with bated breath while he closed the door and, after a moment, mounted the makeshift ladder which led to his bunk.

There was no sound of water or washing. A creature of nature, Luke always washed in the streams. He had done that since he was a small boy.

Rosie fell into uneasy sleep and woke to the sound of the birds outside her window. Peeping through one eye at the clock, she was astounded to see it was already gone eight.

She scrambled out of bed. 'Luke!' she called. Her sleep had been restless, with scenes of blood and mayhem, and Luke always at the centre. 'Wake up, Luke. It's gone eight!'

Small sounds emitted from his bunk. So he was still there, she thought. These days she never knew where he was, or what he was up to.

Annoyed that the best part of a day was already gone, Rosie washed and dressed, and threw open the curtains. There had been a downpour in the night. The leaves were still dripping, and the grass shone like silk. She lingered for a while, her gaze softening as she gazed on the scene before her.

Mentally shaking herself, she set about cooking breakfast. It wasn't long before the air was filled with the warm aroma of frying bacon and brewing coffee.

'Smells good, Mum.' Pushing aside the heavy curtain that separated the cooking and sleeping areas, Luke strolled in. Hair unkempt and face unshaven, he looked a sorry mess. 'Why didn't you wake me earlier?'

Turning the bacon, Rosie said, 'Who would wake you if I wasn't here?'

He laughed in that irritating way he had. 'I'd have to get myself a woman.'

He was a handsome young man with a strong physique, but it broke her heart to see how he was letting himself go. 'She would need to be a special woman to take you on the way you are,' she retorted.

'Oh? And what's that supposed to mean?'

'You have no pride in yourself any more. You scrape a living by killing and selling rabbits, and you have no purpose in your life. What woman would put up with that?'

'You do.'

'That's because I don't know any better!' She carried the teapot to the table, setting it down with such force that the hot tea spurted from the spout. Returning to the cooker, she collected the frying pan and took it to the table. Holding it over the plates, she dished up the bacon, several rashers for him, two for her. 'There's bread if you want it.' She pointed to the pile of crusty fresh slices. 'But there's no butter. I've run out of money.' She returned the frying pan to the cooker.

He glanced up, surprised. 'I thought you sold your drawing.'

'That was last week. Market folk won't pay big

prices.' Rosie loved to pencil sketch. Nothing too grand, just the quiet things of nature all around her.

'You'll have to do more then, won't you?'

'Don't you tell me what to do.' Lately he was getting too big for his boots. 'Besides, the stall-holders are on to me now. They don't take kindly to outsiders getting space for nothing.'

'What, three paving stones wide, against the rubbish bins? It's hardly a prime site, is it?'

'Prime site or not, they don't like it.' She seated herself at the tiny table and poured herself a mug of tea. 'If I push my luck they'll have me thrown off altogether, then where would I be?' Slapping a rasher of bacon between two slices of bread, she sank her teeth into it.

'You'll think of something, you always do.'

And there the subject ended because, as always at eight thirty in the morning, Rosie switched on the radio for the news.

'Must you?' Luke had no interest in the outside world.

'Can't lose touch, Luke.' Much as she loved the life of a wanderer, Rosie didn't care for total isolation.

Finishing the last of his bacon, Luke got to his feet. 'I wish now I'd never found the damned radio. And don't keep it on too long. It drains the van's battery.'

Rosie licked bacon fat from her fingers. 'Haven't you forgotten something?' she asked sternly.

'No, I hadn't forgotten.' Reluctantly digging into his pocket he threw a handful of coins on to the table. 'That's all I have, but I'll have more by tonight.'

'Oh?' She didn't trust him any more. 'I hope you're not doing anything that could bring trouble.' Trouble seemed to follow them wherever they went and, just like in her dreams, Luke was always at the root of it.

'You worry too much.'

'Luke?' Her voice was soft, making him pause.

'What now?'

'Mike Peterson . . . your father. Do you ever think of him?'

He scowled at her. 'Why should I? He means nothing to me.' Yet he did think of him. Day and night he thought of how as a child he had yearned for a father but he was never there. Somehow it had helped to think it wasn't his father's fault, that he had died before his time. Now he knew different and it ate into him like a canker.

'If anything happened to me, he would be your only family.'

'Never!' His features hardened with contempt.

'Do you hate him so much?'

He smiled that cruel, stony smile that struck at her heart. 'You will never know how much.' Thrusting back the curtain, he returned to the front end of the camper. 'If I'm late home tonight, don't come looking for me!'

Rosie's attention was taken by an interesting item of news. 'Luke! Listen to this!' Springing off her stool, she turned up the volume.

'. . . murdered man was named as Dr Roger Edward Carlton, a respected and accomplished specialist in the treatment of psychological and neurological disorders . . .'

Luke's face appeared round the curtain.

'. . . Colleagues at the Landsmead Institute are said to be shocked at the brutal murder . . .'

Rosie stared at her son. 'Landsmead Institute.' She had seen that sign so many times on her lonely vigil. 'That's where Mike is.'

Chuckling, Luke turned away. 'Perhaps he was the one who murdered him.' He laughed.

'Luke! Come back here!' She needed to talk.

'It's no wonder I'm a misfit,' Luke called over his shoulder, 'when I've got *his* bad blood running through me!'

To her horror, Rosie heard the newsreader go on to say that police were investigating the murder of Dr Carlton. There was mention of another murder in the area three years ago . . . Eddie Johnson's killer was still at large.

Rosie ran out of the camper and soon caught up with Luke. Grabbing him by the arm, she swung him round. 'I'm frightened. They might get round to thinking it's the same person who killed *Eddie*.'

'Why would they?' His remark gave nothing away but his nervous expression told Rosie he was troubled by the news. 'Besides, we're a good eighty miles from there.'

'I need to ask you this, Luke . . .' she said hesitantly.

'No more questions!'

'The truth, Luke. Did you go after that doctor?'

He laughed out loud. 'What in God's name makes you think that?'

'I don't know, but you frighten me, Luke. You've changed.'

He shook her off. 'I wonder why!' When he strode off, she made no attempt to stop him.

'Take care, Luke,' she called after him. 'I might follow you and find out what you're up to.'

Deeply troubled, he didn't answer.

CHAPTER NINE

Mike stepped back to admire his handiwork. 'There!' Reaching out, he pulled Susie to his side. 'What do you think of that?'

Susie looked wide-eyed at the Christmas tree; almost filling the hallway, it was six feet tall, bedecked with ribbons and strung with fairy lights. Every branch was hung deep with chocolate novelties and pretty decorations. 'Oh, Daddy! It's the biggest Christmas tree I've ever seen!'

Laughing and dancing, Susie went to fetch Jack who was sulking in the kitchen. 'Come and see!' she urged, and he did, not willingly but because Susie had asked him. All the time their father was away, Jack had taken it on himself to watch out for her, and now he loved her with a fierce, protective passion.

Encouraged, Mike waited for him to get close before asking, 'Would you like to switch the lights on, son?'

'I don't care.' The friction between these two had not lessened.

'Yes! Go on, Jack, light the tree!' urged Susie.

Mike held out the hand-control. 'It's all yours.'

He felt as though he was talking to a stranger. However hard he tried, he could not seem to bridge the deep rift between them.

Hesitating at first, Jack took the control.

'Go on, Jack,' Susie cried. 'I want to see.'

For Susie's sake, he threw the switch, and the lights came on, bright and colourful like a rainbow.

'Ohh!' Clapping her hands to her face, Susie gazed up at the lights. 'It's like fairyland,' she said, and even Jack had to smile.

While Susie and Jack gazed at the tree, Mike watched his son. Though he put on a tough, uncaring front and tried to appear older than his eight years, Mike knew he was desperately insecure. If only he would talk about that night, things would be all right, he thought, but so far Jack had deliberately avoided the subject. If Mike walked into a room, Jack walked out. On the rare occasions when Kerry managed to get everyone round the table at the same time for the evening meal, Mike made every effort to draw Jack into family conversation, but his efforts were in vain. As well as remaining silent, Jack avoided all eye contact with him. Mike had decided that it would have to be Jack who made the first move, and for both their sakes, he prayed it would be soon.

Julie's impatient voice broke the moment. 'Come on, you two. It's time we were off.'

'Look, Grandma!' Susie's excitement tempered Julie's impatience. 'Daddy's made the tree shine.'

'It looks lovely,' Julie said grudgingly. 'But we have to be going now or we'll miss the bus into Doncaster.'

Jack protested as usual. 'I don't want to go to Doncaster.'

As always, Susie used her girlish wiles. 'Please, Jack. We're going to buy Christmas presents. If you don't go, I'm not going either, and I really want to go.'

It did the trick.

Kerry fussed over them, buttoning up their coats, and making certain they had on woolly hats and gloves. 'The forecast is snow before the day's over,' she told them. 'You're to stay close to Grandma. It's Saturday and with Christmas only a week away, it's bound to be very crowded. Hold Jack's hand the whole time, Susie, and do exactly what Grandma says.' She gave them each a kiss, though Jack was not very responsive. 'I shall expect you both to be good as gold.'

Jack began to grow excited at the prospect of going on a bus all the way into Doncaster. 'I want an Action Man,' he declared.

'We're getting presents for Mummy and Daddy, and that's all,' said Julie, which promptly wiped the grin off his face.

With his arm round Kerry, Mike watched them leave. 'I wish Jack would confide in me,' he said. 'I feel I've let him down somehow.'

'He resented you being away all that time,' she answered. 'He was too young to understand. And don't forget, in a different way he, too, was scarred by the ordeal you both suffered. He'll get over it, just as you have, but it takes time.'

Mike gave her his lazy smile. 'You think I'm over it, do you?' If only she knew, he thought.

Kerry answered quietly, 'You must be, or they would have kept you in the hospital.'

'That's right,' he said thoughtfully. 'They would, but they didn't, so everything must be OK.' Three precious years of his life had been wasted, he thought bitterly, and all because no one believed him. If Jack had told them what had happened, the things he had seen that night, they would have had to believe him. But Jack had let the doctors think he had lost his mind. In the end he'd had no choice but to outwit them.

'Except for Jack.'

'What did you say?' With an effort Mike dragged himself back from his private nightmare. He stared at Kerry.

'You just said everything was OK, and I simply said except for Jack, the way he won't let you get near.'

'Oh, Kerry, if only he would talk to me about it.' Sadness clouded his face. 'Sometimes I think he's afraid of me.'

Kerry shook her head. 'Not afraid,' she assured him. 'Jack is wary, that's all.'

'What about you?' His dark eyes enveloped her. 'Are you wary too?'

'Don't be silly.' She didn't like it when he

looked at her in that probing, intimate way. The eyes were windows to the soul, isn't that what someone once said? Mike's eyes were beautiful, but they were also dark and fathomless, a place of untold secrets.

'I do love you,' he murmured, brushing her face with his lips. 'I would never do anything to hurt you, you know that, don't you?' His hand lovingly cupped her breast.

Gently, she pushed him away. 'I'm not ready yet,' she said apologetically. 'I need a little more time.'

'Like Jack,' he sighed. 'I can wait . . . if I have to.'

'We'd better go.'

'You don't have to come. I can go myself. That is, if you trust me with your car.' She had wounded him yet again, and it had struck deep.

'You can take the car any time you like,' she said quickly. 'But I would like to come along. I thought you wanted my ideas too.'

'Only if you really want to.'

'I've said so, haven't I?'

'Good. Then let's go.'

Together they left the house and while Mike brought the car from the garage, Kerry stood in the porch, her coat collar turned up against the biting wind, and a prayer on her lips. 'I want to love him. I so much want it to be the way it was before.' She watched him walking across the drive, a tall, handsome man whom any woman would be proud to call husband. 'What's wrong with me?' she murmured. 'I just can't open up to him. It's as if something is keeping us apart – keeping him and Jack apart too. And it frightens me.'

'Your carriage awaits, m'lady.' Smiling, Mike opened the car door and waited for her to climb in. 'Even with a cold, red nose, you look beautiful,' he said, and everything was so natural she thought the fault must lie with her – and the feelings she still felt for Steve.

As they drove to his old offices, Mike could not hide his excitement. 'I need to get working again,' he told her. 'Too much time has been lost already.' More than anything, he needed to focus his mind on practical matters. That way, he might be able to forget the bad things.

The premises where Mike had built his business were only ten minutes' drive from home. Situated near the harbour of West Bay, they consisted of a yard and a small warehouse. Mike had taken out a long lease on the building and, thanks to Kerry, the lease had been kept going while he was away.

He parked the car outside the office building. In the cold, hard light of day, it looked a bleak place. The overhead sign was rusting, the painted words barely legible: 'Peterson Hire Company. Domestic and Commercial Vehicles. Best terms. Long or Short Hire.'

'Look at that!' Mike pointed through the security mesh at a solitary sorry-looking van parked in the corner of the rear yard. 'All it needs is a new engine, a lick of paint, and I'm on my way.'

Kerry smiled. 'You'll get the business off the ground,' she told him as they walked to the front door.

'You bet I will,' he vowed. Sliding his arm round her shoulders he drew her close. 'Especially with you on my team.'

The look on his face told her how much she meant to him and it made her feel good. Maybe it would be all right after all, she thought. Maybe, once his business was up and running, things would get back to normal – whatever 'normal' was.

The lock on the door had seized up. After three attempts at opening it, Mike abandoned his efforts. 'Stay where you are,' he told Kerry. 'I'll see if there's an easier way in through the back.'

There wasn't; the back lock, too, had rusted and jammed.

Kerry heard the sound of breaking glass and ran round to check on him. Mike had a brick in his hand. 'Stay back!' he called out. One more blow against the surprisingly tough glass in the back door and he could reach in. It was a long stretch down to the interior lock.

'Be careful!' Kerry could see him straining to reach, his arm in up to the shoulder and his whole body pressed tight against the door.

She heard a click as the lock opened. But as he

moved his arm out, there was another sound, a quick, sharp crack as the large remnant of glass slid out of its socket.

Realising the danger he was in, Mike swiftly drew his arm away. The glass shattered to the ground. 'Whew! That was close.' Shaking bits of broken glass from the top of his shoes, he opened the door. 'I'll go first,' he told Kerry. 'Be careful of the glass though.'

When Kerry didn't answer, he glanced at her and was astonished to see her leaning against the wall white-faced and trembling. 'It could have sliced your arm in two,' she said faintly. 'You could have lost your fingers . . . if you hadn't got your arm out in time . . .' She bowed her head. 'I'm sorry. It scared me, that's all.'

He went to her. 'Look,' he spread his hands, 'eight fingers, two thumbs. All present and correct.'

She smiled up at him. 'I'm glad,' she said, and her genuine concern meant more to him than she could ever know.

They went inside. 'Smells musty,' he commented, and Kerry agreed.

'I haven't been anywhere near the place for at least twelve months,' she confessed. 'Some man offered to rent it but then he backed out and I never bothered after that.'

'It's just as well,' Mike told her. 'Renting out is more trouble than it's worth. You can never get the buggers out when you want the place back, and besides, I've got a feeling there's something in the lease about that.'

Proud and excited, he toured the rooms, making notes and calculating how much it would cost to get the place straight and equipped for business.

'There's money in the bank, thanks to my catering business,' Kerry told him. 'Not a lot, but you should be able to buy at least a couple of decent vehicles.'

'What would I do without you?' he said gratefully, and the smiles they exchanged seemed to mark a new beginning.

'We could rip out this old reception area,' Kerry suggested. 'It's too closed in. You want to project space and light, and a sense of prosperity.'

He grinned. 'With two vehicles?'

'Two vehicles to *start* with,' she said. 'Once you get going, there'll be no stopping you.'

'You really do believe in me, don't you?' he said. 'I didn't expect that.'

'Oh?' She wiped her fingers along the desk, trying not to appear embarrassed. 'What did you expect?' She clapped her hands together and a flurry of dust rose like a mushroom before her, making her cough.

'I'm not sure.' He ran his hands through his hair, like he always did when he was unsure of himself. 'Maybe I don't expect you to trust me.' She shouldn't, he thought. That's why he was wary of Julie, because she saw through him, and she knew. No one should trust him ever again.

Misinterpreting him, Kerry said, 'Why ever not? You were always a good businessman. How do you think I managed to do so well with the catering enterprise?'

The wickedness went from his mind as quickly as it had wormed its way in. 'Because you have a good head on your shoulders,' he answered with conviction, 'and because, thanks to me, you were left with a family to fend for.'

'Thanks to you, yes, Mike, because over the years you taught me everything you knew about running a business. It's true you left me with a family to fend for, but it wasn't your fault. You were ill.'

'Crazy in the head, isn't that what you mean?' Anger welled up in him, but he pushed it down.

Kerry shook her head. 'No, that *isn't* what I meant. You were *ill*. We are none of us immune from illness, Mike.'

In the shaft of light that filtered through the dusty windowpane, she looked small, and sad, and so vulnerable, the sight of her made him ache with longing. He went across to her. 'When I was in that hospital, I thought of you every minute of every day. I dreamed about you, and remembered all the wonderful times we had together.'

'Me too,' she murmured. And it was no lie.

He smiled. 'Really?'

'Yes. Really.' During those dark days, he was

always in her mind. Not always in favour, but in her thoughts all the same. Even when she was making love with Steve, her emotions were tainted with other, more uncomfortable feelings – shame, guilt and revenge all mingled together.

His dark eyes grew pained. 'If I thought all that was gone for ever, there would be no point in going on.'

Feeling herself melting beneath those wonderful eyes, she moved away. 'We'd better press on or the kids will be back before we are.'

Mike was aware she had deliberately changed the subject, and once again he suppressed his anger. 'You're right.' He took up his pen and notebook. 'Give me a minute or two,' he said, and resumed his note-taking. 'The whole place needs rewiring,' he muttered. 'I reckon the freeholder should pay towards that.' He remembered the broken window and made another entry in the notebook. 'I'll tell him vandals broke the window, so he can pay for that too.'

'What about new doors?'

'Down to me, I'm afraid. And the decorating, new floor coverings . . . it won't be cheap.'

'Nothing ever is.'

'I don't really want to touch your money. I'll get a job. Put this enterprise on hold for a while.'

Kerry would not hear of it. 'When I was a lady of leisure and you were working, was the money you earned *your* money?'

'No, it was *our* money. We always shared, you know that.'

'Right. So you'll take the money I've saved and use it to set yourself up.'

He looked at her. 'If you're sure that's what you want.'

'I am.'

'I'll put back every penny.'

'That's settled then. Are we done here? Can we go and choose the children's Christmas presents now?'

'Two more minutes, then we're out the door.' He noticed a tattered old cardboard box tucked behind his desk. 'What's this?' Curious, he opened it up, and gasped with astonishment. 'Good God! I wondered where this had got to.' Swinging round he called Kerry. 'You'll never believe what I've found. It's been hidden under here the whole time.' Carefully, he lifted the box and placed it on the desk top. 'I wonder if the battery still works. Hidden behind the desk – can you credit it?' He was like a child with a toy.

'What is it?' Kerry asked, and then smiled as soft music filled the air.

Mike laughed for joy. 'It takes me back, I can tell you,' he said, patting the battered brown radio lovingly.

Kerry recalled the first time they had heard it. 'Peacock's market, wasn't it?' she chuckled. 'The auctioneer played it over the tannoy and we put in a bid for it – two pounds, if I remember right.'

'Three,' he corrected her. 'That bald-headed feller with the lion-head walking stick kept pushing up the price.'

Caught up in the mood, she threw back her head and laughed aloud. 'I remember! When it was knocked down to us, he swore like an old trooper, and some old dear hit him over the head with her umbrella.' She listened to the music. '10cc,' she murmured, swaying to the rhythm, her voice singing along. ' "I'm not in love . . . so don't forget it . . . it's just a silly phase I'm going through . . ." ' It was one of her old-time favourites.

When Mike slid his arm round her waist and began dancing her across the floor, she moved with him. It was like old times, when they were foolishly young and so in love, and nothing else in the whole world mattered. He pulled her closer, drifting to the music and thinking how good it was to feel her in his arms at last. 'God, you're so lovely.'

Looking up into those smouldering eyes, she felt herself weakening. His hands began to move over her body. She didn't have the strength or desire to resist, and why should she? He was her husband, after all.

Gently he drew her down.

Carried along by the mood of the moment, they made love there, on the cold, hard floor, with soft music washing over them and only the heat from their bodies to keep them warm. It was a wonderful, sensuous experience; she opened herself to him, and he took her greedily, tenderly, like he used to.

Afterwards, they were like strangers, not knowing what to say; hardly able to look each other in the eye. 'You don't regret it, do you?' Mike's love for her was stronger than ever.

She was confused, her loyalty split . . . Mike . . . Steve. Which one did she really want? 'No,' she said. 'I don't regret it.'

Yet he was still afraid. Afraid of her; afraid of Jack. Afraid of what lurked out there, in the night, wanting to spoil it all.

Outside, the watching figure crept stealthily away. It had seen too much for its own peace of mind.

It was half past four in the afternoon when Kerry and Mike arrived home. The lights were on and through the window they could see Julie and the children laying newly wrapped presents beneath the tree. 'Oh!' Kerry was disappointed. 'I wanted to get home before they did.'

'It's OK.' Mike took the presents. 'You go in. I'll shoot upstairs with these.'

Mike opened the door and went straight up, while Kerry took off her coat and made her way into the kitchen.

Upstairs, Mike quickly hid the presents in the wardrobe. That done, he would have made his way down but on opening the door he could hear the four of them talking and laughing together.

They didn't need him, he thought, not when they had each other.

Softly closing the door, he sat on the bed, feeling alone and dejected. He had felt at odds with them all ever since coming home but he had never felt as much like an outsider as he did right now.

Today had been wonderful, and yet there was something not quite right. He looked round the room. Nothing had changed. It was all exactly as he remembered, and yet it was like the room of someone he had never known.

He looked again, trying to belong, needing to know that he was back among those who loved and needed him. His anxious gaze drew on these familiar surroundings; the pine dresser littered with Kerry's things – he had bought that for her a week before their wedding day. And the pine bed, with its beautifully embroidered cover. She had persuaded him that a pine dresser needed a pine bed. 'It won't look right otherwise,' she pleaded. They couldn't afford it, but he went ahead and bought it anyway, just to please her. She could always twist him round her little finger.

It was such a beautiful room, he thought. Kerry's room. He smiled. 'In hospital, whenever I thought of her, I would always picture her here, in this room, at the dressing table brushing her hair, or gazing out of the window at the garden.' The smile fell from his face and his eyes grew sad. 'Sometimes I wonder if I'll ever belong here again.' There was a kind of undercurrent whenever he was around; suspicion and fear, that's what it was, and he was the cause of it. Yet he had done nothing wrong and he was not a threat. He didn't want to take over, or belittle what Kerry had achieved. Through what must have been a terrible time for her, Kerry had become independent and he respected that. He knew he had to establish his proper place here, but that would take a long time.

'There are things I have to come to terms with before I can pick up all the pieces,' he mused. 'What Kerry and I have now is too delicate. I can't risk losing it by confiding in her. She wouldn't understand. I hardly understand it myself.' He knew he must confront the strange phenomenon that had changed him for ever alone. He pushed it to the back of his mind and went downstairs.

The evening was enjoyable. Julie helped Kerry lay out the tea and everyone sat down. The children talked about their day with excitement. 'Grandma took us to see the big Christmas tree and there were goblins and Father Christmas and everything!' Susie told them. Kerry said how she and Mike had sung along with the carolers in Bridport, and how the square was filled with people, all singing along to the sound of the brass band. Susie and Jack had an argument about who should have the last fairy cake, and Kerry told a joke that made them all laugh.

Mike was happy with his family all round him, and he never stopped smiling – except when he caught Julie regarding him in that penetrating way she had. She feared him, he knew that. She didn't know it but he feared her too.

At nine o'clock Kerry prepared the children for bed. When they protested as they always did, she chastised them with a warning. 'Don't push your luck, not if you want to stay up late on Christmas Day.'

Susie hugged Mike. 'Will you take me to the park tomorrow?' she begged. 'It's holiday and I've got two whole weeks off school.'

'I might.' He held her close. 'We'll see, sweetheart.'

Julie's voice cut across their conversation. 'Have you forgotten, Susie? You and I were going on the bus to West Bay, to see the boats in the harbour.' She looked disappointed. 'You did promise.'

Susie seemed surprised. She couldn't remember promising but it sounded like a nice treat. 'Oh, all right then.' Addressing Mike, she said, 'I'm sorry, Daddy. I didn't know.'

'It's all right,' he teased. 'That's the way with beautiful young women. You offer to take them out, then find they have a prior engagement.'

Surprisingly, Jack had something to say. 'I'd much rather go to the harbour than walk in the park,' he muttered, casting a glance Mike's way, and before Mike could answer, he was out of the room and on his way up the stairs.

Having cunningly secured Susie's company tomorrow, Julie bade everyone goodnight.

A few minutes later, Kerry followed the children upstairs. After making certain they were safely tucked up in bed, she made her way to her mother's room. Normally she would tap on the door before going in, but not tonight, because tonight she wanted answers.

Julie was putting curlers in her hair. One glance at Kerry's face and she knew she was in the wrong again. 'She *did* promise to come with me to West Bay,' she said defensively.

'You're lying! Why, Mother? You know Mike is trying desperately to get his life together. It's important for him to gain the children's confidence, you know that.'

Casually scooping cream out of a jar, Julie began to spread it over her youthful skin.

'Mother!' Banging her fist on the dressing table, Kerry demanded an answer. 'I asked you why?'

Julie wiped her hands on a pink tissue. She looked her daughter in the eye. 'Because I don't trust him, that's why.'

Flushed with anger, Kerry took her mother by the shoulders and swung her round on the stool, her face so close to her mother's she could see smears of cream on her skin. 'What the hell did you think he was going to do with her? He idolises that child. There is no way he would let anything bad happen to her.'

'If anything bad happened to her, it would be Mike who caused it,' Julie said calmly.

Reeling back as though from a slap in the face, Kerry was momentarily speechless. Behind her shock was the knowledge of her own fleeting suspicion of Mike.

'Why don't you admit it?' Julie insisted. 'You don't trust him any more than I do. You know he should never have been let out of that hospital.'

The only thing Kerry knew at that moment was that if her life was ever to have any meaning again, she must make a stand. Either she believed in Mike, or she listened to her mother who seemed determined to tear the family apart.

'Where did you go this afternoon, Kerry?' her mother asked. 'Where did he take you?'

'None of your damned business!' Her face grew hot as she recalled how she and Mike had made love on the cold floor.

Guessing she had struck a raw nerve, Julie sighed. 'Dear God. Can't you see what he's trying to do? Don't you understand what's happening here?' Relentless now, she went on, 'I wish I knew what really happened on that night.'

'I don't want to hear this kind of talk.' Kerry pressed her hands over her ears.

Julie lowered her voice. 'What about Jack? That poor boy hasn't had one restful night since it happened. What I want to know is, what did Mike do to him? What did he tell Jack to make him so terrified?' She took hold of Kerry's hand.

'He's bad,' she whispered. 'There's something evil about him, and I can't help being afraid for you and the children.'

'I think you'd better go home.' Julie's strange comments were making her nervous.

Julie gasped. 'What did you say?'

'I want you to leave.'

'You're asking me to *leave*? You want me to desert you and the children when you need me most?' Tears rose, and her voice faltered. 'I'm sorry if I frighten you when I say these things about Mike. I know I shouldn't. Please, Kerry, don't make me go. I have to be near you and the children.'

'Why?'

Julie was a crafty soul and knew how to use her wiles. 'I'm lonely, that's why. I can't stand to be on my own. Let me stay, for a while longer at least. Please?' The tears began to flow and Kerry was mortified. Love and hatred, where did she draw the line? 'Please, Kerry?'

Against her better instincts, Kerry relented. 'All right, Mum, but only if there's no more talk of Mike being evil. And no more coming between him and the kids. If you can't agree to that, then you'd better pack your bags right now.'

Julie nodded.

Convinced that her mother had learned her lesson, Kerry planted a kiss on her forehead. 'Goodnight, Mum.'

'Is it all right to take Susie to the harbour

tomorrow?' Feigning humility, Julie gave a half-smile. 'I won't take her if you don't want me to.'

'All right, but I mean it, don't ever try that trick again.'

'No. Goodnight, dear.'

'Goodnight.' Emotionally drained, Kerry returned downstairs.

Mike was watching television, but switched it off when she came in. 'Kids all right, are they?' Getting to his feet he came towards her.

'They're asleep by now, I shouldn't wonder.' Gratefully, she sank into the nearest chair. 'Won't be long before I'm off to bed myself.'

'Fancy a cup of hot chocolate?' He always used to make her a hot drink last thing at night.

She shook her head. 'No. I'm too tired.'

He stood over her, hands in pockets, like a naughty boy. 'About today . . .'

'Don't make too much of it, Mike. Like I said, I'm not ready to make a full commitment just yet.'

'Will you *ever* be?' He was patient, but not a saint.

'I hope so.'

'For the children's sake, or ours?'

She looked up at him. 'It's not that I don't love you.'

'But?' He had a feeling she had been talking to Julie.

'I'm not sure, Mike. I want it to be right. I want it to be like it used to be.'

'It can't ever be like that again. Too much water under the bridge and all that.' Seating himself opposite her, he smiled into her pretty eyes. 'Let's not fool ourselves. I've changed, and so have you. But I still love you just as much as I ever did, and I value our marriage all the more because I thought it was lost to me.'

'You just have to give me time, that's all I need. Time to readjust.'

'You're sure there's no one else?'

Kerry shook her head. 'No one else.'

'Truth?'

She giggled. Now and then she saw glimpses of the old, mischievous Mike and it pleased her. 'Truth.'

In a more serious tone, he asked, 'Just now, when you went upstairs, did your mother waylay you?'

'Why would she do that?'

'Did she tell you how evil I was, and how she was afraid for you and the children?'

'Mother's always had a strange attitude, you should know that.'

'I know she hates me.'

'She's not married to you. I am.'

'Thank God for that.'

'Don't be wicked.'

'Can I be wicked with you tonight?'

'Not tonight.'

'Do you want me to move into the spare bedroom?' He felt so insecure.

'Don't be silly. I hope things never get that bad.'

'We won't let them.'

Kerry got up and went to the fire where she warmed her hands, her face turned away from him as she remarked shyly, 'It was good, Mike. You and me, today.'

'So there's hope?' Coming to stand beside her, he thought how childlike she looked in the soft glow of the flames.

'Yes,' she agreed. 'There's always hope.'

'Take your time. I won't harass you.'

'I know you won't.' If she knew anything, it was that Mike would respect her feelings. 'I'm going up now,' she told him. 'I really am tired.'

'I'll be up later,' he said. 'Don't worry, I won't wake you. I'll be as quiet as a mouse.'

'Be as noisy as you like,' she laughed. 'The way I feel, it would take a truck through the wall to wake me.'

A fond, fleeting kiss and she left him there, staring into the flames and wondering if it would all come right between the two of them. 'Be patient,' he told himself. 'However much she might deny it, she *does* have a lover.' His features hardened. In the firelight the dark eyes glittered. 'One of you will win,' he muttered, 'and one of you will lose.'

He did not intend to be the loser.

It was midnight when he turned out the lights

and went upstairs. As he passed Jack's room, he heard crying. Gingerly he turned the door knob and peeked in.

The room was lit by only the small bulb in the bedside lamp. In the halo of light he could see Jack lying in bed, eyes closed and obviously asleep. He was disturbed, writhing about and thrashing his arms, as if trying to fend off some attacker. 'No! Leave me alone!' he sobbed. 'Get away! *Get away from me!*'

Mike hurried to the bed, his hands reaching out to still Jack. 'Ssh! I'm here,' he whispered soothingly. 'You're having a bad dream. No one's going to hurt you.'

Jack's eyes jerked open. On seeing it was Mike, he opened his mouth to scream, but Mike quietened him. 'I'll go now if you want me to,' he said. 'I was just passing and I heard you cry out.'

It hurt him to look at his son and see the fear in that small, white face. Covered in a film of sweat, the face was twitching. 'I want you to go away.' Jack's wide, stark eyes betrayed a terror that no child should experience.

'All right, I'm going now. Try and sleep.' He wanted to take the boy in his arms and comfort him, but he knew if he did it would only frighten him more.

When he got to the door, a small, trembling voice made him pause. 'I'm sorry I lied.'

Mike looked back. 'It's all right, son.'

'I suppose you want to kill me.'

Shocked, Mike went to him. 'Good God, no! What makes you think that?'

'I dreamed you chased me. You wanted to hurt me . . . because I lied.'

'I would never hurt you. But tell me, why did you lie?' Encouraged by their conversation, Mike sat on the edge of the bed, his dark eyes fixed on that pathetic little face.

Silence.

'Were you afraid they might think you were crazy and lock you away?'

Sullenness.

'I'm sorry I was away for such a long time, Jack, but if you had told them the truth, I might never have been made to leave you.'

'I won't tell!' Sliding under the covers, only his big, frightened eyes could be seen peeping over the top.

'There's no use in telling now,' Mike said. 'I'm home and it's over. You don't have to worry.'

The boy stared at him. 'Won't I ever need to tell . . . about when the skies ate them up and they never came back?'

Mike shook his head. 'Not if you don't want to.'

'And you're not angry?' The small face visibly relaxed.

'No, I'm not angry. It doesn't matter what the others think, does it, Jack?'

'No.'

'We know what we saw, and they don't. So it might be better if we make it our little secret. What do you think?'

'I'd like that.'

'And do you believe I don't want to hurt you?'

Silence.

'Jack! You do believe that, don't you?'

'In my dream you wanted to hurt me.'

'That was just a dream.' Mike stood up. 'I have dreams too,' he confessed. 'But dreams can't hurt you.' Making Jack comfortable, he asked, 'Would you like me to leave the big light on?'

'No.'

'Goodnight then, son.'

'Goodnight. Daddy?'

'Yes, son?'

'Where did they go?'

'I don't know.'

'Will they ever come back?'

'I don't know that either.' The memory flitted across his mind, making him tremble. 'Go to sleep now, and remember, it's our secret.'

Softly, he closed the door and glanced towards the main bedroom at the other end of the landing. 'Can't go in yet,' he murmured. 'There's no tiredness in me.' To lie alongside Kerry, wanting and not having, was a torment he did not enjoy.

Quietly he went downstairs, through the kitchen, then outside, where he lit a cigarette and forgave himself for this lapse. 'I'll give them up tomorrow.' He drew deeply. Then he blew out the smoke in a succession of perfectly shaped hollows. 'Or maybe I won't give them up at all,' he smiled. This was the first cigarette he had smoked since leaving the hospital. He knew it would not be the last.

The boy's confession had woken bad feelings in him. That was when he found it most difficult to cope, when the bad feelings threatened to overwhelm him.

Agitated, he walked to the garden bench and sat down. The cold dampness made him gasp. He drew again on the cigarette, his gaze lifted to the skies – heavy with the promise of snow. It was a beautiful evening all the same. Beneath his feet rotting leaves made a crisp, uneven carpet, and all around the air was curiously quiet, hung with the dry, musty smell that preceded the dawn.

He began to relax, then stiffened when he heard a noise from the undergrowth. Curiosity rippled through him. Then a sense of fear.

He laughed softly. 'You're safe enough here,' he told himself.

But his instincts told him otherwise.

He grew chilly and made his way back to the house where he planned to enjoy a whisky and a hot bath before going to bed.

Outside the back door, he took his last drag of the cigarette. Bending to stub it out in a flower pot, he suddenly felt a shiver run through his blood. *'Mike . . . I'm here . . .'* The eerie whisper washed by him like a gentle breeze. *'Don't be afraid.'*

Shocked, he swung round, burning his fingers on the tip of the cigarette. 'Who's there?' Peering into the darkness he thought he saw a shadow.

'It's only me.'

Deeply shaken, Mike took a step forward. 'Come out where I can see you!' He had always suspected they might be watching him, and now he knew.

The silence thickened.

'Don't hide from me.' Fear trembled through him.

'I must go now.'

The rustle of leaves underfoot brought his attention to the darkest corner of the garden. 'No! Don't go,' he pleaded. 'We should talk.' Softly, so as not to frighten, he approached. 'Why are you here? What do you want from me?'

There was no answer. Whoever it was had fled into the spinney.

Cautiously at first, Mike followed.

It was dark in the spinney, but he knew every track, every hide-out; before he was put away, he and the children used to play the hiding game in these woods. A person could disappear in here and never be found. 'Don't run away,' he whispered. 'Tell me what you want with me.'

Aware that someone was very near, he stood perfectly still, listening so intently he could hear his own heart beating.

The silence was tangible, like the night. All around him the trees formed a guard of keepers, a stark reminder of the prison he had lived in for the past three years.

Panic took hold, closing his throat so he could hardly breathe. Gasping for air, he wanted to run out of the darkness and into the open, but he dared not move; could not. Trapped by his own fears, he stood transfixed, frantic eyes peering into the darkness.

It seemed an age before he heard a sound, the softest, quickest sound, only an arm's reach away – and there it was! A dark, shapeless thing, making good its escape. 'No! Wait!' Excited now, he pursued it through the woods and along the lake, his feet slipping and sliding as he ran over the soft, muddy ground. There was a thrilling moment when he thought he could reach out and take hold of his tormentor, but then he was alone, lost in the dark, with only moonlight on the water to guide him home.

When he got back to the kitchen, he found Kerry waiting for him. 'I woke up and you weren't there.' She eyed him with suspicion. 'I wondered where you'd gone.' Her curious gaze went from the jagged tears on his shirt to the mud on his shoes. 'What happened to you?' Fear marbled her voice.

'There was ... *something* out there, in the garden.' Going to the sink he washed the sweat from his hands and face. 'I went after it.'

'What was it?'

Drying himself, Mike shrugged. 'I don't know. I didn't get close enough to see.' He didn't want to talk about it.

'Mike?'

He peered at her over the towel. 'Yes?'

'Are you . . . all right?' She could hardly look him in the eye.

He laughed softly. 'You mean, am I going crazy again? Did I just imagine it?' Murderous anger fired through him.

'No. I meant exactly what I said, are you all right?'

'I'm fine,' he said.

She smiled at him. 'Come to bed.' Her fingers crept into his, her lips parting sensuously as she reached up to kiss him. 'I missed you.'

His grin was sheer delight. 'You did?'

She nodded, eyes smiling. 'Yes,' she murmured. 'I did.'

He saw the desire in her eyes and was thrilled. 'Are you sure about this?'

'No.' Tantalisingly, she licked his lips. 'I'm sure I'll regret it in the morning.'

Her answer made him smile. 'I hope not,' he murmured. This was a moment to cherish, he thought. Who knows? There may never come another. 'I love you.' Ever so tenderly, he kissed her.

'I know you do,' she answered softly. That was why she had to give their marriage every chance.

That was why she tried so hard to put Steve out of her heart. It wasn't easy, and in the end she might not be able to give him up. But, for now, she needed loving, and Mike was here, warm and willing.

Hand in hand they went upstairs.

From her room, Julie heard them making love. Long after they had grown silent she lay awake. 'I saw you,' she whispered, 'out there, calling to the night like the madman you are.' Her eyes glittered with hatred. 'You may be worming your way into *her* affections, but I know you, Mike Peterson. I'm watching your every move.'

Sleepy now, she snuggled beneath the bedclothes. 'I promise you,' her gaze shifted to the door, *'before I let you hurt this family, I'll see you in hell!'*

The nurses' residence was not too far away from the hospital. A proud, worn remnant from Victorian times, it nestled behind a high wall off the main street.

At this late hour, there were few lights burning in the tall, narrow windows. Late-shift nurses were working, and the ones who had already delivered a full shift were too bone-tired to stay up late, so they went to bed and slept the sleep of the righteous.

The breeze had gathered in strength until now

it blew leaves and bracken before it. And one lone figure.

The figure was that of Nurse Alice Henshaw. She seemed greatly agitated as she rushed in through the main entrance. Hurrying up the stairs, she hoped no one would see her come home so late.

But she was out of luck. Her house-mate, Sally Jenkins, was tucked up on the settee with a bag of sweets and a book; the television was on low, so she didn't hear Alice come in. But she saw her as she tried to sneak into the kitchen. 'Oh, Alice, there you are!'

Alice swung round. 'Sally!' Lying came easily. 'I didn't see you there.'

Sally followed her into the kitchen. 'You're out late, aren't you?'

Alice inwardly groaned, though her ready smile did not betray her feelings. 'Sorry. I didn't mean to disturb you.' She wasn't in the mood for conversation.

Sally noticed how unkempt Alice was, and her shoes were covered in mud. 'Look at you,' she laughed. 'I was about to ask if you'd had a good time but now I can see you have. What did he do, roll you over in the mud? Kinky, was it?' She laughed so much she almost choked on a barley twist.

Alice played along. 'No, it wasn't kinky,' she answered. 'Just . . . different.' She giggled wickedly, hoping Sally would leave her alone.

'Sounds interesting.' Heaving herself on to a stool, Sally winked. 'Want to tell me about it?'

'No, I don't. So bugger off and let me get cleaned up.'

'Is it anybody I know?' Curiosity was her middle name.

'No. Now do as I ask, and bugger off.'

Realising she was not wanted, Sally clambered off the stool. 'See you in the morning,' she sighed resignedly, 'when you're in a better mood.'

When Sally had gone, Alice made her way upstairs where she bathed and got ready for bed. But she was too agitated for sleep.

Restless as a cat, she walked back and forth, her bare feet padding the carpet and her flimsy nightgown billowing as she walked. Her hair was washed and shining, and her pretty eyes bright from the evening's excitement. Her pale skin was prickled by the cold air that came in through the window, yet she made no attempt to close it. She didn't seem to mind, didn't seem to feel it. What she felt was a sense of loss, and it was eating her alive.

Suddenly she stopped pacing and stood with her back to the wardrobe, her stricken eyes staring across the room at a small framed photograph beside her bed. It was a group picture, of all the nurses and patients at last year's Christmas party. The original picture was hanging in the dayroom at the hospital, alongside all the others taken over the years. Alice had wanted a copy of this one, 'Because it's my first Christmas here,' she'd explained. No one questioned her reason. No one knew of her obsession with Mike – except for Sally who was a busybody but never a telltale. Besides, in her longer nursing career, she had seen it all before.

After a while Alice crossed the room to her bed. Taking the photograph into her hands, she fondled it, like a woman might fondle a lover. Tears ran down her face as she gazed at the face in the centre. 'I miss you,' she whispered. 'I want you so much. She's not for you. You were mine, and she took you away.'

Carefully, she took the picture out of the frame. Creasing it on either side of the face, she tore it from top to bottom, so she had a strip showing only those familiar features – Mike's features.

Kissing it lovingly, she placed his picture under her pillow and climbed into bed, her fingers curled round the strip as she drifted into an uneasy sleep.

In the quietness her voice was like that of a spoiled, angry child. 'I don't want to hurt her,' it murmured, *'but I don't know how much longer I can wait.'*

PART THREE

1984

Secrets Will Out

CHAPTER TEN

Rosie was pegging out the washing when she saw Luke coming out of the woods. He had a string of fish on his belt and a sack over his shoulder. 'Poaching again!' Rosie feared that one sorry day Luke himself would be brought home strung over somebody's shoulder. 'Have you no sense? You know how keen the landowners are to catch the poachers – shoot first and ask questions later, that's what they were saying down at the pub.'

'The landowners aren't wily enough to catch me.'

'Don't get too clever, son. They have their ways. What's more, the law is on their side, and the last thing we need is to get tangled up with the law.'

Throwing down his catch, Luke sat on the van steps, arrogant as ever. 'Don't worry about it,' he said with a sly grin. 'I've hammered out a good deal today.'

Knowing how foolhardy he was, Rosie's nerves tingled. 'What kind of deal?'

'Never you mind. But if anybody gets shot by the gamekeepers, it won't be me.'

Striding over to him, she demanded, 'I want to know, Luke. What kind of deal?'

'You're a nosy devil.' Plucking a piece of grass, he tore at it with his teeth. 'I don't have to tell you everything.'

Feigning indifference, she returned to her washing. 'OK. Please yourself.' She knew he would tell her in time, especially if she pretended she didn't care whether he told her or not. 'I haven't got time to chat. Some of us have got work to do.'

Her instincts proved right; when she went to pass him with the wash basket, he casually remarked, 'Me and Bob Willet have come to an understanding.'

She stared at him. 'Bob Willet? Isn't he the warden from the Sorenson Estate?'

'The very one.' He grinned. 'He fetches me the goods and I dispose of them. That way we both win. He gets half the proceeds and nobody's any the wiser. All he has to do is claim it was a poacher. I've got a ready buyer, and he knows how to keep his mouth shut.' Pleased with himself, his grin widened. 'Clever, don't you think?'

Irritated, Rosie pushed by. 'You're an arrogant bugger, that's what I think, and it'll serve the pair of you right if you're caught and locked up for a good stretch.'

He followed her into the camper. 'You don't mean that.'

She looked at him consideringly, his lanky

figure and baby eyes and the way he had of worming his way into her heart, even when she wanted to throttle him. But, good or bad, he was her son and, for the moment, God help her, all she had in the world.

Taken aback by her seeming lack of compassion, he said, 'I know I've not been the best of sons, but you've not been the best mother either.'

She nodded. 'I know that.'

'So don't be hard on me, eh? We both do the best we can. Isn't that the truth of it?'

She bowed her head. 'Yes, son.' She sighed. 'That's the truth of it.'

'And you wouldn't really want to see me locked up, would you?'

She laughed. 'For a while maybe, until you mended your ways.' Catching a whiff of him, she swung her basket at his head. 'Phew! You stink rotten! Get them clothes off and wash yourself. How many times have I told you about fetching the smell of death in here?'

Protecting his head with his arms, he backed away. 'All right! All right! No need to split my head open, woman.' In two strides he was out of the door and down the steps. 'I'll wash when I get back. I'd best get this lot down to the pub. The landlord's waiting, money at the ready, and if I don't collect it, somebody else a bit quicker off the mark might do it for me.'

Slinging the sack over his shoulder, he went away whistling.

* * *

It was gone two in the morning when Rosie heard the commotion outside. Having been restless because Luke wasn't yet back, she had only just drifted into a fitful sleep.

When the footsteps stumbled up the steps, she suspected it might be him, though it didn't sound like him. 'Is that you, Luke?' Sitting up in bed, she lit the lamp and peered towards the door, her heart bumping. What if it wasn't him? What if it was a ruffian looking for an easy target? Or, worse still, the police.

'Answer me, Luke, you bugger!' When there was no answer, she scrambled out of bed and went softly across the room. 'What the devil are you playing at?' Taking up a thick stick used for propping open the door on sunnier days, she flung it open, crying out when he fell inside. 'You're bloody drunk!' she wailed. 'Get out of here!' Incensed, she bent to push him down the steps, when suddenly she noticed blood on his face. 'Oh my God, Luke, what have you been up to now?' Instinctively, her eyes went to the night outside but she could see no one.

'Let's get you inside,' she muttered angrily. 'I want some answers from you, my boy.'

She got him to the bench, then boiled a pan full of water. After cleaning and dressing the gash on his temple, she sat beside him. 'Who did this to you, and why? The truth now!'

Still dazed from the incident, he denied anyone

was involved. 'I thought someone was after me,' he said. 'It was dark. I took off through the spinney . . . I didn't see the loose branch. It came down heavy on me.' Fingering his head, he winced. 'It knocked me out for a while.'

Rosie knew him well enough to know when he was lying. 'I asked for the truth and you give me a cock-and-bull story!' she retorted angrily. 'What really happened, Luke? Tell me who did this to you.'

Luke clung to his story. 'There's nothing else to tell,' he insisted. He gave her a strange look, as if wanting to confide in her. But then he thought better of it. 'I'm tired.' Standing up, he took a moment to steady himself. 'Goodnight, Mum. We'll talk tomorrow.'

Rosie sighed, 'Aw, Luke, you make so many enemies, you worry me sick.'

'No need to worry. I know how to look after myself.'

'I wonder if you do.' She knew he wouldn't tell her the truth, but she knew it was bad. 'Go on to bed. Like you say, we'll talk tomorrow.'

'Goodnight.'

'Goodnight, son.'

Long after he had gone to his bunk, Rosie lay awake. 'I'm to blame,' she whispered. 'It was wrong of me to tell him about Mike. All those years he believed his father was dead. Now he knows different, and he can't live with it.' She had done it for the best, and lived to regret it.

'Luke was a good boy,' she murmured. 'Now, because of me, he's wild and wilful, and I'm so afraid he'll come to a bad end.'

She could hear him moving about, restless, like a caged animal.

'Somebody hurt you tonight.' Her voice was strangely hushed, eyes glittering with a kind of madness. 'Whether he likes it or not, Luke is Mike's boy. Before I'll let anyone harm him, I'll see them dead!'

CHAPTER ELEVEN

Mike came down the stairs two at a time. He felt good. With Christmas over and the New Year already one week old, he felt there was much to look forward to.

Making straight for the frying pan he took up a plate and served himself two eggs and a rasher of bacon. 'Looks good enough to eat.' Winking at the kids, he waited for Kerry's sharp retort, but it never came. She was sitting with her head in her hands, eyes downcast, as if she had the world on her shoulders. 'What's wrong?' he asked her.

Without looking up, Jack answered. 'She's miserable.'

Susie went to her mother's defence. 'No, she's not!'

'All right, you two, that's enough.' Mike was in no mood for arguments. 'Go and get ready for school.'

Jack threw his toast down. 'Didn't want breakfast anyway!' Sliding down from the stool he slunk out of the room.

Susie ran after him. 'Wait for me, Jack.'

Kerry looked up. 'I'm sorry,' she said. 'I don't

mean to be miserable. It's just that I've got a lot on my mind this morning.'

Mike cut into his bacon. 'Do you want to talk about it?' He stuffed the bacon into his mouth and began chewing.

'Not really,' she answered. 'It's to do with work.'

Part of her problem was Steve. She still had strong feelings for him, and she was finding working with him a strain.

'I'd like to help.' Enjoying his breakfast, Mike came up with an idea. 'If you wanted, I could always forget the hire business and come in with you.'

Kerry's answer was swift. 'Not a good idea.' Though they were growing closer, she felt it would take months, maybe years, before she felt totally secure with him. 'I think it would do you good to restart your own business.'

'Just a thought.' He felt rejected.

Smiling, she added, 'Besides, I don't want you muscling in on my little kingdom. I sweated blood for that independence.'

'Muscling in was not my intention,' he assured her. 'But I know what you mean.'

Kerry finished her tea and stood up. 'I'd best get the kids off to school, then it's back to the grindstone.'

'Me too.'

His remark surprised her. 'Oh? Sounds like you've got plans.'

172

'It's time I saw about buying a couple of sound vehicles.'

It was just what she had been waiting for. 'I'm glad,' she said. 'And the money's at your disposal, as I told you.'

'I'll put it back, I promise.'

'When you're ready.'

Mike had a question. 'That guy you work with . . .'

Shocked that he should mention the very man who was playing on her mind, she answered, 'You mean Steve?'

'Get on all right with him, do you?'

'Yes. Why do you ask?'

He shrugged. 'Just wondered, that's all.'

'I must admit, though, I've been thinking of letting him go.' The words were out before she could stop herself, and with Mike's next comment, she knew it was a silly thing to have said.

'Giving you trouble, is he, this Steve?'

Angry at his remark, Kerry snapped, 'I didn't say that, and no, he is *not* giving me trouble. Steve is a good bloke. He's hard-working and reliable, and staff like that are hard to find.'

Taken aback by her outburst, Mike put up his hand in mock self-protection. 'Whoa! I only wondered if he was causing problems.'

'I don't know what you mean by problems.' She was on the defensive and that was her second mistake.

'You said it was *work* making you miserable. I

know you love what you do, so naturally I wondered if it might be a clash of personality between you and this Steve. From what you tell me, you've recently given him more responsibility. Sometimes promoting staff can lead to trouble. They begin to imagine they know more than you do. It causes trouble. I've seen it happen all too often.'

'Well, you're wrong about this one.'

'So why are you thinking of letting him go?'

She was tempted to say, 'Because he was my lover for three years, and part of me wishes he still was,' but she kept her cool and sidestepped the question. 'I'm not thinking straight this morning. Steve isn't the problem. I'd better go and see to Jack and Susie.'

Kerry went up to the bathroom where she found Julie was already in charge. Satisfied that they had cleaned their teeth properly, Julie gave them a smile. 'That's very good,' she said. 'Downstairs now, and get your coats on.'

After they'd gone, she tackled Kerry. 'I heard the two of you arguing,' she said.

Another time, Kerry might have snapped at her for interfering, but not this morning. This morning she needed someone to talk to, and what she had in mind was not for Mike's ears. 'If I confide in you, can you keep it to yourself?'

'Of course. That's what mothers are for, isn't it?'

'Not now though,' said Kerry. 'There isn't time.'

Julie had already guessed. 'It's to do with Steve, isn't it?'

'No, it's *not* to do with Steve. It's to do with Mike.'

'You love him, don't you, this Steve?'

Kerry's thoughts were already at the ware-house, with Steve. She had to make a decision, and it was tearing her apart. 'What did you say? Sorry, I wasn't listening.'

'Steve. You're in love with him, aren't you?'

'We'll talk later.' It was always the same. She began a conversation, and then regretted it. Her mother's bluntness set her nerves on edge.

'Haven't you ended your affair with him?'

Horrified, Kerry rushed to the door and softly closed it. 'For God's sake, Mother! Do you want Mike to hear?'

'Hardly!' Julie snorted. 'If he knew what Steve meant to you, he'd probably go out and kill him – you as well, if my suspicions are right.'

'Look, don't start insinuating that Mike's a killer. It's *me* we're talking about. I should have had more sense than to think you could talk about anything without bringing your hatred of Mike into it.'

'I'm sorry,' Julie lied. 'I'll guard my tongue, I promise.' But she wouldn't guard her thoughts.

'I've got myself in a bad situation,' Kerry groaned, 'and I don't know what to do.'

'Do you love Steve?'

Kerry took a moment to think about that, and

there was only one answer. 'Yes, I love him.' Before her mother could gloat, she went on, 'I love Mike too, but in a different way. At first, Steve was just another employee. We became friends, and before too long we were lovers. I never meant that to happen, but I don't regret it. With Mike away, bills piling up, all the worry . . . the awful loneliness . . .' Beneath her mother's searching gaze she felt awkward, like a child. 'I needed someone and he was there,' she finished lamely.

'And now Mike's back, you have to make a choice.'

'I thought I'd already made it. But I still need Steve . . . it will take longer than I thought.' She took a deep breath. 'Things are getting better between me and Mike. Jack's even beginning to accept him again.' She paused. 'Whatever you think of Mike, he's my husband and the father of my children. We were a family, and can be again, I know it. I just have to keep Steve at arm's length.'

'Don't be too hasty,' her mother urged. 'Talk to Steve. Tell him you have to give Mike a chance, but don't shut him out of your life altogether or you might live to regret it.'

Kerry looked at her enviously, thinking how strong-willed her mother was, and how whenever she wanted anything she grabbed it with both hands and damn the consequences. 'You don't understand,' she told her. 'I'm not like you.

I can't juggle two men at once. I have to make a choice, and live with the consequences.' If only she was strong enough to stand by the choice she must make, but so far she was weak.

'What if Steve won't go quietly?'

Kerry wanted the conversation over. 'Don't concern yourself, Mother,' she said. 'I'll deal with Steve.'

Outside on the landing, Mike listened intently, his back pressed to the wall and his heart sinking with every word he heard. Kerry's confession thundered through his brain until he thought he would go crazy. All the time he was shut in that damned place, she had had a lover. How could she do that to him? He didn't care how lonely she was, or how the bills piled up, she ought to have had the strength to be faithful. The time spent away from her had been torture. All he could think of was her, how he longed to hold her, needed to feel the warmth of her body in his arms, yearned to be with her. All that precious time. Every minute of every day, he had loved her until it was like a physical hurt. And all the while she was lying with another man.

The man's name glowed in his mind like a beacon. Steve, a friend then a lover, that's what she had said. And she loved him.

He heard them moving towards the door. Quickly he ran down the stairs and into the kitchen. 'Are you kids ready?' The tone of his voice belied the rage inside him.

A few minutes later, he saw Kerry and the children on their way. 'Are you sure I can't give you a lift into town?' Kerry asked.

He shook his head. 'Thanks all the same. The walk will do me good. I need the fresh air.' What he really needed was to let the rage settle so he could think straight.

But the rage didn't settle. Instead it hardened inside him. With each step he took, he recalled everything she had said, how she had deceived him, how she still loved him. He mimicked her voice: 'I love Mike too, but in a different way . . .'

What way was that? Was her mind on Steve when she made love with him? Mike's face twisted with murderous rage.

Kerry had avoided Steve all day, but now, with only half an hour before finishing, and everything running smoothly, she knew he would seek her out.

She left the office and went on a tour of inspection.

As always, even after the baking was done and both ovens cleaned out, the wonderful aroma pervaded the air, conjuring up fresh bread, meat pasties and jam doughnuts. Warm and thick, the smell filled the nostrils and tickled the senses. In the morning the room was piled high with racks of delicious food waiting to be delivered or collected. In the afternoon, when they were all gone, that wonderful, unique smell hung in the air, like a special kind of perfume.

'It's been a rush.' Trudy had been with Kerry the longest. She always had something to say, and today was no different. 'The orders are all out and everything's ready for tomorrow.' Proudly, she showed Kerry the newly cleaned oven and the pile of spotless baking trays beside the sink. 'I've just got to put it all back together. Then it's home to a cuppa and my feet up.'

Her colleague laughed. 'You can say that again!' she quipped. 'Mine feel like two puddings on the end of my legs.'

Kerry chatted to them for a few minutes. 'You've done well,' she said. 'Finish up now, and I'll see you tomorrow.'

Trudy, the older of the two women, drew Kerry aside. 'You look tired ... if you don't mind me saying.'

After a long, hard day, Kerry would have brushed aside the remark, but Trudy went on, 'Why don't you get a young girl in to do the packing?' she suggested. 'You've got more than enough to cope with. I mean, the phone's going every minute of the day, and there's all that paperwork – some days I can't see you behind the pile of stuff on your desk.' She shook her head. 'Honest to God, I don't know how you do it all.'

'I like to be busy,' Kerry told her. 'Besides, I can't afford to take on a girl.' Especially not with Mike needing money to start up again, she thought. 'I'm already stretched with four wages to pay as it is.'

That last remark stirred Trudy to answer, 'I understand. I'm sorry. I just thought you looked tired, that's all.'

Kerry assured her she hadn't taken any offence. 'You know it's always chaotic on the first day back after the holidays. Everyone wants their delivery at the crack of dawn. It's been all hands to the deck today, but tomorrow won't be so bad. You'll be able to bake and pack as usual, and I'll be free to chase the orders and catch up on a mountain of paperwork. But there will be no girl.' She smiled. 'We've always managed before and unless we suddenly get some huge, fabulous contract that brings in a fortune, we'll just have to cope as we are.'

As Kerry walked away, Pauline, the younger of the two women, said cheekily, 'I told you, Trudy. I said she wouldn't have no work for your sister. You heard. She's stretched to pay our wages as it is.'

'Hmh! I don't believe a word of it. She's making a small fortune out of us, and all we get is a measly bonus at Christmas.'

'And a wage all the year round, and a job that we enjoy doing. You do enjoy working here, don't you, Trude?'

'Course I do.'

'There you are then. Let your sister find her own job.'

'You're a cheeky young bugger, you are.'

'Have to be,' came the reply, 'or people will walk all over you.'

Lowering her voice, Trudy edged nearer. 'If I tell you something, do you know how to keep your gob shut?'

'Try me.'

'I reckon she's carrying on.'

'Never!'

'I'm telling you. I reckon her and that Steve Palmer have been having it off for years.'

'Don't be daft! She wouldn't look twice at him, especially now that dishy husband of hers is home.'

'I'm not so sure.' Trudy glanced at Kerry and Steve as they made their way up to the office. 'I could be wrong, but they always seem to be closeted together in that poky office.'

'So? What's wrong with that?'

'Temptation, that's what.'

'They have to work closely or nothing would run smooth, would it, you silly cow?'

'Hey! That's enough of your lip!'

'Well, if you ask me she hasn't got time to be having it off with anybody. I wouldn't be surprised if she hasn't even got the energy to have it off with her own husband when she gets home of a night. In my book, she's a real grafter and she deserves what she's got.'

'I'm not denying that.'

'Then leave her alone and stop making up

stories about her and Steve Palmer.' Angrily, Pauline slammed a tray back into the oven, cursing when she broke a nail on her little finger. 'Anyway, why would Steve want to look at a married woman when he can have any girl he chooses?'

'What? Including you?'

'Don't be so bloody daft!'

Trudy looked at her in astonishment. 'Well, I never, you're jealous!' she teased. 'You fancy him, don't you? Go on, admit it. You'd like to have your wicked way with him, wouldn't you?'

'You silly old bat! Is that all you can think about, other people's sex lives? You must be kept short at home if you need to fantasise about what everybody else is doing.'

'Don't talk so bloody stupid!' The remark had cut too close to the bone. 'Me and my feller have got a very healthy relationship, I can tell you that.'

Pauline knew she had hit a nerve. It made her sad in a way. 'We'd best get these ovens finished,' she said casually, 'or we'll be here till kingdom come.'

After Kerry and Steve had gone through the papers, arranging the deliveries and order of route, Kerry organised the rota for baking and packing, and adjusted the work charts. Satisfied that his duties were done for the night, Steve asked Kerry if he might take her for a drink. 'We need to talk.' Things had been playing on his mind. Lately he had felt her slipping away from him, and he meant to keep her at any cost.

'We can talk here.' Filing the papers in the relevant trays, she deliberately turned her back on him. 'Look, Steve, there's something I have to tell you.'

'I thought there might be.' He sounded dejected.

Without turning round, she said softly, 'I'm sorry, and I wish there was any other way, but . . .' she swallowed hard, 'I really don't think we can work together any more.' With the truth out in the open, she turned to face him. 'I'm sorry, Steve. I'll give you a first-class reference. You've earned that, and a month's pay in lieu of notice.'

Shocked, he stared at her with his mouth open. 'You want me out of here altogether, is that what you're saying? You can't mean it, surely. And even if you did, where would you find a replacement by the end of the week?' His face stiffened. 'Unless you've already found somebody to take my place.'

She shook her head. 'No, I haven't, but I will. If it comes to it, I can always get a temporary driver.' She didn't want him to think he was indispensable, even if he was. 'We've had one before, when Jason was off, and there was no problem.'

'Please, Kerry, think what you're doing. You and me, we belong together. I love you . . . I thought you loved me.'

'It doesn't matter what either of us feel.' Being alone with him like this was a mistake. She began to falter. 'I don't want you to go, and I don't want you to stay. It's too much of a temptation – for both of us.'

In two strides he was across the room, his hands on her shoulders. 'Come away with me,' he begged. 'Sell up here, and I'll take care of you. Bring the kids too if that's what you want, but don't turn me away. Not after what we've been to each other.'

'It's too late for all that.' She felt suddenly threatened. 'Don't cause trouble, Steve. Please, just accept things the way they are.'

'I can't.' His hands gripped her shoulders so hard, the pain made her wince.

Steeling herself, Kerry told him in a firm, quiet voice, 'Look, Steve, the last thing I want to do is hurt you. We had a wonderful relationship, but we both knew the time would come when it would have to finish. That time is now. What we had is over, that's all there is to it.'

'You never loved me, did you?'

'What?'

'You *used* me!' Anger flashed in his eyes. 'You never loved me.'

Kerry shook her head. 'That's not true. I did love you . . . I *do* love you. But there are all kinds of love. Some last, some don't.'

For a long, agonising moment he stared into her eyes, a parade of emotions flowing between them. Suddenly, in a move that took her by surprise, he grabbed her to him and kissed her, a long, passionate kiss that reminded her of what she and Steve had before, and what she may never have with Mike.

To the watcher who stood on the outside looking in, it seemed as if she was willing him on. 'Bad woman!' The harsh whisper rippled through the quiet evening. 'Bad, bad woman!'

'What was that?' Breaking from Steve's arms, Kerry shrank against the wall. 'Did you see it?'

Confused, Steve followed her gaze to the window. 'What? What did you see?'

'A shape . . . a shadow. I'm not sure.' Guilt shivered through her. 'Someone's watching us. Please, you'd better leave now.'

Squaring his shoulders, he told her, 'I'm not going anywhere until you see sense. Just now, when we kissed, I know you wanted it as much as me.'

Clenching her fists, she said through gritted teeth, 'Just leave me alone!'

'Never!' Wrapping his hands round her small fists, he kissed each one. 'I'm going outside to make sure no one's out there, and then I'm coming back.' He grinned. 'You won't get rid of me so easily.'

Realising he would not be reasoned with, Kerry waited until he was out of the room and down the stairs before grabbing her bag and belongings.

Softly, she went down after him. As he went

out the front, she went out the back. Her car was parked by the back door. Quickly she got inside, started the engine and was on her way down the road before he even realised.

'Damn the man!' she muttered as she drove. 'He won't give me any peace. He'll never accept that it's over between us.'

Distraught that she had got away, Steve sat down at the desk, head low and eyes closed. 'I can't let her go,' he murmured. 'She still loves me, I know it.' Alone and unsure, he began to cry; softly like a man cries, angry and ashamed at the same time.

He laid his head down and let his emotions run free, until after a while he was exhausted. 'Tomorrow,' he murmured. 'It'll be all right tomorrow. She'll see how wrong she's been.'

At the top of the stairs he switched off the light to Kerry's office. As he turned to close the door, he thought he saw a shadow. 'Who's there?' The silence was intimidating. He switched on the light but could see nothing. Peering downstairs, he searched the ground floor with his eyes but could see nothing untoward. 'She's got *me* jittery now.'

He waited a moment, then stepped forward, beginning his descent to the ground floor.

He didn't hear the intruder. He couldn't know the hatred in that intruder's heart. He didn't see the arms that stretched out, nor the hands that reached to spread themselves on his back.

All he knew, as he tumbled to his death, was

the violence that sent him downwards. And the face of his murderer as it stared down on him, a kindly, smiling face.

And those wicked eyes. Alive with madness.

Sergeant Madison was convinced. 'It's Peterson all right,' he insisted. 'Think about it, sir.' Making sure he got his facts right, he paced the floor, running it through his own mind before putting his ideas to the inspector. 'It all fits together. The first murder was that of Eddie Johnson, and we know that he was Rosie Sharman's boyfriend.'

'So?' Inspector Webb was new to this division, and if there was anything he hated more than coming in at the tail end of an unsatisfactory investigation, it was raking over cold ashes.

'Well, we also know that Rosie Sharman was seen with Mike Peterson at the public house the day the storm sent him over the edge.'

'I see. And because both Eddie Johnson and Peterson knew Rosie Sharman, you think you can tie Peterson in with Johnson's murder?'

'If both men were attracted to the same woman, yes, it's a possibility.'

'Have you read the notes on this case?'

'Over and over.' Until his eyes were red and his mind was dizzy.

'Good. Then you must know that at the time of Eddie Johnson's murder, Mike Peterson was still in the hospital.'

'We only have the nurse Alice Henshaw's word

for that: nobody else saw him for at least an hour either side of the murder. He could have got out of the hospital, committed the murder and got back before anybody realised.'

'Are you saying the nurse was lying?'

'Mistaken, maybe.'

'Hardly.'

'Then she lied.'

'Why would she do that?'

'I'm still working on that one.' It was a puzzler. 'Maybe she was soft on Peterson, and turned a blind eye when he wanted to go missing.'

'And what about motive?'

'Sharman and Peterson might have had something going, and Eddie Johnson found out. According to those who knew him, he was a violent, moody sort of a bloke. A man capable of murder. It's likely he was in a jealous rage . . . looking to kill Peterson. That could account for him having the knife when he was found.'

'It couldn't account for him being dead when he was found though, could it?'

'Peterson might have had the same idea. He went out looking for Eddie Johnson and, if I'm right, he found him and killed him.'

'If any of that were true, it would have been uncovered during the investigation.'

'They didn't dig deep enough.'

'You're skating on thin ice, Madison. What has all this got to do with this latest death anyway?'

'Peterson keeps turning up like a bad penny,

and I'm not just talking about the Eddie Johnson killing. When Dr Carlton was bumped off, once again Mike Peterson is somewhere in the picture. He was Dr Carlton's patient for three years. That man must have known more about the workings of Peterson's mind than anybody else.' Anticipating the inspector's objections, Madison hurried on, 'He might have discovered that Peterson had murdered Eddie Johnson. Or maybe Peterson even confided in him. It's possible, a doctor is like a priest, oath of secrecy and all that. So we have murders, and two links with Peterson, and both murders unsolved.' It gnawed at his peace of mind. 'Now we come to the latest death, Steve Palmer.'

'I know, I know. That makes the *third* link with Peterson.' Inspector Webb realised he was beginning to think like the sergeant.

'And, in my opinion, the strongest link of all,' said Madison. 'Steve Palmer worked closely with Peterson's wife all the time he was in the hospital. Imagine how he must feel, knowing his wife is seeing another man day after day, year in, year out. And Palmer was unmarried and a good-looker.' He paused, his thoughts rolling back over the years. 'Do you remember how she looked when we questioned her . . . nervous . . . glancing at Peterson out of the corner of her eye. I said at the time she looked guilty as sin.'

'So you think Peterson found out they were carrying on and killed him?'

'It's another possibility, that's all I'm saying. Who could blame her if she was tempted to find comfort in the arms of another man? If she did, it's possible that Peterson found out and went after Palmer.'

Webb shook his head. 'But Palmer's death was an accident.'

'I don't think so. I don't go along with the coroner's findings, that he fell down the stairs. He knew those stairs like the back of his own hand – that's what the women said, and they should know because they watched him run up and down them every day. Even Peterson's wife had to agree that it seemed unlikely he should have lost his footing.'

'There's no evidence that Peterson's wife and Steve Palmer were having an affair.'

'I'm still working on it.'

'Well, when you have hard proof, I'll back you all the way. But you know as well as I do, we can't make a case on possibilities and theories.'

'Yes, sir.'

When Inspector Webb left, Madison sat at his computer and called up one file after another. Finally, he came to Rosie Sharman. His eyes narrowed. 'Now there's a mystery. Never found. Never questioned.'

After a while, he switched off the computer and sat there thinking and wondering. 'She must be out there *somewhere*. And if I'm right, she must know something. Or why did she go into hiding?

And for so long.' His mind was made up. 'Find Rosie Sharman,' he told himself, 'and I guarantee she will lead you right back to Mike Peterson!'

CHAPTER TWELVE

Even in January, the city of Dublin was magical.

On this Friday evening, everywhere was lit like Christmas all over again; every window was plastered with 'SALE' signs, and every shop filled with people. Some were spending, some browsing, others just wanting to get out of the house for a while. Ordinary, God-fearing people, with ordinary ambitions and ordinary lives.

But there was nothing ordinary about the middle-aged couple who entered a small café in the cobbled side street.

If every face told a story, their faces told of torment, and fear. The man was small and shrivelled before his time; the woman was haggard though her strong, classical features betrayed a certain faded beauty. They seemed nervous, occasionally glancing about, as though worried someone might recognise them.

Hurrying into the café, they chose a table far from the glare of the street, somewhere they could talk and not be overheard.

No one noticed them. No one cared. How could they know that this middle-aged pair were a couple in hiding, in fear for their lives? Dressed in warm coats and gloves, there was nothing special about the pair save for their quiet, sad faces, and the troubled eyes that hardly dared look up.

'What can I get youse?' asked the waitress in her broad Irish accent. Red-haired and green-eyed, she had a smile to charm the fairies. The woman had just laid a single page from an outdated newspaper on the table. The waitress's curious gaze was drawn to a certain article out-lined in vivid red pencil.

The woman noticed her interest and quickly folded the page and returned it to her shopping bag.

'Poor devil!' said the waitress. 'Imagine dying from falling down a flight of stairs. Would yer believe I used to run up and down the cellar here in high heels. Sure I musta been mad!' She pointed to the flat, dark shoes adorning her feet. 'They're ugly, so they are, but it's better than ending up with me neck broke, don't yer think?'

'Very sensible,' the woman replied and was relieved when the girl took their order and hurried away.

The man was angry. 'What in God's name are you doing, carrying that article about with you and laying it out for everybody to see?'

'I have to keep them close,' she replied simply, 'so we never forget what danger we're in.'

He held out his hand. 'Give it to me.'

Glancing about, she dropped her voice to a

whisper. 'I've got them *all* here.'

Disbelief flitted over his features. 'Good God, woman!' he groaned. 'Have you gone mad?'

'Please, Tom, don't be angry,' she whispered.

Quietly now, he apologised. 'I'm sorry.' If she had gone mad, he couldn't blame her. There were times when he thought they might both be better off locked away in some secure place. Or six feet under the ground. But he needn't worry on that score, he thought caustically, because the way things were, the murderer might come for them at any time.

'Two teas, piping hot.' The waitress placed the tea before them. 'Would you like anything else?' she asked. 'We've got some fresh doughnuts, and a slice or two left of the chocolate gateau.'

When they declined, she went away, softly singing.

'Give me the paper.' Once more he held out his hand. 'I won't lose it,' he promised. 'It'll be safe with me.'

'I've got them *all*,' she repeated.

He looked at her, thinking what a small, pitiful thing she was when only a few years ago she had been a strapping, handsome woman, with a sense of humour and a quick, inquisitive mind. But that was before the monster showed its true face.

'Can't I keep them?' she quietly pleaded. 'So I don't forget.'

The sigh came from deep down. 'Aw, Emma, what am I to do with you?'

'Love me,' she murmured, 'like you used to, when we were first married.'

'When we were first married,' he echoed. It seemed a lifetime ago, when in fact it was only, what? Twenty-eight years. Yes, he had loved her then. And he loved her now, and when he spoke, the love showed in his voice. 'Keep them hidden,' he told her softly. 'It wouldn't do for people to know you carried such things with you.'

Smiling, she secured the page and closed her bag. Then she held out her hand and he placed his over it. 'We'll be all right, won't we, Tom?' she asked.

Tom nodded. 'That's why we moved away.' He dared not promise they would be safe. How safe could they be against the cunning mind of a murderer?

Thinking of the articles Emma carried with her, and the madness that pursued them, he grew restless. 'I think we'd better go.' He gulped his tea down. 'Quickly, Emma. It's getting late.' While she finished her drink, he nervously took a long, official-looking white envelope out of his pocket.

'What's that you've got there?'

'Just a bill,' he lied. 'Nothing for you to worry about.' He carried it everywhere with him, just in case.

The waitress returned. 'Anything else?'

He pulled out his wallet. 'No, we'll pay now,' he said. 'We're in a hurry. We've got a bus to catch.'

From the counter, the waitress watched them leave. 'Such nice people,' she told her colleague, 'but they look worn out.'

A rush of customers kept her busy for a while. By the time she went to clear their table, they were long gone. 'Oh, they've left something here!' Rushing to the door, she glanced up and down the street. There was no sign of them now. She slipped the envelope into her apron pocket.

At the counter, she mentioned it to her colleague. 'I don't know what to do with it.'

'If it were me, I'd post it,' she said. 'It's the only thing you can do.'

'There's no stamp on it.'

'So put one on.'

'What? They didn't even leave a tip!'

'Send it without a stamp.' She grinned. 'I often do that. Nobody ever makes me pay.'

Intent on getting his beloved wife to safety, the man had not missed his letter. It was only one of many all the same, not to be posted, but kept safe, just in case.

A short time later they boarded the bus back to the outskirts; at every stop along the way they peered out of the windows, searching for a certain face in the darkness. *Praying they would never again have to look on it in the flesh.*

Their small, nondescript house was hidden down a narrow lane. It was their retreat, their 'hidey-hole'. Here they could pretend the outer world and all its terrors did not exist. When the door was bolted, and the curtains closed against the shadows, they even dared to think they might be safe.

Creatures of habit, their routine never varied. On entering the house, Emma would remain by the door while Tom did his rounds. First he searched in every cupboard and corner, under the bed, and even behind the curtains. That done, he would return downstairs to reassure Emma.

While she went into the kitchen to make them a night-time drink, he would check that the alarm had not been tampered with in any way. The shopping was quickly packed away. After that, Tom would follow Emma up the stairs with the tray.

The room where they slept was more like a sitting room than a bedroom, and it had an *en suite* bathroom. Two comfortable armchairs, a small round table, and a television on a small sideboard made the bedroom cosy and welcoming. The bed stood away from the window, in the darkest corner. It was a calculated precaution, like the many heavy bolts that had turned the house into a fortress, and the alarm which had cost them a small fortune to install.

On entering the room, he set the tray on the table, then, while Emma poured the chocolate, he closed and bolted the bedroom door. He drew the curtains and went to the wall behind the bed where he flicked a small switch to activate the alarm. Instantly, in all four corners of the room, small red lights glowed. 'You can relax now,' he told her.

But she couldn't. And neither could he.

Sitting there, in their self-imposed prison, they talked about the way their lives had evolved. They spoke of their earlier achievements, and the mistakes that followed, and the way all their dreams had come to this.

Emma took out the newspaper pages and laid them side by side on the table. 'Tom, tell me the truth. Do you think she really did kill all these people?' Her voice trembled.

He thought for a moment. 'Yes, I think so,' he answered. 'It all adds up, do you see? She was there, in the area, and she probably believed she had reason enough to kill them.' Swivelling the articles round to face him, he pointed to each one in turn. 'See? Mike Peterson. His name crops up in every one.'

'You think he was the reason?'

He nodded. 'You know how jealous she can be, and how overwhelming her rages are.' He shook his head forlornly. 'And she has an appetite for killing. We know that.'

She pointed to the article on Steve Palmer. 'They say this one was an accident.'

He laughed. 'They're wrong.' The laughter died away. 'They don't know her like we do.'

The woman bowed her head. 'If I'd known before . . . I swear I would never have let her live.'

Reaching over, he held her hand. 'Don't torture yourself, Emma.' He got up then, and walked to the window where he gingerly raised the curtain, peeped out and quickly dropped it again. 'Besides,' he continued, 'you're a kind, gentle woman. You could never inflict hurt.' His voice thickened with hatred. 'Not like her!'

They finished their drinks. Tom prepared for bed.

'I think I'll have a bath,' Emma told him. 'I need to be quiet for a while, to soak my bones, and think . . . about things.'

'All right, sweetheart.' He kissed her on the cheek. 'Call me when you need me. I won't be asleep.' He didn't sleep much these days; always on the alert, half awake, half asleep. Listening. Frightened. *She* had done that to him. She had done far worse to Emma.

While Emma soaked in the adjoining bathroom, he lay on the bed, thinking back over the years and wondering where it all went wrong. 'Too late now,' he mused aloud. 'The badness is out.'

The minutes passed. He could hear Emma shifting in the water, that muffled, splashy sound that made a body feel oddly comfortable. 'Emma?'

'Yes?'

'Do you need me to help?'

'Not yet.'

He waited a moment, reflecting on her answer – given too quickly, sounding too urgent. He wondered, and the wondering became unbearable.

Climbing out of bed, he went quietly across the room. Pushing open the bathroom door, he went inside. Emma was lying with her back to him. She seemed to be reading something. Softly, he went forward. 'Emma? Are you all right?'

Startled, she let something drop and it slithered to the bottom of the bath.

'What are you up to?' He had not meant to frighten her. Reaching down into the water, his fingers curled round the hard edge of a picture fame. Raising it to the surface, he saw what it was, and his face darkened. 'I thought we agreed you would destroy this.'

Panicking, she snatched it from him, her sobbing pitiful to hear. 'I tried,' she confessed, 'but I can't destroy it. I can't!'

'All right, keep it if you must.' As she turned it over, his eyes caught sight of the face in the picture. Once he had loved that face, that person. Now, all he felt was repugnance and loathing. 'But don't let me see it ever again,' he pleaded. 'It haunts me, Emma. Can you understand that?'

'How did she come to be so bad?' Emma murmured. With a mother's fondness she gazed at the picture, a kind of pride filling her eyes as she regarded the young woman. Dressed in nurse's uniform, and with a black and tan puppy at her feet, she seemed deceptively innocent. 'She was such a sweet little thing and, oh, I did love her so.'

'Don't, Emma. Please.'

Looking up at him with appealing eyes, she asked, 'Do you remember how beautiful she was?'

'The beauty was only skin deep.'

'And how she always longed to be a nurse. Do you remember that?'

'I remember how she slaughtered the small creatures that innocently strayed into our garden.'

'Hurting them to make them better, that's what she used to say.' She smiled through her tears.

'Don't say any more!' Thumping his fist on the wall, he swung round, his face red with anger. Suddenly he, too, was crying, all the hurt pouring from him. 'She killed your puppy. Do you remember *that*, Emma? Do you?'

Struck silent, she stared at him. Slowly, her whole face crumpled with pain. 'Why did she do that, Tom?' she cried. 'Why did she like to hurt things?'

Bending to his knees, he took her in his arms. 'Because she's wicked,' he whispered. 'Her mind was always twisted.'

'Was it my fault?' Like any loving parent, she thought herself a failure in some way she did not understand.

'Oh, no. Not your fault, or mine,' he assured her lovingly. 'It's the way she was made, that's all.'

'I wonder . . . should we tell?'

'And I wonder if we haven't suffered enough

already.' He knew their daughter's loathing was such that she would never admit to their being alive. For some mad, inexplicable reason known only to herself, she had wanted them dead long ago. If they went to the police and told them she was the one they were looking for, it would drag him and Emma into a nightmare worse than any they had already suffered.

They would have to look her in the face, see themselves mirrored in her eyes. People might not understand that he and Emma were victims too. They might be condemned as being bad parents, and that was never true, they had always done their best, even when they knew it was hopeless. And through the nightmare of everyone knowing they had bred a monster, Emma would shrink and die before his eyes.

His mind shrieked in protest. He could not let that happen. Far better for them to remain silent.

'Emma?'

'Yes?'

'If we did tell them, and all they did was lock her away, I'm afraid she might get out and come after us.'

'We must never tell them then.'

'I agree.'

'I need your help now.' Handing him the bar of special cream, she let him gently help her forward.

With tender, circular strokes, he moved the bar across her back, occasionally dipping the bar into the water, so the cream would foam and soften her skin. Every time she flinched, he waited patiently until she could let him go on.

When it was done, he cupped his hands into the water and threw the warm, soothing liquid over her back to wash the foam away.

What he saw made him want to cry. Emma's back and shoulders were a criss-cross of deep, vivid scars, jagged at the edges. Below her right shoulder blade, the scars became tangled where the bone had poked through. She never complained, but then she was not one for complaining.

'Maybe she got the badness from me,' he whispered.

'Why do you say that?'

'Because of what she did to you. And because, if she was here now, I would kill her with my bare hands.'

Emma turned to kiss him. 'No,' she smiled. 'It was a long time ago. Don't be vengeful. Don't let her win.'

'You're a good woman, Emma,' he told her, 'and you're right. We must not let her taint the future the way she tainted the past.'

Later, when they were lying in bed, Emma heard a noise. Tom got out of bed to peer through the window.

'What was it?' she asked.

'Only the wind,' he replied. 'Nothing to be afraid of.'

She lay in his arms for a while longer, neither of them able to sleep. 'Tom, I'm not afraid when you're here with me.'

'I'm glad.'

A pause, then, 'She won't ever find us, will she, Tom?'

There was a long moment of silence before he answered. 'We've done all we can,' he said. 'We moved here to Ireland. We found this hideaway and made it secure from intruders. No, I don't think she'll find us.'

Satisfied, she fell into a restless sleep.

Some time later, Tom walked the floor, his heart quickening with fear at every sound.

Pausing, he gazed down at her sleeping face. 'I've done all I can to keep you safe,' he whispered. *'Now, all we can do is pray.'*

CHAPTER THIRTEEN

Rosie woke to a beautiful morning. Through the partly opened window she could hear the sound of birds squabbling, and when she sat up in bed to peep through the curtain, she was thrilled to see a robin perched on a branch outside her window. 'Aw, you little beauty,' she cooed, and was sorry when the sound of her voice frightened it away.

Rising from her bed, she shivered when the cold winter air wrapped itself round her nakedness. 'Luke!' Going to the front end of the camper van, she called again. 'Luke, wake up, you lazy bugger. We need some wood chopped and a fire going before we freeze to death.'

When there was no answer, she drew back the curtain and looked up at his bunk. 'Luke, are you up there?' Still no answer. She took a closer look. His bed had not been slept in. 'What the devil's he up to now?' She returned to her own area and she scraped together what pieces of wood were lying in the tiny hearth. With that, she managed to get a small fire going, enough to boil the kettle and make herself a pot of tea.

Seated on the mat, cross-legged, the warmth

flowing over her, she stared into the flames, sipping her tea and wondering what would become of him. 'You're a real worry to me,' she muttered. 'I never know where you are or what you're doing.'

The minutes ticked away and still she didn't feel like moving.

When the fire burned out and it got so cold that she couldn't stop shivering, she stretched her arms above her head and groaned. 'What I wouldn't give for a little house and a proper chimney, with a fire to curl my toes over and a kitchen where I could sit and dream.' Her smile deepened. 'With Mike beside me, I'd want for nothing.' At heart, she was no different from the girl she was years ago.

She went to the sink and drew out a basin from the cupboard beneath. Into this she poured a little of the hot water and a sprinkling of cold. Then she stripped down to her skin and washed all over.

Searching out a clean jumper and jeans, she quickly dressed, tied back her auburn hair, and pulled on the floppy denim cap Luke had bought her for Christmas. Then she donned her duffel coat and boots and went out.

Luke always kept a good supply of kindling. Every day, he would come back with an armful of fallen branches. When they were chopped small enough to fit in the tiny stove, he would fill the wooden scuttle, and stack the remainder in a box which he had swung from the belly of the camper.

Rosie went to it now, grabbed a bundle of kindling and hurried back inside to drop the wood into the scuttle. She took off her coat and boots and slipped her feet into a pair of blue and white trainers. Three years old and worn virtually every day, they were a sorry sight, though deliciously comfortable for slopping about in.

A short time later, when she had made her bed and cleaned the living area, she took a short walk to see if Luke might be making his way back. Cutting through the snow, she went down by the spinney and out along the brook, but there was no sign of him. 'Damn you, Luke! You'll have me old before my time.' Hoping he might have come home another way, she made her way back.

He hadn't.

Inside the van she got the fire going until the little place was warm as toast. She made herself a coffee, and took out her painting materials. Unable to concentrate, she returned them to the cupboard and restlessly paced the floor, pausing only to stare out of the window to see if he was about.

After a while, she sat and did some thinking. 'What am I doing with my life?' She felt very isolated. 'I'm going mad here, forever worrying about Luke. Living from hand to mouth, never sure whether we'll have enough to keep body and soul together, hiding from the police and trembling at every knock on the door.'

She didn't want much out of life but contentment always seemed to elude her. 'I was just a kid when Mike left me pregnant, not caring whether I lived or died.' Because of what he did, her life had been hard. 'Not a day passed when I didn't want to kill him,' she admitted. 'We had it all, but he didn't want a baby. He said he wasn't ready for all that.' Regrets overwhelmed her. If she didn't do something about Mike soon, it would be too late.

She remembered the advert she'd found in last week's newspaper. Going to the far end of the settee, she grabbed up the cushion and plucked the advert from its hiding place. For the umpteenth time she read it: 'Urgently required, general domestic help. Apply in the first instance to the Staff Manager, Landsmead Institute, Priory Street, Bridport, Dorset.'

Rosie held the cutting in her hands, pressing it to her heart like a balm. 'I could change my appearance and if I got this job, I would be nearer to Mike . . . find out all there is to know. Hospitals keep records. I could watch the house where he lives, choose my moment. He probably has to attend hospital regularly. I could gain his confidence . . . be his friend.' A look of anger distorted her features. 'I could tell him all the awful things I've done because of him!'

Suddenly she saw herself in the mirror and was shocked. Bent over like an old witch and talking to herself, she seemed like a crazy thing. 'Watch out,' she told the image in the mirror, 'or you'll be going off your rocker good and proper. His fault!' she hissed. *'His fault!'*

Standing there, looking at herself, she was a girl again; sixteen years old, pregnant and abandoned. She remembered it all, the anguish and the uncertainty after he had gone. 'You did me wrong, Mike.' She smiled sweetly. *'And really, you should be punished!'*

Rosie decided to take her paints and easel down to the spinney. When the snow lay heavy on the boughs it was the most magical sight and she wanted to try and capture the scene. Wrapped in her duffel coat, and with her rich, auburn hair peeking out from beneath the denim cap, she looked a pretty enough picture herself as she sat and painted.

Suddenly she heard the cracking of twigs and her heart turned somersaults. She snatched up her paints and easel and hid behind an old oak tree.

Waiting with bated breath, she watched to see who was about. A figure emerged, stumbling and bleeding. 'Luke!' Even from where she was, she could see he was badly hurt. His arm was hanging limply by his side, and one of his eyes was badly swollen. Shuffling painfully along, he didn't hear her cry out.

In a minute she was by his side. 'Who did it?' She grabbed his good arm. 'Who did this to you, Luke?'

He just stared at her dully.

'It's all right,' she soothed. 'Take it easy. I've got you.' Abandoning her belongings, she helped him slowly home.

'You're lucky your arm isn't broken,' she said when she got him inside the camper van. 'You'll be right as rain once I've cleaned you up, but you'll not be out shooting and poaching for a while, I can tell you that!'

She boiled some water and poured a generous measure of disinfectant into the bowl. 'This will sting,' she warned him, and when she dabbed the liquid on his open wounds, he almost leaped from the chair.

'You've a cut here needs a stitch or two,' she said, raising his fist to clean the knuckle. 'But it's too dangerous for you to show your face at the hospital.' Flattening his hand against her knee she cut lint and a strip of plaster and pulled it over the wound as tightly as she could. That done, she covered it with a bandage. 'Don't bend your fist,' she told him, 'or the wound will open again.'

When the washing and binding was done, she made him a hot, sugarless drink and gave him two painkillers to take with it. Then, sitting beside him, she demanded to know, 'Who have you been fighting with? And don't lie to me, son.'

They were both startled when another voice answered, a voice familiar to Luke but unknown to Rosie. 'He hasn't been fighting,' the girl said. 'He was attacked, and it's all my fault.'

Knowing Rosie was nervous of strangers, Luke told her, 'It's all right, Mum. This is Anna.'

Cursing herself for having left the door open, Rosie stared at the girl. She was small and pretty, with long, dark hair, and the sweetest, sorriest face.

'I'm sorry, Luke,' Anna said from the door. 'I didn't know he sent them after you . . . I overheard them talking, and I had to find you.'

Impatient, Rosie looked from one to the other. 'Will somebody tell me what's been going on?'

'Let her in,' Luke urged. 'She's taken her life in her hands coming here.'

'Come in then,' said Rosie, 'and close the door behind you.'

Anna sat down close to Luke.

'Right.' Rosie pointed to the girl. 'I'll hear your side of the story first, young lady, and be quick about it.'

The story tumbled out, and Rosie was shaken by it. 'So.' Her gaze shifted to Luke. 'All this time, when I thought you were out poaching, you've been having your way with this girl, and now you've made her pregnant, you thoughtless bastard!'

'It's not like you and . . . *him*,' Luke protested. 'I won't run out and leave her to face it all on her own.'

'We're not talking about *me*,' Rosie said angrily. 'It's *you* we're talking about, you and her.' Looking at Anna, she asked in a quiet, firm voice, 'You say your father's the head warden hereabouts.'

Anna nodded. 'If he finds Luke, he'll shoot him dead.'

'And he knows you're pregnant, does he?'

Afraid to answer, the girl clung to Luke, the truth betrayed by the fear in her eyes.

'How old are you, girl?'

'Nearly eighteen.'

At least Anna was not a baby – not like she was when Mike abandoned her.

'Luke says he won't leave you. What do you say to that?'

'I love him.' She gazed at Luke, and there was no doubt she was speaking the truth. 'I just want to be with him.'

'What about your parents?'

'My mother died four years ago. There's only my father, and he hates Luke. He hates anybody who gets near me. He would never let me have friends, and now he's found out about me and Luke, he means to split us up.' Her voice broke. 'Please don't let him. Luke and I want to be together. We want the baby . . . we want to be a real family.'

Luke confirmed every word she said. 'Help us,' he pleaded. 'Tell us what to do.'

Rosie looked at these two youngsters and felt the years roll away. She knew how it was. What was happening now was not Luke and Anna. It was her and Mike. But things were different then. This girl was not her. Anna was not alone, not like she had been. Alone and frightened, thrown on to the streets by her shamed parents. Anna was luckier. She had Luke. She had a chance to make something good come out of all this.

Rosie made up her mind. 'I have a plan which might suit us all.'

For days now she had been thinking about making her way back to Bridport but so many obstacles stood in her way, the main one being Luke who would have argued about the dangers in going back. She had even thought about letting him go his own way, but she knew only too well what it was like to be cut adrift at such a tender age. So in spite of the troubles he had brought her at different times, she had dismissed the idea of turning him out. But now she could see he was not the child she believed him to be. Here was a young man with a sense of commitment. It was plain to see he loved Anna, and Anna clearly adored him, and though her father might think differently, Rosie thought they had every right to be together.

She decided to help them, not just for their sakes but for hers too. Here was her chance to break away and carry out her plan. Right or wrong, she had to find Mike and do what she had always intended to do.

Luke listened to her plan and was torn two ways. 'If you let me and Anna have the camper van, where will you go? What will you do?'

'Let *me* worry about that,' she answered. 'I've

been on my own before, and I know the pitfalls.'

Looking at her face and seeing the light in her eyes, he suddenly realised. 'You're going back there, aren't you? You're going to *him*.'

'Yes.' There was no point in lying. 'Your father and I have unfinished business.'

He didn't know what she meant. 'I've never been sure whether you love him or hate him.'

She laughed. 'Both. The line between love and hatred is very delicate.'

Anna was intrigued. 'You never mentioned your father, Luke. I thought he might be dead.'

Luke looked away. 'He might as well be. He's a bastard!'

'Like mine. He's a bastard too. Where will we go, Luke?' This was her man and she carried his child. All she could do was trust him.

'As far away from here as possible.' He tried to raise his arm; the pain was excruciating. 'But if I can't drive, we won't be going anywhere.'

'I'll drive,' she offered. Luke argued that she had never driven anything bigger than a Ford Escort but she managed to convince him it was not a problem.

A few days later they left.

The parting was bitter-sweet. Rosie stood by the kerb, wrapped up against the cold, suitcase in hand, and a small wad of hard-earned money in her bag. 'You look after her now,' she told

Luke, and he promised he would.

Anna thanked her for her help. 'I'm not sure we should be letting you do this.'

'You've got no choice,' Rosie responded. 'And you'd best make tracks, before your father comes looking for the pair of you.'

'How will I know where you are?' Luke asked.

Rosie regarded him for a moment. 'You're not to worry about me, son. You've got someone of your own now, and a baby on the way. You think about them, and let the rest take its course.'

'You're going back to punish him, aren't you?'

'Like I said, your father and I have unfinished business. That's all you need to know. Now go on,' she urged. 'Anna's waiting.'

'Come with us, please.'

'I can't.'

The determination in her eyes and the defiant toss of her auburn head told him Rosie would not be persuaded from what she needed to do.

Reluctantly, he climbed in beside Anna. 'Take care of yourself,' he told Rosie. 'When the baby's born, we'll come and find you.'

Rosie watched them go with a heavy heart. 'I don't even know if I'll ever see you again,' she whispered, and not for the first time that day, the tears ran down her face. But she didn't regret her decision. Not for a minute. Not when she had Mike in her sights at last.

For two days, Rosie slept rough. She ate what

Nature provided, drank and washed in the streams, and made the fields her home.

She spent her time thinking, and at last she was ready. 'It's now or never,' she told herself.

Hitching a lift into Weymouth, she found a chemist shop in one of the side streets and bought black hair dye, small, sharp scissors, and a hand mirror.

When the items were paid for, she went down the street, scouring the shops until she found one suitable for her purpose. In here she selected a plain brown skirt and grey, long-sleeved blouse, with a woollen cardigan to match, and a dark duffel coat with a hood. At the back of the shop, she rummaged through boxes of shoes. The brown, flat-heeled ones were perfect for her new image.

In the changing room she inspected herself in the long mirror. Saddened and shocked to see how frumpy and old she looked, Rosie comforted herself with the knowledge that it was all part of a greater plan.

Having bought the clothing, she headed for the seafront. She felt closer to Mike now than at any time over these many months. At the promenade she hurried down to the ladies' toilets.

Just beyond the cubicles was a small washroom. 'That'll be 20p.' The attendant held out her hand. 'Face and hands only, and you bring your own soap.'

Rosie paid and entered. She waited until the

woman disappeared back inside her cubby-hole and then took out her scissors. Snip by devastating snip, she began hacking off her beautiful auburn hair. Not daring to look in the mirror, she cut until the wastebin was full, and her hair so close to her scalp it felt like a feather cap on her head.

Gathering her courage, she raised her eyes and looked at the image in the mirror. What she saw made her catch her breath in horror. 'Oh, Rosie!' Shocked by the image staring back at her, she whispered under her breath, 'How many more sacrifices must I make before it's over?'

She turned the hot and cold water taps on. When the sink was half filled, she took out the bottle of dye and placed it on the shelf beside her. The sooner she had washed and dyed what was left of her magnificent mane, the sooner the transition would be complete.

She had just applied the black hair dye, when a shriek from behind gave her a fright. 'What d'yer think you're doing?' the attendant demanded. 'Face and hands only, I said! Now, get out of here before I have the police down on you.'

'All right! All right!' Wiping the liquid from her eyes, Rosie splashed her face clean. 'I'm doing no harm,' she pleaded. 'Let me finish.'

'Why should I?'

When danger was about, Rosie had learned to think quickly. 'Do you like my clothes?'

The woman was taken aback. 'What d'you mean?'

Rosie fingered her jumper. 'My clothes. Do you like them?'

The woman took note of Rosie's attire – the smart jeans and attractive green jumper with its roll collar and pretty flower emblem. The leather ankle boots. The long dark woollen overcoat Rosie had worn on her way in was hanging on a peg beside her.

'Well?' Rosie saw the interest in the woman's eyes.

Wary, the woman answered, 'What if I do like them?'

'Let me finish here and you can have them.' When the dye began to drip in her face, she quickly wiped it away. She had never used dye before and was afraid it might stain her skin if she didn't hurry.

The woman turned her shifty gaze on the coat. 'That too?'

Rosie nodded. 'Is it a deal?'

'OK.' When she had started this job a week ago, she wasn't too keen. The other attendants had told her there were perks to be had if you kept your eyes peeled. Now she knew what they meant. 'You'd best wash that dye off your face and neck,' she suggested drily, 'or you'll be marked for weeks.'

She gave Rosie a bigger towel with which to dry her hair and from her tiny office she kept her

eye on her. She watched her comb her hair, and
she saw her dress herself in those awful, drab
clothes. And she wondered what trouble the
young woman had got herself into, to do such a
dreadful thing.

When Rosie handed over the bag of clothes,
the woman looked her up and down. 'It's got
nothing to do with me,' she said, 'but you must
be mad. I can't understand why anyone would
want to change these clothes,' she held up the
bag, 'for those.' She gestured at Rosie's new,
unattractive attire. 'What's more, if I had hair
like you've just dropped into that wastebin, they'd
have to murder me before I'd let them cut a single
strand of it.' Shaking her head, she asked sadly,
'Why ever did you do it?'

The woman seemed friendly enough now but
Rosie decided it would be unwise to get involved
in conversation with her. 'You're right,' she said
stiffly. 'It's none of your business.' She thanked
her for the towel, and her help. 'You've got the
best of the bargain.' Rosie glanced at the bag the
woman was holding.

The woman nodded. She had no cause to
disagree. 'Are you in some sort of trouble?' she
wanted to know.

Rosie laughed. 'I've been in trouble all my life,'
she said, and before the woman could question
her further, she made good her escape.

A few moments later, when she caught sight
of herself in a shop window, Rosie almost didn't

recognise herself. 'That's good,' she thought. 'From now on I can be whoever I want to be.'

The manager of the Landsmead Institute did not suspect Rosie was anything other than what she professed to be.

Seated behind his desk and wearing a look of authority, he allowed her a few minutes of his precious time. 'You do realise the work is . . .' he paused, wondering how to describe the filthy jobs she would have to carry out. 'What I'm saying is, we need a general help, and that means doing everything from cleaning out the patients' rooms to scrubbing the kitchen floor.'

'I understand, sir.' Rosie had perfected the humble approach. 'I'm not afraid of hard work.'

'Hmh.' He stared at her until she felt uncomfortable. 'And you say you haven't worked for some time?'

'That's right, sir. I've been looking after my aged mother. After she'd . . . gone . . .' she looked suitably upset, 'I sold the house and took to the road. Now I want to settle, get a proper job and somewhere to live.'

'Well, as I've already explained, the only accommodation we can offer is a small bed-sitting room behind the nurses' quarters.'

'That will suit me fine, sir.'

'And you say you can't supply me with any references whatsoever?'

'No, sir.' It was no good lying. The only way

was to convince him that she was the person for this job. 'But I'm honest, and I'll work long hours. I'm not worried about working in a hospital,' she assured him. 'I looked after my mother for so many years, I'll probably feel at home here.'

He stared at her shabby clothes and pretty face, and that awful crop of black hair, and he felt a pang of compassion. 'Normally we insist on references, but I have to admit, there are very few people who want this sort of job. The work really is demanding.'

'It doesn't bother me, sir.'

'Look, Miss . . .' His brow furrowed. He was never very good with names.

'Miss Downham,' she answered. 'Sheila Downham, sir.'

'Yes, well, Miss Downham, as you are the only person to reply in three weeks of advertising, I think I might give you the opportunity to prove yourself.'

Rosie smiled. 'Thank you very much, sir,' she answered humbly. 'You won't regret it.'

He smiled for the first time since she had come into the room. 'I don't know about that,' he said. 'Matron usually interviews new recruits but as she's not here for the next fortnight, the duty falls on me. I'm prepared to give you a trial, until Matron returns. After that, we'll see. How does that suit?'

'Thank you, sir.'

'Sixty pounds a week, plus overtime.' He

consulted his notes. 'Or forty pounds a week if you live in.'

'I'd rather live in, sir,' she answered. 'It'll be easier, especially if I'm working overtime and such.'

'How soon can you start?'

'Tomorrow, if you like, sir.'

'Good. Things have been difficult since the last woman left.' Bloody impossible, more like.

'Could I move my things in tonight, do you think?' The sooner she was settled in, the better.

'That seems perfectly reasonable to me.' He pressed a button on the telephone pad, and almost immediately a clerk came in. 'Show Miss . . .' Flustered, he looked at Rosie.

'Downham, sir.'

'Yes, of course.' Addressing the clerk, his manner softened. 'Miss Downham is starting work here tomorrow and she would like to see where she'll be living.' He gave the clerk a smile that was too intimate. 'The same room as before,' he said. 'Take her along now, would you? I believe she wants to move her belongings in tonight.'

The clerk returned his smile. As Rosie followed her down the outer corridor, she suspected there was more going on between those two than met the eye.

Nobody knew better than Rosie that things were rarely as they seemed.

CHAPTER FOURTEEN

From the other side of the kitchen table, Julie kept a keen eye on her daughter. Since Steve Palmer's death, Kerry had been morose and withdrawn. She had little time for her family, but where the business was concerned, she drove herself harder and harder, until the weight fell off her and her face grew haggard. 'You've got to let up,' Mike told her. 'You'll make yourself ill.'

She never listened.

In spite of knowing about her affair with Steve, he still loved her. 'Stay home today,' he urged now. 'Go back to bed – one day off won't hurt.' Striding across the room, he leaned over her. 'Let me keep an eye on your business, at least for today.' When she didn't reply, he leaned down to put his arms round her. 'I promise not to ruin you,' he teased. 'I do know a bit about running a business.'

'No!' Realising how harsh she sounded, she gave a half-smile. 'Thanks all the same,' she said, 'but I have to be there. I'm interviewing a new man today.' That would be hard, she thought, finding someone to take Steve's place. 'Anyway, I thought you had an important meeting with the sign-writer.'

'That can wait.'

'No, it can't. Not when you're so close to seeing it all come together at last.'

He didn't need much persuading. Excitement had mounted all week. Now that the office was ready and the two hire vehicles were at the sign-writer's, he couldn't wait for that first phone call to kick it all off. 'Are you sure?' He was always prepared to put Kerry's needs first.

'I'm fine,' she told him, with a glance at her mother who was silently listening. 'You get on with what you've got to do.' She pecked him on the cheek, eager to be rid of him.' Go on. You don't want to keep the sign-writer waiting.'

'OK. See you later then.'

He finished his coffee, said goodbye to the kids, and left for his appointment.

After he'd gone, Kerry sent the children upstairs. 'I want you down here, dressed and ready for school in ten minutes.' She looked at the clock. 'And no wasting time,' she warned. 'I've a busy day ahead of me.'

Julie waited until the children were out of earshot. 'I rarely see eye to eye with Mike,' she said, 'but this time he's right. Keep on the way you are and you'll run yourself into the ground.'

Kerry rounded on her, 'Leave it, Mother!'

'I can't leave it,' Julie persisted. 'It's painful to see you this way. I know how shocked you were by Steve's death, and I understand what you're feeling now.'

'Really?' Hostility rose like a bitter taste on her tongue. You don't know anything, she thought.

'Let me guess. You and Steve rowed, and now you can't forgive yourself, is that it?'

'Mind your own business.'

'I thought so.' Julie suspected there was more to it than that, but for now she was keeping her suspicions to herself. 'You rowed and then he died. You mustn't blame yourself. Guilt will drive you insane.'

'It's not *me* that's guilty.'

'What do you mean?'

Just then Susie came bounding into the room. 'Jack won't give me my PE kit. He keeps hiding it.'

A small, white bag came hurtling through the air, with Jack walking sedately behind. 'I did *not* hide it,' he protested. 'It was in your cupboard all the time. You didn't look properly.'

After inspecting them to make sure they were suitably washed and combed, Julie ushered them towards the hallway. 'No arguing, you two. Get your coats on.'

They were out there only a minute before the arguing started. 'I'd better go.' Taking her cup to the sink, Kerry rinsed it.

Julie couldn't leave it at that. 'What did you mean when you said it wasn't you that was guilty?'

Angry, Kerry swung round. 'It doesn't matter.'

'You think Steve was *murdered*, don't you?'

Kerry dried her hands and swept by, her head deliberately turned from her mother. 'Right, you kids!' she called to the bickering pair. 'In the car with you.'

'Kerry!'

'You don't give up, do you, Mother?'

Julie lowered her voice. 'You think Steve was murdered. And so do I.'

Kerry stared at her.

'And we both know who's capable of murder, don't we?'

Kerry shook her head. 'You don't know what you're saying.'

'Think about it. If it was obvious to me that you and Steve were still involved, what makes you think Mike didn't realise it as well? The way Mike is, there's no telling what he might have done.'

Kerry was silent. The same thought had crossed her own mind, but she had no intention of admitting it to her mother. She couldn't believe Mike really was a murderer, and neither did the police, evidently. They had asked a lot of routine questions, but nothing that suggested they suspected foul play. And the coroner had declared Steve's death accidental. Who was she to question the verdict?

Foot-weary and needing a bath, Rosie stacked

the mop and bucket in the cupboard.

'I'm glad it's Friday.' The patient was a homely-looking girl by the name of Mavis. Admitted to the hospital with manic depression, she had been here almost a year. 'My mum comes to see me on a Friday.' She smiled her lopsided smile.

Rosie had taken a liking to her. 'Hello, Mavis,' she said. 'What are you doing all this way from the ward?'

In the two weeks she had been here, Rosie had quickly learned the routine. She knew the patients and they knew her, and if they followed her from the ward, it was her responsibility to call someone in authority to deal with them. But she rarely did that. Instead, she would take them back where they came from herself – unless of course they were violent, and then she would press the bell and chat to them until someone arrived to take charge.

Mavis was easy. As Rosie headed towards her ward, Mavis followed.

'I know where you live,' she told Rosie. 'I came to see you yesterday and you weren't there.'

Not believing her for one minute, Rosie humoured her. 'How can you know where I live?'

'I followed the nurses, and I saw you through the window. You live at the back of the house, in that horrible little room.'

Rosie chided her. 'That's very bad of you, Mavis. You know you're not supposed to wander away from the ward.'

'Sometimes, when the nurses are busy, I go for a long walk. When I come back, they think I've been to the toilet.'

Rosie couldn't help but smile. 'One of these days they'll catch you at it and you'll be in real trouble.'

'You won't tell, will you, Rosie?'

Rosie promised. 'No, Mavis, I won't tell.' But she added a warning. 'I might, though, if I know you've been snooping on me or the nurses.'

'I like you.'

'Thank you, Mavis.' It was good to be liked.

'I like Nurse Jenkins too.' Her face crumpled with fear. 'But not Nurse Alice. She hurts me.'

Rosie stopped; Mavis stopped. 'Do you mean Alice Henshaw? When did she hurt you?' Rosie knew Henshaw had a violent temper.

'When I dropped the washbowl. She squeezed my arm and told me I was a lazy, wicked thing.' Rolling up her sleeve, she showed Rosie a long bruise on her arm.

Rosie was shocked. 'You'll have to be more careful, won't you? Then she won't have reason to hurt you.'

'She hurt you too. I saw her.'

'Did you?' Rosie didn't think anyone had seen.

'She slipped on your wet floor, didn't she?'

Rosie didn't like Mavis knowing. 'It was just an accident, Mavis. I put the notice out but she didn't see it.'

'You had the mop in the bucket.' Mavis

screwed up her face in concentration, trying to remember exactly what she had seen. 'She pushed the mop hard, and it hit you in the face.'

Rosie shrugged it off. 'We'll *both* have to be more careful then, won't we?' She would have to be doubly careful now that she knew Mavis had been following her.

'It's Friday.' Both incidents already forgotten, Mavis's face lifted in a smile. 'My mum comes to see me on a Friday.'

Rosie pushed open the door to the ward. 'In you go, Mavis.'

Satisfied the nurse had seen her, Rosie left her there and hurried away to her own tiny quarters. She hoped the bathroom was free so she could enjoy a long, lazy bath; a rare luxury for her.

The nurses' quarters were situated at the back of the hospital. Made up of four terraced houses, they each had a sitting room, two bedrooms, kitchen and bathroom. Built on the back of the last one, with its own access to the outside, Rosie's bedsitter had once been an outhouse. It consisted of one long room that doubled as a sitting room and bedroom, and it had a tiny scullery where she prepared her frugal meals. There was also a toilet, but no bathroom, so if she wanted a bath she had to take pot luck behind Nurses Jenkins and Henshaw.

Grabbing towel, soap, and a bottle of shampoo, Rosie wanted to get to the bathroom before they finished their shift. She went through the ground floor of the house and up to the bathroom. Pressing her ear to the closed door, she called out, 'Is anyone in there?' Since bursting in on Alice Henshaw, Rosie had been warned to shout before she opened the door; the bolt was broken and, so far, the caretaker had not found time to fix it. She called again, but there was no answer.

Delighted, Rosie went into the bathroom and turned on the taps. While the bath was filling she went to one of the two cupboards mounted on the wall, one marked 'Jenkins', the other marked 'Henshaw'. Opening the door marked 'Jenkins', she peered inside; there was a bar of blue soap, a flannel, and two tubes of toothpaste. 'Hmm. Nothing here worth nicking!' Then she looked in the one marked 'Henshaw'. Here she found a pretty bottle containing green bath oil. 'Go on, Rosie,' she urged. 'She'll not miss a drop or two, and you want to look your best, especially if you're seeing Mike tonight.'

Unscrewing the bottle, she poured a measure of oil into the water; she watched it froth and dance, before turning her attention to the door. 'You'd think *somebody* would fix the bloody bolt,' she grumbled. 'Any pervert could look in here.' She rammed the chair underneath the handle.

Stripping off her overall and undergarments, she stood before the mirror, naked but for the gold pendant round her neck. Heart-shaped, with a tiny centre diamond, it had been a gift from Mike. 'Look, Mike,' she murmured. 'Do you see how close I keep it?' Caressing the pendant, she spoke to him, holding his image strong in her mind. 'I remember the day you brought it to me . . . the day after I told you I was pregnant.' Sadness clouded her eyes. 'That night you went away, and I couldn't find you.' A tiny smile lifted the corners of her mouth. 'I've found you *now* though, haven't I? *And I won't ever let you leave me again.*'

She took the pendant off and placed it lovingly on the pile of folded clothes. Glancing up, she caught sight of herself in the mirror again. Taking a moment to regard her nakedness, she recalled how she used to look; young and firm, with all her life ahead of her. Knowing those times could never return, she gave a little shrug. 'If I wanted to, I could still turn a few heads,' she said smugly. 'But I don't want any other man. Mike is the only one I've ever wanted.' Finding him had been an uphill struggle, and even though she had him in her sights, he was still out of her reach. But not for long, she thought.

Half an hour later, she hurried back to her own quarters. 'They're not back yet,' she congratulated herself. 'You couldn't have timed it better.'

Safely back in her room, she reached under the bed and drew out a carrier bag. Opening it on the bed, she took out some clothes and a pair of pretty blue shoes. 'If that lavatory attendant hadn't forced me to give her my other clothes,' she muttered, 'I wouldn't have had to spend my last week's wages on these.'

That little incident had left a bitter taste in her mouth. 'When this is all over, I've a good mind to go back and teach her a lesson!' But she knew she wouldn't.

When she was dressed and looking her best, she twirled before the mirror. 'You look good, Rosie.' The satisfied smile fell away. 'Except for your hair. Mike always used to love your long, red hair. Remember how he would stroke it, and wind the curls round his finger?' She turned from the mirror. 'When he sees what you've done, he'll be so disappointed.'

A few minutes later, she was ready to leave, her heart pounding at the idea of seeing Mike once more. After checking the address, she tucked the little brown notebook into her bag. 'This hospital is not very secure,' she tutted. 'Not when a common cleaner can get access to patients' confidential files.' She chuckled. 'But then Rosie Sharman is no common cleaner. She's used to getting what she wants.' A hard look flitted over her features. 'And woe betide anyone who gets in her way!'

Discreetly slipping out the back way and down the alley, she made her way to the high street where she hailed a taxi. 'Harbour Lane, West Bay,' she told him briskly.

Climbing into the back, she caught him eyeing her long legs. Looking in the mirror, he smiled at her, thinking she might keep a man warm on a lonely night.

The chilling look she gave him soon cooled his ardour.

At the harbour, Rosie took a minute to get her bearings. 'I hope you're not playing games with me!' She glared at the driver through the window. 'This is the harbour front. I asked for Harbour Lane!'

Unperturbed, he held out his hand. 'That'll be two pounds. You'll find Harbour Lane right in front of you.' He pointed to the corner. 'It's easier for me to turn round here, and anyway it's right there, just a few steps away.'

Rosie paid the fee and hurried away. 'Bastard!' Anger came quickly these days. 'I'll walk back,' she decided. 'Two pounds for a couple of miles – it's daylight robbery!'

She thought of Mike and how they would soon be together. And the anger melted away.

Locating Mike's home, she positioned herself on the wall opposite; tucked into a recess, it was the perfect place from which to see and not be seen. With the lights on, and the curtains open, Rosie had a clear view of the inside. Somehow she had not imagined Mike in a house with traditional furniture and chintz curtains; when she had known him, he was like her – like all the sixties children, wild and wanton. 'The passing years change everything,' she thought sadly. But it didn't change the way she felt about him. Nothing could do that.

With dinner over, the children in bed, and Julie watching TV in the kitchen, Mike and Kerry had escaped to the lounge.

Building up the fire with more logs, Mike glanced at his wife. Hunched on the settee, she looked so small and vulnerable. Going to sit beside her, he asked, 'Are you all right?'

'Yes. Why shouldn't I be?' She didn't look at him. There was too much guilt in her eyes. Her mother had strengthened the idea in her mind that Steve's death was no accident, and that maybe, just maybe, Mike *was* a murderer after all.

'Is it something I've done?' He sensed her fear and it puzzled him.

She looked at him, her steely gaze unnerving. 'I don't know, Mike. *Have* you done something?'

'I've spent the whole day chasing my tail,' he replied lightly, 'trying to get the business going. I've seen the accountant, I've chosen the signs, and I've placed several adverts for a mechanic. I've decided I can manage on my own at the desk, until we get going properly. I've got another appointment with the accountant next week, and a few days interviewing candidates for the mechanic's job. Meanwhile I have to get the licence back before I can start trading. And that's it. In a couple of weeks, three at the most, I'll be my own boss again.'

Reaching out, he took hold of her hand and squeezed it. 'It's all thanks to you,' he said gratefully. 'I don't know how you did it, but like I said, I'll pay back every penny.'

'Mike, can I ask you something?' Seeing him all excited and keen, she could not believe he was capable of taking a man's life.

He nodded, his face serious. 'Ask away. I knew there was something on your mind. You've been too quiet all evening.'

'Do you think Steve was murdered?'

The abruptness of the question took him aback. 'I hadn't really thought about it,' he said cagily. 'Didn't the coroner say it was an accident?'

'I still find it hard to believe he fell down those steps.'

'What's triggered all this off?' He sensed Julie might be behind it. 'Has someone suggested he was murdered?'

Kerry felt like a traitor. 'No,' she answered too quickly. 'It's just that he knew those steps so well – I've seen him run up and down them in the dark, and never lose his footing. The power went off one night some time ago. Steve was in the office. It was late and everywhere was pitch black, but he ran down the stairs, found his way to the fuse box and had the whole place lit up again in no time. How could he do that but fall down and break his neck on those same stairs?'

'Did you tell all this to the police?'

'Yes, but they didn't take much notice. In fact

that miserable inspector said that sometimes it can be easier to find your way in the dark.'

'He's right, you know.' Mike truly agreed with that. 'In the dark, all your senses come into play. In the light, you tend not to concentrate so much.' He knew that from his time at the hospital. Sometimes, in the dark, he had felt he had the eyes of a cat and always he could hear his own heart beating. In the daylight, outside influences interfered with his senses.

'You didn't like Steve, did you?'

'I didn't know him well enough to like or dislike him.' In fact, knowing what he knew, he resented him immensely. 'You mustn't let Steve's death play on your mind,' he urged. 'Torturing yourself won't bring him back.'

Alerted to the subtle change in his voice, she looked into his eyes. 'I'm not torturing myself. Why should you think that?'

'I know you were fond of him.'

She sat up, nervously wringing her hands together. 'Look, Mike, there's something you should know.'

Raising his hand, he gestured for her not to say any more. 'I think I already know,' he said. 'But it's over now, isn't it? We mustn't let it come between us.' He had to choose his words carefully. 'I had an idea you and Steve were having an affair, but I didn't want to confront you with it. If you were working up to making a choice, it had to be *your* choice. I didn't want to destroy any future we might have together by issuing ultimatums, and anyway, what right did I have to do that?'

Kerry was ashamed. 'You had every right. You're my husband.'

'Not for the past three years.' How he wished he could turn back the clock. He had to hear it from her own lips. 'Would you have chosen him, do you think?'

She took a moment to answer. When she spoke, he knew she was telling the truth, and he was filled with regrets. 'I had already told Steve we were finished. I said I had to make a go of it with you. That the affair we had was because I was lonely; that it didn't mean anything more than that.' She paused. 'I turned him away . . . told him he would have to find other work.' Tears filled her eyes. 'That's why I'm so obsessed with what happened. Because I feel partly to blame. If he really did fall down those steps, it was because his mind was on me and what I'd done to him.'

'I don't deserve you.' Hooking his hand beneath her chin, Mike raised her face to his. 'And if you were that lonely, I can't blame you for turning to someone else for comfort. We have so much going for us, Kerry. Don't let anything spoil it. Not now.' When she smiled, his heart soared. She was his at last. 'Dry your tears,' he murmured. 'I'm taking you out.'

She laughed. 'Where?'

'I don't know. Anywhere! We can take a boat

out and sail all the way to the horizon or, if you're not feeling that adventurous, we can stroll down to the Fisherman's Inn and have a quiet drink by the log fire.'

Greatly relieved that her secret was out in the open, she threw her arms round him. 'We can do that here,' she suggested meaningfully.

'You brazen hussy!'

'You're not complaining, are you?'

The look he gave her was charged with emotion. 'Never!' Gently pushing her away, he told her, 'Stay right where you are. I'll be back in a minute.'

He went out of the room and returned moments later. 'Close your eyes,' he said, and when she did as she was bid, he came across the room. She felt his weight push down beside her. She felt his hands on her shoulders, and his breath gentle on her face. 'I love you so much,' he murmured; kissing her passionately, he made her shiver with anticipation.

Outside, in the cold night air, Rosie watched them kiss, and her heart was dark with hatred.

She saw him release her, and she waited with morbid fascination while he took the small white box out of his pocket to show her. She saw Kerry's face open with delight. Mike took the gold pendant out of the box and placed it lovingly round his wife's neck.

Rosie was devastated. 'You bastard!' she hissed.

'You can't give her a pendant. You can't do that to me . . .' Her voice trailed away in a sob. 'Oh, Mike, I thought it was a special thing, between you . . . and . . . me . . .'

Hurt and disillusioned, she reached to her neck, fingers searching for her own gold pendant. *It wasn't there!*

Frantic, she tore at her clothes, shaking them loose, thinking the pendant might have got caught up inside. 'I can't have lost it!' On her hands and knees she scoured the ground, breaking fingernails and grazing her knees.

Frustrated, she stood up and ran off down the street. 'It's in the bathroom. I must have left it in the bathroom.' Her only thought was to get it back. The prospect of losing it was too crippling to contemplate. She ran down to the harbour, not sure which way to go. Seeing a cruising taxi, she hurried towards it, not realising it was the same driver who had dropped her off earlier.

'You're lucky I'm here,' he said as she got in. 'I just dropped a fare off . . . stayed on for a quick pint at the pub.' Then in the half-light he saw her face. 'Blimey, it's you!' A swift glance at her dishevelled clothes and smudged make-up, and he assumed she was on the game. 'Got a rough one, did you?' he chuckled. 'Myself, I'm always gentle as a lamb . . .'

He was stopped short when she flung open the door and would have scrambled out. 'Hold on, you silly cow! I don't mean anything by it. Tell me where you want to go and I'll have you there before you know it.'

She sat on the edge of the seat. 'Landsmead Institute,' she panted. 'And for God's sake, hurry!'

As he drove off, he glanced at her face, wild and mad-looking. 'Landsmead Institute, eh?' he muttered. 'I should've known.'

He would have drawn up outside the institute but because she didn't want to risk being seen, Rosie told him to drive on and drop her a short distance away. She paid him and then ran back along the road. He shook his head forlornly. 'Mad as a bleedin' hatter!' He didn't linger and, fares or not, he did not come back that way again.

As Rosie ran along the darkened street, a slight scuffling sound made her look round. There was no one there. A few moments later, she heard footsteps behind. When she looked again, the street was deserted. 'You're jumping at shadows,' she told herself, yet she couldn't help feeling that someone was following. Fear made her run all the faster.

Somewhere along the way she lost a shoe, but she didn't stop for it. Instead she kicked off the other one and didn't halt until she reached the trees. From here, she could sneak in the back way and no one would be any the wiser.

Anxious, she looked back. No one there. No one ahead either. The way was clear.

In the hallway she took a moment to catch her breath. 'Of course. Jenkins is off to her family this weekend, and Alice Henshaw is down to work night shift.' She had seen the shift rota when cleaning Matron's office. 'So there's nobody here but me – at least until eight o'clock tomorrow morning.'

In the camper van she was rarely nervous, but here, whenever she was alone at night, she was always restless. Shivering from head to toe, she wondered about being here all alone until tomorrow morning. 'What's the matter with you?' she muttered. 'Stop acting like a scared kid. It's not as if somebody's going to creep up on you and slit your throat.' The idea did little to ease her mind.

She went quickly up the stairs and headed for the bathroom. She glanced behind her. The feeling that she had been followed still lingered.

Pushing open the door to the bathroom, her searching gaze went straight to the chair where she had piled her clothes, with the pendant on top. There was no sign of it now though; not on the chair or beneath. 'It's *got* to be here,' she groaned. 'It can't be anywhere else.' Dropping to her knees she searched every inch of the floor. 'It's gone.' She was devastated. 'But where could it have gone?' She ran through it all in her mind. 'I put it on top of my clothes . . . afterwards, when I'd had my bath, I got dressed and went down. But I don't remember seeing it after I left this room, and I didn't miss it until I got to Mike's place. I *must* have lost it here . . . The towel!' She ran down the stairs and into the laundry room at the back of the house. 'I brought the towel down and put it in the wash basket!' she cried. 'I remember I put it down on the chair while I dressed. The pendant could have been caught up in the towel!' It was her last hope.

Flicking on the light as she went in, Rosie went straight to the laundry basket, and there, nestling on top, was the pink towel she had used. Carefully she took it out and laid it on the floor. On all fours, she went over every inch of it. Finally, she had to concede that it was not there. She then tipped the laundry basket upside down, sorting through the dirty washing: frilly briefs, towels stained with mascara and hair dye, all the usual, mucky things. 'It's not here.' Dejected, she put everything back. She thought of the pendant Mike had just put round his wife's neck, and for one wicked moment she wished it had been a hanging rope.

At the sink, she washed and dried her hands. As she turned away, out of the corner of her eye she caught sight of something glittering.

She went over to the worktop. What had caught her eye was part of a gold chain dangling from inside a small wall cupboard. Gingerly, she opened it. There was washing powder, fabric softener and such inside, and tucked right behind these was her precious pendant.

Elated, she snatched it up and pressed it close to her heart. But how had it come to be here?

'Somebody *took* it.' Who? Nobody was in the house. No matter. She had it back now, and that was the most important thing.

She put the pendant on and swung round, arms out, softly laughing. Suddenly she stopped, eyes wide and heart fluttering. 'What was that?' It was coming from outside, the very same sound she had heard before – soft, urgent scuffling. She backed away, instinct warning her she was in danger.

She hid in the laundry cupboard and waited, frightened eyes peeping out through the narrow chink between the doors. 'Don't let them come in here,' she whispered. 'Please, don't let them come in here.'

The soft shuffling footsteps slowed, then came right into the room. Inside the cupboard, hardly daring to breathe, Rosie remained absolutely still. She could see very little; a strip of wall, a patch of floor, and that was all. But there was nothing wrong with her hearing. She heard the familiar click of the door being closed and, soon after, the key being turned. Then came the sound of the washing-machine door being opened.

Rosie stretched her neck to try and see what was happening. By leaning her head over to the right, she got a blinkered view of the washing machine. Yes, the door was open, and she could see someone's back – a long, dark coat, and brimmed hat. Whoever it was wore gloves ... small hands. A woman? The gloved hands reached down to raise a bundle of washing. Strange, thought Rosie, why would anyone wear *gloves* to handle the washing? Unless . . . Oh, dear God, who was it out there?

Now the bundle of washing was in her sight, and her nerves froze. *The washing was covered in blood.*

Not just a trickle of blood, or a dark, meandering stain such as she had seen on hospital sheets and operating gowns. It was far more sinister than that. And the garments were not hospital gowns. They appeared to be a woman's clothing – a blouse; items of underwear, and what could have been a skirt.

Suddenly, Rosie did not want to know who was out there. She closed her eyes, every sound deafening to her heightened senses.

She heard the washing-machine door close, then the little drawer open and that peculiar woosh of washing powder being poured in. The machine started and the water began running; all was familiar to Rosie, but not comforting. Not like this.

Now she could hear the sound of the tap running in the sink. A shadow crossed her line of vision. Returning to the spot from where it had collected the bundle of washing, the figure bent down and began scrubbing the flagstones . . . Scrub, scrub, scrub – the sound grated on Rosie's nerves. There followed a flurry of activity, doors being opened and closed, slammed in anger, she thought; and then, as it passed the cupboard, the figure paused, its dark shape blotting out the light. It seemed to be listening, watching for something.

Inside the cupboard, Rosie was sweating so much it ran down her neck. She was convinced she was about to be discovered.

Abruptly, the figure moved and the chink of light reappeared. Rosie heard the outer door being unlocked, then the light was switched off, plunging her into total darkness. There came the sound of receding footsteps, and once again Rosie was all alone.

It took a few moments before she mustered the courage to emerge from her hiding place. Even then, she came out cautiously. She fumbled her way to the door and peered out. There was no one to be seen. Sagging with relief, Rosie's hand went instinctively to the pendant round her neck, drawing comfort from the feel of it. It brought her nearer to Mike. And Mike was her strength.

Daring to switch on the light, she looked at the washing machine; the clothes were tumbling, like any other wash, yet not like any she had ever seen. Her fearful gaze went to the sink, where a river of red water was being pumped down the drain.

Unable to watch any more, she shut her mind to it all and hurried back to her room. Once inside, she threw home the bolt on the door, turned the lock and checked all the windows.

Suddenly, she froze. 'There's somebody outside!' Flattening herself against the wall, she
watched the shadow pass the window. 'Oh, God!'
Her throat closed tight and her tongue stuck to
the roof of her mouth.

When a moment later a knock came on the
door, she thought she would die there and then.
Then a voice she instantly recognised said, 'Rosie.
I know you're in there. Please, Rosie, let me in.'

Terror turned to rage.

Rosie hurried to the door. 'Mavis, is that you?'
Even though she was certain, she was loath to
open the door.

'Let me in!'

Rosie unbolted the door and flung it open. 'You
bugger, Mavis!' Grabbing her by the arm, she
dragged her inside. 'What the hell are you doing
wandering about this time of night? You scared
me half to death!'

'I came to see you,' Mavis was clearly distressed. 'I couldn't find you.'

Mavis was wearing a long dark coat and
expensive leather gloves.

Horrified, Rosie was half afraid to ask, 'Mavis,
were you in the nurses' laundry room just now?'

Confused, Mavis shook her head. 'I don't think
so.'

Rosie pointed to the coat. 'The coat and gloves,
are they yours?'

Worried, Mavis shook her head.

'Where did you get them?'

'I found them. I didn't steal them, Rosie, honest. I found them. I want to keep them.' She began crying.

Convinced Mavis was no danger to her, Rosie closed and bolted the door. 'Sit down, Mavis,' she invited. 'We have to talk.'

When the two of them were seated opposite each other, Rosie gently quizzed her. 'The coat and gloves, Mavis, where did you find them?'

Mavis pointed to the window. 'Out there.'

'Where exactly? Did you find them in the hospital bins?'

Mavis shook her head. 'In the woods.' She laughed. 'I saw somebody.' Preening herself in the coat, she lowered her voice to an intimate whisper, 'They were hiding them, but I saw.'

'Who did you see? Who do these clothes belong to?'

Mavis stiffened, a look of fear in her eyes. 'Not telling.' Scrambling out of the chair, she backed away. 'Stop asking me bad things.'

'It's all right, Mavis.' Carefully, Rosie got out of the chair. 'I don't want to frighten you. I want to help.'

Continuing to back away, Mavis whimpered, 'I want to go now. Somebody might miss me. I'll be punished.'

'I'll take you back.'

'No!' She ran to the door and tried to unbolt it. 'I have to go. Let me go!'

Rosie tried to calm her but Mavis managed to

unbolt the door and fled into the night. Alarmed that Mavis might hurt herself, or that someone else might want to hurt her, Rosie went after her.

From a distance, she saw her run through the back doors to the hospital; the porter stopped her and appeared to be talking to her, probably giving her a good telling off, Rosie thought. Mavis would be safe now, she decided, and made her way back.

In her room, Rosie leaned against the door. 'I should call the police,' she murmured. 'But I daren't. They'll say I'm involved. They'll blame me for Eddie's murder, and lock me away for life.' She shook at the prospect. 'I can't call them, I can't!' There was only one thing to do. 'I'll talk to Mavis tomorrow and find out what I can.'

For the third time that night, she checked that the door was secure. That done, she went to the settee and settled down. She didn't turn off the light. She didn't undress, nor did she wash. The truth was, she didn't feel safe.

Lying there, she stared at the ceiling, her mind in chaos. She glanced at the window, making sure the curtains were tightly drawn. Then she looked towards the door, and noticed something on the floor next to it. She got up and went to pick it up. It was a small blue book, much like the notebooks the nurses used. 'Mavis must have dropped it when she was struggling to unbolt the door.' Taking it back to the settee, Rosie opened it and began to read.

It was a diary – *containing the thoughts of a mad mind.*

After the first page she slammed it shut. 'This can't be Mavis's,' she muttered, horrified. 'It must belong to whoever hid those clothes.' The same person who had put those bloodied clothes in the washing machine. The same person, she was sure, who had stolen her pendant. 'Why did they take my pendant? Maybe they meant to blame me for something terrible.'

She daren't think what.

'Go on then.' The porter scowled at Mavis. 'Get yourself back to bed or Matron will have your hide!'

'You won't tell, will you?' Mavis pleaded.

'I should do,' he told her firmly, 'and I will if I find you sneaking by me again.'

'I'm sorry.' She really was.

'You will be. Especially if you cause trouble. The nurses haven't got time for trouble.'

'Can I go now?'

'Mind you think about what I said, no more sneaking out at night.' Looking her over, he wondered how she came by such an expensive coat. 'Go on then,' he said more kindly, 'and behave yourself in future or I'll have to tell them what you've been up to.'

Alarmed by his remark, she started crying. 'I haven't been up to nothing!'

'Hey!' He tried to make amends. 'I didn't mean

it, Mavis. I wouldn't get you in trouble but you have to understand, it's wrong of you to be roaming about at night. You see, it's my job to keep an eye on things. I have to make sure nobody goes in or out. But you caught me napping. If I told them that, I could easily lose my job. Now, we neither of us would want that, would we?'

'I don't mean to roam about. I can't help it.'

Some way off, the shadow stayed hidden, waiting for the moment.

While the porter lectured Mavis, softly it advanced, slithering by until, with a satisfied sigh, it was safely inside the building. On silent footsteps, it went towards the stairway, and there it stayed. With blackness in its heart.

'Goodnight then, Mavis.' The porter urged her away. 'I'll say nothing about it this time.'

Mavis made her way along the passage and on towards the stairs.

The shadow moved. Like a spider after its prey.

When Mavis got close to the stairway, she paused, wary. 'Is someone there?' It was so dark under the stairs. She never liked coming this way at night.

When it happened, it was so swift, she didn't even have time to cry out. Out of the blackness, the hand clamped roughly over her face. She felt herself being bodily lifted. 'You saw me, didn't you, Mavis?' The voice was low, shivering with hatred. 'You'll wish you hadn't.'

Outside, the night was thickening; only the sound of owls disturbed the air.

Inside, the door from the boiler room creaked open, then quickly closed again. A figure emerged, carrying a long, dark coat.

After making certain there was no one to see, the figure ran across the lawns and into the spinney. From here, it went over the banks and down to the river. Then it stood for a time, staring at the icy-cold water; its hypnotic flow mesmerised even the most chaotic of minds.

The coat was raised high, the gloves taken from the pocket and thrown, one at a time, into the growling water. Then the coat. The softest of laughter rose on the air. The figure watched the garments bobbing and diving in the water. Then they were gone, swept out to sea.

All done, the figure went on its way.

Try as she might, Rosie couldn't sleep. She heard the owl outside, and though it had never disturbed her before, tonight it made her shiver.

At five minutes to one, she heard footsteps approaching; afraid but curious, she lifted the curtain and peered out. Emerging from the direction of the hospital was the figure of a woman. Head down against the cold wind, the woman moved quickly, until she was close enough to recognise. Rosie gave a sigh of relief. 'It's Alice Henshaw!'

She turned away, but then hesitated. 'Maybe I should go and ask her if Mavis got back all right.' The temptation receded. 'No, I'd better not. If Mavis was caught, it would have been Henshaw who got it in the neck. After all, she was on duty. She should have known Mavis was likely to run off.'

Thinking Henshaw might be in a foul mood, Rosie dropped the curtain, believing herself fortunate that she was not responsible for looking after those who couldn't look after themselves, though she felt ashamed to be thinking it.

She brewed herself a mug of coffee, and sat thinking about the events of the night, turning the mug round and round in her hands until the coffee grew cold and undrinkable. Emptying the coffee down the sink, she re-boiled the kettle and made herself another.

Her eyes were drawn to the diary. She went over and apprehensively picked it up. 'It *can't* be Mavis's!' The more she thought about it, the more she believed Mavis was incapable of such shocking thoughts. She put it down and drank her coffee while it was hot, deliberately averting her gaze from the little blue notebook.

After a while, she finished her coffee, placed the mug on the floor, and with renewed determination opened the notebook. She leafed through it, not reading it continuously, just a passage here and there.

* * *

One day, I must kill them both. I have tried to love them, but the hatred is too strong. Last night, I crept into their room and watched them while they slept. He had his arm round her, and she didn't even know! I hate her for that . . . hate her!

One day soon, I'll make them pay for what they've done to me. I'm ugly, I know that, but it's their fault. They made me ugly. They were too old. The other children would tease me . . . 'Is that your grandma?' they'd say. I told them, yes, but they laughed at me. They knew I was lying.

Daddy said I was bad because I didn't work hard enough at school. He said I would never amount to anything. When I told him I passed my exams, he didn't believe me. He laughed. Mummy didn't tell him not to laugh. She'll be sorry for that! They'll both be sorry.

When I was little, I heard them rowing. He told her I needed to be disciplined. I heard them talking later . . . about how they should never have got me from the bad man. I don't know who 'the bad man' is, but I'll find out. Then they'll wish I hadn't.

They were always wanting me to make

friends. They think I don't know why, but I do. It's because they want to be rid of me. But I won't leave. I must punish them first. Besides, I need to find out about 'the bad man'.

They say some people are mad, but sometimes I think I'm madder than any of them.

4 August 1980. This is a special day. At long last, I think I've found someone who understands me. He never tells me I'm ugly, and he never laughs at me; not like they do. I haven't told him because he might not like it. I'm so ugly, I don't suppose he could ever love me, so I'll always protect him, and he will never know.

I have them under my thumb now. There was a time when they ordered me about, but now they have to do what I tell them, or they know what might happen. When they realise what I have in mind, they'll beg me for mercy. They'll have to suffer for a while, before the time comes to put them out of their misery.

The time is very near.

Still holding the book, Rosie let it rest in her lap. She had read only snatches of what was written but it was enough to make her aware that, not too far away, was someone who thought nothing of committing murder. It was a woman, someone who had lost all sense of reality; some poor, wretched soul, who was, in her own words, 'madder than any of them'. Strange that, Rosie thought. Madder than who?

Sitting there, alone with her thoughts, Rosie drew comfort from the slight noises emanating from the upper reaches of the house. 'Sounds as if I'm not the only one having trouble getting to sleep,' she remarked.

If Alice Henshaw had been any sort of an approachable being, she might have gone up and shown her the diary. But common sense prevailed. 'See Mavis and find out where she got this diary,' she told herself. 'Then we'll decide what's to be done. But I'll have to be careful how I go about it. I can't risk attracting attention to myself. Not when the police are probably still itching to get their hands on me.'

One thought led to another, and soon she was thinking of Luke and his new girlfriend. 'I wonder where they are now,' she mused. 'On the open road somewhere, where I should be if it wasn't for Mike.'

With Mike's name on her lips she lay back against the cushions. Closing her eyes, she gave herself up to thoughts of him. 'Oh, Mike, if only I had you, everything would be worthwhile.' But she hadn't got him – at least not yet.

Mike filled her mind, the book slipped to the floor and soon she was sleeping; a shallow, unsettled sleep, disturbed by pain and emotion.

It was the sirens that woke Rosie.

Sitting up in the chair, it took her a moment to gather her wits. 'Police!'

Her first thought was that they had found her. Scrambling up, she ran to the window. 'Oh, my God!' The scene outside was chaos. Two police cars flanked the hospital entrance; there were uniformed men everywhere, and Matron was looking more serious than Rosie had ever seen her. Slowly shaking her head, she was talking to a police officer.

The sirens Rosie had heard grew louder, and then the ambulance came screaming in, drawing to a halt close to the side entrance. Two paramedics leapt out, one going to the back of the ambulance, while the other ran across to speak to the approaching police officer.

Still dazed from sleep, all Rosie could understand was that they were not here for her. But something bad had obviously happened.

She saw the porter. Seated alone on a bench, he looked pale and ill, puffing on a cigarette as if his life depended on it.

Rosie quickly dressed. Surveying herself in the mirror, she decided it would be hard for anyone to recognise her as Rosie Sharman. 'You've done such a good job,' she told her image, 'your own mother wouldn't recognise you.'

She let herself out and made her way to the porter. She sat down beside him. 'What's happened, Tom?' she asked. 'Why are the police here?' While she spoke, she kept a keen eye on their movements.

Tom looked deeply shocked. 'I've told them all I know,' his voice trembled, 'I need to sit quiet for a few minutes . . .' He patted his chest. 'My old heart ain't what it was.'

Rosie was gentle. 'It's not Mavis, is it? Don't tell me she's run off again?'

When he stared at her, she sighed. 'Oh, Tom, isn't she a bugger, eh? I told her to go straight back and I watched her come across to the hospital. I saw her talking to you.'

When Tom looked up, she saw he was crying and her heart sank. 'What's happened, Tom? Tell me!'

'It weren't my fault. I warned her, go straight back to your ward, that's what I said. Like you, I knew she'd be in real trouble if Matron found out. I'd have got the sack too. She knew that. That's why I was so sure she'd gone back to her ward.' Overwhelmed by it all, he bowed his head. 'I never dreamed she'd gone downstairs.'

'Downstairs?' Rosie was impatient. 'The boiler room, you mean?' Why would Mavis go down to the boiler room?

Covering his face with his hands, he sobbed helplessly. 'I went down there first thing . . . same as always. On a winter's morning it's nice to warm your arse. Me and the maintenance man like to sit and have a chat when it's quiet, and besides, it gets lonely in my little office. He makes us a brew and it breaks the day, if you know what I mean.'

'But what about Mavis?' Rosie said impatiently.

Tom closed his old eyes and put his hand over them, as if fending off some terrible thing. 'She was . . .' he shuddered. 'Oh, dear God!'

'Tom! What are you trying to tell me?'

His voice calmer now, he went on, 'Like I said, I went down, same as I always do first thing of a morning. There was no sign of Bob. I called out, but it was that quiet, only the sound of the boiler churning away. I thought he'd gone out for a minute or two, so I filled the kettle and put it on, and I waited . . . I didn't see him, not at first. Lying on the floor, he was, right by my feet, and I didn't even see him.'

'What? You mean he was hurt? Had there been an accident?'

'Lying in a pool of blood, he was.' Tom gulped hard. 'I could see he were dead straightaway.'

'*Dead?*'

'I panicked. I ran out . . . went to get help.' He gave a low, shuddering cry. 'That was when I saw her.'

'Who, Tom? Not Mavis. Tell me it wasn't Mavis.' The look on Tom's face confirmed what she knew in her heart.

* * *

Detective Inspector Webb watched the body being carried to the ambulance.

'Too late for this one,' the officer remarked. 'A heavy blow to the back of the head. He wouldn't have known a thing.'

'What about the other one?'

The policeman looked as if he was about to throw up. 'Don't know, sir. They're down there now.'

'Are you all right?'

'No, sir.'

'Bit of a shock, eh?'

'Yes, sir.' He looked grey. 'Can I take a few minutes out, sir?'

'Go on. Five minutes, then I want you back here.'

He went at a run. A short time later he could be heard pewking in the bushes.

'Poor sod.' Sergeant Madison had finished taking notes from Matron. 'Green behind the ears.' He gestured towards the shrubbery. 'He'll get used to it.'

DI Webb glared at him. 'Not on *my* patch, he won't! Whoever did this is a bloody psycho. I want him caught before he can do it again. Get every available man on to it,' he ordered. 'I want results, and I want them fast!'

'Yes, sir.'

Webb glanced at Madison's notebook. 'Right then, what have we got?'

'The woman is Mavis Dewhurst, a patient at

the hospital. According to Matron, she had a habit of absconding but they always got her back.'

'Not this time, eh?'

'Well.' He consulted his notebook. 'It seems she went missing again last night. It was only when the morning shift arrived that they saw her bed had not been slept in.'

'What about the *night* shift? Why didn't they realise she was missing?'

'There were two nurses on last night, Nurse York and Nurse Henshaw. We've spoken to them both and neither had any idea she'd gone. Nurse Henshaw said she checked Mavis Dewhurst's bed while doing her rounds. It would have been Nurse York's job to check after lights out, but by all accounts they had a bad night.' He tapped his notebook. 'Apparently one of the more violent inmates decided to go on the rampage.'

'York and Henshaw – you got them out of their beds, did you?'

'You could say that.' He laughed. 'Nurse York wasn't too happy to be woken up early. I pity the poor sod who marries her. The other one, Henshaw, was woken by the sirens. She came across to see what was going on.'

'Where are they now?'

'In the dayroom. PC Hawkins is keeping an eye on them.'

'What about the man who found the bodies?'

'That's him over there.' He pointed to Tom. One of the nurses was with him now. 'I feel sorry for the old bugger. Fancy stumbling across that lot down there, eh?' He whistled through his teeth. 'Got a dicky heart too. It's a wonder it didn't finish him off.'

'What sort of a monster would do a thing like that?'

'God knows.'

'He's got to be demented, to cut up a young woman like that.' He shook his head. 'I've seen some things in my time, but . . . We've got to pull out all the stops on this one.'

'Don't worry, sir, we'll get the bastard.'

At that moment, two paramedics came out of the boiler room. The stretcher they carried was rigged with drips and all manner of life-saving equipment. Lying there, white as death and unmoving, Mavis looked a terrible sight.

Webb followed them. After they put her in the ambulance, he asked, 'Do you think she'll live?'

'Your guess is as good as mine.' The taller of the two closed the doors. 'It's a miracle she's alive at all.'

From not too far off and well out of sight, Rosie heard every word. She decided to put as much distance between herself and the police as possible. No one saw her there. No one saw her leave.

Just then there was a flurry of activity when Hawkins reported to Webb that one of the nurses had gone missing.

'What the bloody hell do you mean, gone

missing? I thought you were on watch!'

'I was, sir! I never moved from the door.'

'Then how the hell did she get out?'

'There's a window, sir, small and high up. It's the only other way out.'

'*Which* nurse?'

'Henshaw, sir.'

'What about the other one?'

'She stayed put, but didn't let us know till Henshaw had gone.'

'Right. Get over to Henshaw's quarters with Sergeant Madison. I want that place searched from top to bottom.'

'Right away, sir.'

In Alice Henshaw's room, they found nothing of interest, apart from a torn photograph.

'Wonder who this is?' said Hawkins idly.

Madison took it from him. He stared at the face in the picture. 'I know him,' he said.

'Oh? Who is he then?'

'I'm sure it's Mike Peterson.' Madison was delighted. Now DI Webb would have to take him seriously.

Later that day, Mike opened the door to DI Webb and Sergeant Madison. 'Are you Mr Peterson?' It was Webb who asked. 'Mr *Mike* Peterson?' In fact, he recognised him from their enquiries the year before.

When Mike confirmed that yes, he was Mike

Peterson, they showed him their identity cards and asked to come in.

'What's this about?' he asked as he showed them into the lounge where Kerry had just got back from work.

First, they had more questions. Did Mike know a Nurse Alice Henshaw? Did he know the injured woman? When was the last time he visited Landsmead Institute? There were other questions too, questions that prompted Kerry to intervene.

'It seems to me you should explain what you want,' she told them angrily. 'Why exactly are you here?'

'We're investigating a very serious crime,' DI Webb explained. 'Yesterday a man was murdered and a woman seriously injured – she may yet die. We're questioning everyone who might have known them.'

'Mavis was a patient at Landsmead Institute for at least as long as I was there,' Mike told them. 'Of course I knew her.'

'And you knew Nurse Henshaw?'

'Well, yes. I was in her care for most of the time.'

'I see.'

'What has Nurse Henshaw got to do with any of this?'

'How well did you know her – *personally*, I mean?'

'If you mean what I think you mean, not at all! I knew her strictly on a professional level, and that's all.'

'Where were you between the hours of eleven p.m. yesterday, and seven a.m. today?'

'Where all good boys should be.'

'Don't get clever, Mr Peterson!'

'I was here.'

'And your wife will vouch for that?' Webb glanced at Kerry.

'Mike was here with me all night. I'm a light sleeper and if he so much as moved, I'd know. Besides, none of us had much sleep last night. Susie woke with a toothache. While I calmed her down, Mike made us a hot drink. What with all the noise and fuss, Jack woke up too. We must have been up for all of two hours.'

'We'll need to talk to the children.'

Mike agreed. 'But I don't want them interrogated.'

'We just want them to verify what you've told us.'

'Okay, but go easy. They're in the kitchen with their grandmother.'

They all crowded into the kitchen where Julie and the children were engrossed in a jigsaw.

'Jack, Susie,' Kerry said, 'these gentlemen would like to ask you some questions.'

Julie looked quizzically at her but remained silent when Kerry gave her a warning glance.

Remembering how it was before, when he and his daddy were rescued, Jack decided to be difficult. However, when he saw that Susie was quite happy to talk to them, he opened up and confirmed that yes, Susie had had a terrible toothache and everyone was awake half the night.

Afterwards, Mike showed the policemen out. 'Sorry we couldn't help you,' he said with the slightest of smiles.

'Sly bastard!' Sergeant Madison declared on the way back to the police station. 'I know he's involved. I just *know* it!'

'You heard.' Inspector Webb was yet to be convinced. 'He's got a watertight alibi.'

'We're missing something.' Like a dog with a bone, he didn't intend to let it go.

Behind them in the house, tension was building.

Alone in the sitting room with Mike, Kerry said, 'You *did* go out late last night. You were gone for over an hour. I know because I heard the front door close and couldn't go back to sleep. Soon after you came back to bed, Susie woke up.'

'So?' He hadn't realised he'd been missed.

'So I lied for you just now, and I don't like being a liar. Where did you go, Mike? I have to know.'

'Couldn't sleep so I went for a walk. I had some thinking to do.'

'Did you go to the hospital?'

'Why should I want to go there?' Anger flushed his face. 'Good God, Kerry! You don't think I had anything to do with the *murder*?' When she turned away, he took her roughly by the shoulders and spun her round. 'Do you?'

She hesitated, then she muttered, 'No.' Pushing him away, she said she had to see to the children.

As she opened the door to leave the room, Mike caught a glimpse of Julie scurrying away. 'Old witch! She was listening,' he muttered, and he suddenly felt afraid.

It was the sunniest day so far this year. Merrily whistling, the postman parked his van in the lane. Reaching over to the passenger seat, he collected the parcel and got out. Taking a breath of clean, fresh country air, he went up the path to the house.

Still whistling, he knocked on the door.

While he waited, he glanced at the parcel. Small and square, and unusually heavy, it was marked 'Ironmongery'. 'Could be a safety chain, or door bolts.' Having delivered parcels for thirty years, he prided himself on identifying what might be inside.

Growing impatient, he knocked again.

'It's no use you knocking there.' Mrs Lewis was a dear old soul who walked her dog along the lane most days. 'They've gone away.'

'Oh?' Retracing his steps, he paused at the garden gate. 'That's all right. I can always bring it back tomorrow.'

'No point doing that,' she said. 'They'll be away for a fortnight – gone to visit an ailing aunt in the North. Their friend told me. Nice person, very well dressed.'

'Is that right?' He wasn't really interested. He had more on his mind than delivering this parcel. A widower these past few years, he was taking a lady to bingo this evening, and who knew *what* it might lead to.

'They're a quiet couple, you know. I hardly ever see them. Keep themselves to themselves, they do.'

'Can't blame them for that.' Opening the back door of his van, he placed the parcel inside and then scribbled on a card. He went back up the path.' Just to let them know there's a parcel waiting for them,' he said.

Popping the card through the letter box, he drew back as if from something repugnant. 'Phew!' He glanced down at the mat he was standing on.

'What's wrong?'

'I reckon a stray cat must have emptied its tank here.' Taking the mat by one corner, he threw it into the garden. 'They'll not be too pleased to find the doormat stinking when they get back.'

The old woman laughed. 'I'm afraid we're plagued with stray cats. It's bound to rain before long. That'll wash it clean, don't worry.'

'Oh, I'm not worried,' he chuckled. 'My job is to deliver parcels. They'll have to collect it from the depot when they get home.'

Lonely for company, the old woman chatted on. 'I had to stop the milkman yesterday,' she said. 'There were two pints on the doorstep. He swore he hadn't been told, but I said he must have been. I mean, they *must* have cancelled the milk.' She sighed. 'Unless they're like me and tend to forget things. I went away for a week last summer, cancelled the papers, put the cat in the cattery . . .' She gazed fondly at her little dog. 'I didn't put *him* away though. He comes everywhere with me.' She frowned. 'What was I saying?'

Impatient to be gone, he moved to the front of the van. 'You were saying how you wouldn't put the dog in the kennels.' He opened the door and prepared to get in the van.

'Oh, yes.' She followed him. 'I thought I'd done everything but I hadn't, you see. I forgot to cancel the milk; it didn't matter in the end because when I got back the milkman had done it for me. It wasn't the same milkman we've got now though,' she said disapprovingly. 'He's a young sort, got his head too full of football and pop stars.'

After a time they parted company. 'I think I'll take him for a longer walk today,' she said, patting the dog's head. 'It's such a pleasant day.'

Day passed and night fell.

Emerging from the undergrowth, all manner of creatures came out to forage. Dogs barked and from somewhere in the distance the strains of music floated from a parked car – the woods were a favourite haunt of young couples.

After the quietness of day, the night seemed to come alive.

Inside the house, there was nothing alive. Only the rhythmic ticking of the clock disturbed the silence.

The man lay face down on the floor, still and white, fingers stretched above his head as though reaching out for help. Above him, the woman kept vigil, eyes wide and shocked, her body spreadeagled on the wall, held there by the nails in her bloodied hands and feet.

CHAPTER FIFTEEN

However hard she tried, Kerry could not change her mother's mind. 'He didn't mean it. What with the police questioning him, it's only natural that he's touchy.'

'That's no excuse for the way he rounded on me this morning. He told me I wasn't wanted here, said I was snooping, listening at keyholes.' Exasperated, she banged her fist on the table. 'And *you* let him talk to me like that. You didn't even stand up for me!'

'I didn't have a chance. With you two shouting at each other, I couldn't get a word in. Then he stormed out, and the chance was gone. Look, stay, please. I'll talk to him as soon as he gets home.' She went to fetch her coat. 'I'll go to the office and talk to him now if it will make you stay.'

Julie shook her head. 'Will you get rid of him, send him away from you and the children, before something terrible happens?'

Kerry was shocked. 'Mother, what are you talking about?'

'I'm frightened for you. Tell him to leave, and I'll stay as long as you like.'

'Are you asking me to choose between you and Mike?'

'I don't see it like that. It's quite simple. You have to shut him out of your life. *Please*, Kerry.'

'I can't do that, and why should I?'

'Well,' said Julie, 'after the cruel things he said to me, I couldn't possibly stay. I can't bear to be under the same roof as him any more. You can't see him for what he is, but I can. Last week when the police came, he lied to them. You know he did, and you backed him up. You may live to regret that, my girl!'

'Oh, come on, Mother! You know as well as I do he had nothing to do with that awful business.'

'I don't know any such thing, and neither do you.'

'You're talking nonsense. Mike is no killer.'

'I fear for you and the children, but if you're determined not to listen to me, I have to leave.'

'But you'll be lonely at home, you've said so yourself, many a time.'

'I shall only be at home for one night, just long enough to pack a suitcase. My neighbour will go on keeping an eye on the house.'

'What do you mean, pack a suitcase?'

'Your father left me comfortably off. I haven't had a proper holiday in years, so now I've decided to take a long holiday in the sunshine.'

'You're really serious, aren't you?'

'Never more so.' Throwing on her coat, she hurried to the front door; the children could be heard arguing in the garden. 'I promised I would take the children to the pictures. I've kept them waiting long enough, I think. I'd rather you didn't tell them I'm leaving,' she added. 'It might be best if I do that myself.'

Kerry followed her. 'Please, Mother. Don't be hasty.'

'My mind's made up, Kerry. I'm sorry. You know how much I love you and the children, but I can't – *will not* – stand by and see him use you.'

Kerry stood at the door until her mother and the children had turned the corner. She felt uneasy. 'I hope you're wrong about Mike,' she whispered. 'My God, I hope you're wrong.'

A short time later, she turned her mind to work. Glancing at the clock she realised just how late she was. 'Oh, sod it!' Grabbing her bag and keys, she ran out of the house, jumped into the car and was soon away down the road. 'They're bound to be wondering where I've got to!'

When, a short time later, she arrived at the unit, there was a problem already waiting. 'I've been trying to get you for the last ten minutes.' The new transport manager was in his early fifties; responsible and experienced, he ran the place like clockwork. 'I guessed you were on your way,' he said, leading her into the office. 'We have an urgent order.' He thrust the telephone message under her nose. 'A wedding reception tonight. They've been let down and wonder if we can do the catering for them. I said you'd ring back in half an hour.'

Casting her eyes over the list, Kerry gasped. 'We'll never do this,' she said. 'Not unless Pauline and Trudy are prepared to stay on late – and it's Saturday.'

She ran down to speak to then, cringing when she recalled how, not too long ago, Steve had lain lifeless at the foot of these very steps.

At first the women protested but when Kerry told them she would roll up her sleeves and help, they relented.

'Aw! I was looking forward to a night out with Kevin!' wailed Trudy.

'You'll have to wait till tomorrow for your bit of nooky then, won't you?' Pauline laughed. 'Think of the overtime money. You can buy him an extra packet of johnnies and bonk away to your heart's content.'

Kerry ran back to the office and spoke to the bride herself. 'You can relax. We'll have the food set out at the hotel by eight o'clock.' There were tears of gratitude at the other end. 'Anybody would think it was the end of the world,' she said, replacing the receiver. 'I wonder if I was ever that emotional.'

The manager smiled. 'It's her special day,' he said. 'I'm glad we could save it for her.'

Seated at his brand-new desk, Mike looked around the office with pride; bright and new, with pictures of classic cars on the walls, it was everything he had dreamed of. 'I've waited for this for so long,' he murmured, 'and now it's here, I can hardly believe it.'

'Talking to yourself, is it?' The Irish voice sailed across the room. 'They say that's the first sign of madness, so they do.' Having come from the Emerald Isle only weeks ago, he knew nothing about Mike's background. Smiling warmly, he wiped his feet and entered.

Unsettled by his innocent remark, Mike got up to greet him. 'Are we all ready then?'

'Aye. Ready as we'll ever be.' He pointed to the two vehicles. 'The van needed a complete new exhaust system, and the estate had two bald tyres. But nothing too bad. So, there they are, serviced and washed, and ready for the road.' He laughed. 'A jack of all trades, master of none, that's me.'

Smiling, Mike dismissed his remark with a gesture of the hand. 'Don't give me that. I've seen your papers, remember, and now I've seen the results of your handiwork. As far as I'm concerned, I made the right choice in you. The fact that you're willing to wash cars as well is a bonus for me.' He observed the vehicles with gratitude. 'Thanks,' he said. 'I think you and I are going to get along just fine.'

'Will ye be wanting me to stay, or is it all right if I make my way home?' he asked. 'There's a horserace I want to see.'

'No, you can finish for the day,' Mike said. 'I'll be leaving myself as soon as our customers collect the van.' Handing him a wage envelope,

Mike told him, 'You've earned that.'

'See you Monday then.' Pleased with himself, he went on his way.

At precisely midday, as arranged, the couple came to pick up the van. After going through the procedure – insurance, deposit and such – Mike saw them away. 'I don't envy you the house-moving,' he told them. 'Still, you've got a good van there. As long as you don't load it to excess, it won't let you down.' He hoped!

Half an hour later he was just about to shut up shop and go home when the phone rang. Snatching it up, Mike put on his best business voice. 'Mike's vehicle hire, can I help you?'

It was a woman with a dog. 'No, I don't mind you carrying your dog in the vehicle,' Mike answered. 'Yes, I do happen to have one estate car in the yard . . .' In the whole fleet of two, he thought sardonically. 'Yes? Twenty minutes, that's OK. I'll be here.'

Replacing the phone he punched the air. 'You've done it!' he yelled. 'On the first morning of opening you've emptied the yard.' He laughed aloud. 'Seeing as we've only got two vehicles, I don't suppose it's much of an achievement.' But it was a start. 'A bloody good start!' And he was as thrilled as a puppy with two tails.

Fifteen minutes later, the woman and her labrador were delivered in a silver Ford Cortina. Ten minutes after that, she drove off in Mike's newly polished estate car, with the dog looking decidedly nervous in the back. 'Hope it doesn't decide to cock its leg all over the place,' Mike said aloud. 'Still, if it does, I'll charge her for the cleaning.'

At twenty minutes to one, he slipped the cash deposits in his wallet, locked the office, and drove away.

From her hiding place she watched him drive by, her heart aching to go with him. 'Be patient,' she told herself. 'Your time will come.'

Going to the back of the building, she let herself in without too much difficulty. Once inside she went to his desk. With a sigh of pleasure, she sat where he had sat. She touched the things he had touched, the wonder alight in her crazed eyes, and in the way she stroked each article, tender fingertips trembling as they travelled from one inanimate object to another. Such joy!

Such wanting!

Sighing, she leaned forward. Laying her head on his desk, she groaned with bitter-sweet pleasure.

Eyes closed, dreaming of him, she gave herself up to sleep.

The evening was difficult.

Kerry had rung to tell her mother that she would be late, and Julie had promised to wait until her daughter came home.

The moment Kerry walked through the door, Julie wanted to know, 'Have you been thinking about what I said this morning?'

Kerry answered that, yes, she had been doing a lot of thinking.

'And have you changed your mind?'

'No.'

'I see.' Julie went to the telephone and called a taxi. When the taxi arrived, she said her goodbyes, deliberately ignoring Mike who had wisely stayed in the other room.

Julie gave Kerry one last, lingering look, hoping even now she might change her mind.

The look on Kerry's face was her answer. 'Goodbye, Kerry,' she murmured, and with tears in her eyes she departed.

Behind her, she left a mixture of emotions: Kerry was angry, the children cried, and Mike was just glad she had gone out of their lives – for good, he hoped.

Later, when the house was quiet and the children fast asleep, Mike lay awake, all manner of things going through his mind. Julie had been a thorn in his side for too long. He was glad she had gone. He was sure that she was the one who had turned Jack against him. He thought of Susie and smiled. 'Little angel,' he murmured. 'It would take more than her grandma to turn her against me.'

'What?' Half asleep, Kerry rolled into his arms.

The touch of her soft flesh against his was stimulating. Tenderly, he kissed her on the mouth, his hand reaching down to caress her secret parts. 'Want to love me?' she murmured. 'Now?'

The shaft of moonlight coming in between the curtains bathed her face in softness. 'You're so lovely,' he whispered. Awake now, she smiled up at him.

They played for a time, touching and kissing, exploring each other's bodies. After a while he pulled her on top of him. Aroused, she pushed down, engulfing his erect member. Gasping with delight, he placed his moist lips round her nipple, teasing it with his tongue. Sometimes, when emotions are high, lovemaking can be the most satisfying. It was like that now; anger, regrets, emotions joined them together in the most exhilarating union.

When it was over, Mike slept the sleep of exhaustion.

Still excited from the loving, Kerry lay on her side, gazing at his handsome face. 'Is my mother right?' she whispered. 'Are you a murderer?'

Suddenly he stirred. Alarmed, she turned her back to him and eventually drifted into a restless sleep.

The following day, relations were strained between them. 'She won't come back now,' Kerry told Mike angrily. 'I know her. She can be a hard woman when she's put out.'

Suggesting it was probably all for the best, and reminding Kerry how she herself had found it difficult with her mother under her feet all the time, he tried to calm her. 'And it won't be that hard,' he promised. 'One or the other of us will take the children to and from school. Where the housework is concerned, there are any number of domestic agencies with women on their books who can do every bit as good a job as your mother – and not be half the trouble.' Only last week she had a row with the binman, and now he leaves a trail of rubbish all the way down the garden path. If you ask me, it was time she left. Sliding his arm round Kerry's shoulders, he said with a grin, 'Admit it, she's a disaster area.'

Kerry had to laugh. 'She is a bugger,' she chuckled. 'And maybe she will relent. When she gets where she's going, the sun will be too hot, or the food too spicy. Knowing her, she's bound to upset everybody from the manager to the cleaners. You're right, I'm probably blowing it all out of proportion.'

They sat for a time, arms round each other, watching a cartoon with the children. When it was finished, Kerry got up to make Sunday lunch. 'What say we get out of Mum's way for a couple of hours?' Mike had offered to help in the kitchen but Kerry had suggested he take the children out instead. 'We could go to the park,' Mike said now.

'Don't want to go to the park!' As usual Jack was a pain.

'Down to the river then. We could watch the fishermen.'

Reluctantly, Jack agreed. 'Only if I can catch a fish.'

A few minutes later, armed with bread for bait

and apples for themselves, they set off.

Mike looked up at the darkening sky. 'We'd better not be out too long. Looks like we might be in for a downpour – a storm even.'

Puckering her face, Susie stared up at the sky. 'I *like* storms,' she said, blindly skipping along. A moment later she skipped into a cowpat; Jack laughed, and she burst into tears.

'It's all right. No need to get upset.'

Wrinkling his nose, Mike took off her shoe and wiped it on the grass. 'Now, look where you're going.'

While the children ran in front, Mike kept nervously glancing at the sky. 'It's like before,' he muttered, growing increasingly uneasy. 'Just like before.' Crippling images filled his mind, carrying him back to the day when he and Jack were trapped. 'Jack, where are you?' The boy had gone from his sight. '*Jack!*'

Jack emerged from behind a tree, Susie by his side.

'We were hiding from you.' Susie came skipping up to him. 'Me and Jack were going to jump out and scare you.'

Taking her by the hand, Mike laughed; what a fool he was. 'You did scare me, sweetheart,' he admitted.

Keeping his distance, Jack stared at him. Something about today reminded him too. 'We're not babies,' he told his father. 'There's nothing to be frightened of.'

'Well, of course not.' Realising he might be in danger of alienating Jack with his own paranoia, Mike apologised. 'I didn't mean to spoil your fun.' It was so rare these days for Jack to be interested in childish 'fun' that Mike wished he had not shouted like that.

Still eager to play a game, Susie insisted, 'We can play the hiding game.' Jumping up and down on the spot, she squealed with delight. 'Me and Jack will hide, and you have to count to ten.'

To appease Jack, Mike agreed. 'Go on then.'

'Turn round.' Susie knew the rules of the game.

Mike turned round and began counting, 'One . . . two . . .'

Jack's stern voice interrupted. 'You have to put your hands over your eyes,' he said. 'Otherwise it's cheating.'

Mike did as he was told; with hands over his eyes, he began again. 'One . . . two . . . three . . .' His mind was on the storm, and everything that had happened since. He wondered if he would ever be able to stop torturing himself. 'Four . . . five . . .' He softly laughed, thinking how he had almost lost control just now. What in God's name was he thinking of? If he went into a panic every time a storm threatened, he might as well give up. 'Six . . . seven . . .'

Startled by a clap of thunder far off, he paused. Opening his eyes he peered out at the dark, threatening skies. Just like before, they appeared to be closing in, rolling and heaving, like a living, breathing thing. Another clap of thunder, nearer now.

Suddenly Jack was running across the field. 'I'm frightened!' Pale and shivering, he clung to Mike. 'I want to go home!'

Trying desperately to stay calm for the children's sake, Mike smiled at him. 'All right, son.' He spun round, looking for Susie. There was no sign of her. 'Jack, where's Susie?'

Tears streaming down his face, the boy only stared at him.

Panic began to set in. 'Jack! Where's your sister?'

Covering his face, Jack would not answer.

Mike took hold of his hand. 'We have to find her!' Going at a run towards the spot where he had last seen her, Mike called out her name. 'Susie!' The wind howled back at him. 'Susie! Where are you? Call out to Daddy, sweetheart.'

His heart rose like a bird inside him when he heard her voice; faint and frightened, it rode the breeze and took him by surprise. 'I'm here, Daddy . . . please, come and get me.'

'Where?' He spun round but could see nothing. 'Susie! Tell me where you are, sweetheart. I can't see you.'

Frantic, he searched everywhere. He ran between the trees; went up the hill and into the valley below . . . He called along the spinney edge, but she was nowhere to be seen.

Twice more she called out, and each time he

followed the direction of her voice, but whenever he got near, the voice was further away.

Pausing to catch his breath, he took Jack by the shoulders, more scared than angry. 'Jack, before the thunder, when I was counting and you were hiding, you and Susie were together, weren't you?'

Tears still streaming down his face, Jack nodded.

'When the thunder came and you ran back to me, was Susie still with you?'

Again, Jack nodded.

'Where did she go?'

The sobbing increased. *'The sky took her!'*

Breathless with fear, Mike took a deep, painful gulp of air. *'No*. The sky did *not* take her. What happened, Jack?'

Jack was too distraught to speak.

'All right, son. Don't worry, we'll find her.' He pressed Jack close to him. 'We'll search once more. If we don't find her this time, I'll have to get help.' His voice shook. 'Dear God! Don't let her come to any harm.'

Again, they went through the spinney and out across the field, searching every ditch. Still they could not find her.

But they could hear her, a plaintive, frightened voice crying in the wind, and when she cried, they cried.

Two long hours later, exhausted and desperate, Mike stopped searching. 'I'll take you home,' he told Jack. 'I have to get help.'

Back at the house, Mike let himself in. Going straight to the phone, he dialled the emergency services. When the voice at the other end asked which service he required, he quickly explained what had happened. Frustrated, he answered the questions as calmly and coherently as he could. All he could think of was Susie, out there all alone. 'For God's sake, hurry!'

When he put the phone down, he stood for a moment hunched and weary, his head bowed. Susie's voice echoed in his brain – 'I'm here, Daddy . . . I'm here.'

Kerry's voice startled him. 'Where on earth have you been?' she demanded. 'I was just about to come looking . . .' Suddenly she noticed how bedraggled he was, and how Jack was quietly sobbing at the foot of the stairs. Instinctively she looked for Susie. 'What's happened, Mike?' A sense of horror took hold of her. 'Where's Susie?'

'She's lost.' Two simple, desolate words that struck the fear of God in her. For a second, the silence was unbearable. Then Kerry ran at him, hitting him with her fists. Holding her off, Mike tried to explain. 'We were playing the hiding game . . . she was there, but we couldn't find her . . . *We couldn't find her!*'

Grabbing hold of Jack, she backed away. 'Where is she, Mike? What have you done to my baby?' Though her eyes were wild, her voice was ice-cold. 'Bring her home, Mike. *Or you'll wish to God you'd never been born.*'

CHAPTER SIXTEEN

Just when he thought he had got it all together, Mike's world fell apart.

The search was relentless. With the whole town out to watch, police cordoned off the immediate area. The river was dredged, and every square inch for miles around was finger-searched. Overhead, helicopters scoured the area, and everyone who could walk or crawl volunteered to help.

Finally, they had to admit defeat; Susie Peterson had disappeared without trace.

Mike was taken in for questioning. Weary and sick with worry, he sat at the table and answered their questions. Over and over, he told them what had happened, and still they persisted. 'What do you mean, you could hear her?' They asked. 'How could you hear her, Mike? She wasn't there. Tell us again what happened, Mike. Were you and the boy within sight of each other the whole time?'

At one point, he stood up and screamed at them, '*Do you think I imagined it all?*'

'Of course not,' they said. 'But you imagined it all before, didn't you? There was a storm that day too. We never found the young couple.'

'I did not imagine it,' he insisted. 'We could hear her, for God's sake. Ask Jack!'

'We're asking *you*, Mike. What happened when you sent them to hide? Maybe you didn't stay there counting . . . maybe you can't remember. You've been ill before, you could be ill now. We've spoken to the doctor. He says a relapse is not out of the question. *Think*, Mike. Did you go after them? Did you go after Susie?'

Horrified, he stared at them, eyes bloodshot and heart breaking. 'My God! You think I murdered her, don't you?'

'Did you?'

On and on it went, until he thought his brain would split in two. Finally, they let him go. 'We'll be watching you, Mike,' they warned.

'If it wasn't for that boy's statement, I'd nail him here and now.' Sergeant Madison was desperate to prove that he had been right all along.

'He's not the one we want.' Inspector Webb was older and wiser.

'How can you be so sure?'

'Instinct.' He had been up all night, scouring murder files and trying to put two and two together. 'There's nothing I can put my finger on yet,' he murmured, 'but Mike Peterson is not the one, I'd bet my pension on it.' All the same, he hoped he wouldn't have to.

They couldn't prove anything against Mike, especially as Jack had confirmed his story. Yet

Madison still suspected him. So did Kerry. She moved out and took Jack with her. 'Don't come after me,' she warned.

And, knowing their marriage was over, he didn't. Instead he spent his lonely days wandering the valley, calling out for his lost daughter. Each night he wandered home, weary and broken. He didn't sleep. How could he sleep when he knew she was out there somewhere. And always the inspector's words came back to haunt him: 'Are you sure you didn't follow her? Maybe you can't remember.'

And Kerry's cutting words: *'What have you done to my baby?'*

For the first time ever, he began to ask himself if he really was mad.

Stubbing out his cigarette on the heel of his shoe, Sergeant Madison took a deep breath. 'They've told us nothing that we didn't know before, sir.' He threw the stub in the wastepaper bin.

At that moment Matron swept in. Sniffing the air, she glared from one to the other. 'This is a hospital!' she informed them stiffly. 'We don't allow smoking here.'

When Inspector Webb humbly apologised, Madison knew he would pay the price later.

'I believe we still have two more nurses to see.' Webb ran his finger down the list. 'Nurses Jenkins and Barker.'

'I'll send them in one at a time,' Matron said.

'After that, I hope you can leave us in peace. The patients have been disrupted enough. It isn't good for them to see police all over the place.' With that she flounced out.

'How can we be all over the place,' Madison muttered, 'when there's only two of us?' A swift scowl shut him up.

Nurses Jenkins and Barker knew no more than anyone else. 'Have you no idea at all where Alice Henshaw might have gone?' Inspector Webb asked them.

'I got on all right with her,' Jenkins said, 'but I didn't really know her outside the hospital.'

Nurse Barker said the same. 'She could be a funny devil if things didn't go her way, and she was a bit too pally with the patients, but she was a good nurse. I've never seen anyone more dedicated.'

'What now?' asked Madison.

'Back to the station. There are a couple of things I need to check.'

'You're checking Peterson's statement again, is that it?'

'Wrong. I've already been through it with a fine-tooth comb.'

And if Madison thought he had escaped having his knuckles rapped, he was wrong again, because all the way back to the station he was lectured on everything from his manners to his habits.

Back at the office, Inspector Webb reported to his superior.

Needless to say, the chief inspector was not too pleased. 'What the devil have you been doing?' he wanted to know. 'Henshaw has to be found. She's out there, planning God knows what, while you're chasing your tail and getting nowhere!' Before he dismissed Webb, he warned him, 'Your neck's on the line. Step up the hunt, widen the search. Whatever needs doing, bloody well get on and do it!'

Downstairs, Madison was chatting up the new recruit who had been put in charge of postage distribution. She was a friendly, pretty young thing. 'There's one here without a stamp, Sergeant,' she said, holding out the long, official-looking envelope.

Taking it from her, he grimaced. 'It's covered in chip fat or something just as disgusting!' He read the handwritten address: 'To whoevers in charg, The Police Dipartment, Bridport, Dorset.' He grunted. 'No stamp, and this one can't spell. We get a lot of these. They're mostly nutters.' Not for the first time, he observed her long, slim legs. 'I wouldn't waste your time on it,' he said, 'but you can waste time on me any day.'

The inspector's voice right behind him startled him. 'It might be a better idea if you stopped wasting *your* time!' he bellowed. 'I've just been told my neck's on the line. Well, I've got news for you, Sergeant. So is yours! Move yourself. We've got work to do.'

A short time later, the postal clerk came

rushing into Webb's office. 'Please, sir, I think you ought to see this . . .' She had a letter in her hand, and her hand was trembling.

'What is it?' He took it from her.

'It came this morning . . . no stamp. The sergeant said you get a lot of them . . .' She had tears in her eyes. 'I nearly threw it away . . . then I read it, and wondered if it was a prank.' Breathless, she watched him read. 'I don't think it's a prank, sir, I think it's the real thing.'

The inspector wasn't listening.

As Webb read the letter, his face drained of colour. 'Good God Almighty!' He hurried out of the office. 'So the sergeant told her to throw it away, did he? The bloody fool!'

Old Mrs Lewis was walking her dog when the cars screamed up the road. 'Good Lord above, whatever's going on?' Taking the dog in her arms, she moved closer to the hedge. 'It's the police!' The sight of police down here was rare.

Within minutes they had broken in; the first officer reeled back, his hands over his mouth. 'Jesus! What's that awful stench?'

In the hallway, Inspector Webb threw back the curtains. 'Can't see a bloody hand in front here.' Opening the windows, he took a breath of fresh air. Advising caution, he moved forward with his men. 'Easy now.' There was no telling what they might find. He had an idea what the stench was.

Long years in the force got a man used to certain things.

But he wasn't used to the sight that greeted him now, the sight of two people, mutilated and left to rot. 'God rest their souls.' Discreetly, he made the sign of the cross. 'Upstairs!' he told the men. 'Search the house from top to bottom, and when you've finished there, mount a search party round the area – though I should think the bastard's long gone by now,' he added to himself.

He was right. She was long gone.

But the letters were there, hidden around the house; even one under the floorboards. 'Look here, sir.' Sergeant Madison had unearthed a small tin box. Inside was a small amount of money, a number of documents and a copy of the same desperate letter that was sent to the police.

'As nasty a business as I've ever seen,' the doctor murmured to Webb. Pointing to the man, he said, 'A swift blow to the back of the head . . . I think the post-mortem will show he died instantly.'

Webb looked at the other one. 'What about her?'

He shook his head. 'Slow and agonising, I should say.'

On the strength of what they found in the house, particularly the damning letters, there was no doubt of the murderer's identity.

* * *

Nurse Sally Jenkins was duly arrested and charged with the murder of her parents. She also confessed to three other murders: those of Eddie Johnson; Dr Carlton; and more recently Steve Palmer.

Despite endless questioning, she remained adamant that she had had nothing to do with Susie's disappearance. 'If she's dead it was somebody else who killed her, not me.'

For her dreadful crimes she was committed indefinitely to a safe institution for the criminally insane.

The inspector and his sergeant found themselves a corner table in the bar. Over a cool, refreshing lager, Sergeant Madison admitted he had been wrong. 'To think Jenkins killed five people.' Even now he could not fully understand it. 'I don't suppose we'll ever know the whole story behind it all.'

'She killed all those people . . . her parents; Eddie Johnson; Dr Carlton, and Steve Palmer . . . all because of *Mike Peterson* . . . because he bore a resemblance to her real father. In a way you were right all along.'

'How's that, sir?' Compliments! He could hardly believe it.

'You said every murder was linked to Mike

Peterson. But as we now know, he wasn't the guilty one. As far as we can tell, his only crime was to be the image of Jenkins's real father. When she first saw him, she got this crazy notion in her warped mind that he was very special, and had to be protected.'

'Her real father was hardly a saint though, was he?'

'No. He was a drunk and a bastard. He couldn't cope when his wife died and he was left to look after Sally on his own. He heard how the Jenkins were desperate for a child so he sold his daughter for the price of a ticket to America. It was all written down, by their own hand, and in the diary handed in by Rosie Sharman.'

'That diary!' Madison blew out his cheeks. 'Whew! What she did to that innocent couple was beyond belief.'

'I agree, but they weren't all that innocent, were they? I mean, they did take her from her father and kept the truth from her, for many years. Bad though he was, they did her a terrible wrong. But they should not have had to pay for it the way they did.' He shuddered. 'And then to drive back to the nurses' quarters, covered in their blood. Then to calmly wash the clothes in the machine as if it was an ordinary wash day.'

'And poor Mavis, happening to see her when she buried the long coat.'

'But at least she's on the mend. Not like the others.'

'And yet the Jenkins showed her nothing but kindness and love. Hardly seems fair, does it?'

'Not when you think how she made them suffer the way she did, poisoning their food just enough to make them ill, drowning their pet dog, threatening to tell the authorities how they had stolen her. She made them her prisoners. She hated them so much, it turned her mind. They were the enemy in every sense of the word, and she had to control them, whatever it took. Hatred. Revenge. Terrible, powerful emotions.'

'But why kill Eddie Johnson?'

'Because she was watching Rosie Sharman. She'd noticed Rosie hanging about the hospital and she knew an auburn-haired woman was somehow involved in Mike's breakdown. She was afraid Rosie might harm Mike. And you heard what Rosie Sharman said in court – she and Eddie had a terrible row that night. Well, I think Jenkins was watching Rosie and when Eddie Johnson went out to get Mike, he was carrying a knife, remember? She wasn't about to let him harm Mike, so there's your motive.'

'OK. What about Dr Carlton?'

'That's an easy one. He discharged Mike, and she didn't like it. She wanted him where she could keep an eye on him at the hospital.'

'And Steve Palmer?'

'Steve Palmer and Kerry Peterson were having an affair – we know that now. Sally Jenkins was sure that Peterson's wife would leave him for

Palmer, and she couldn't let that happen. She needed to know that he was being looked after. She just couldn't stand by and see Peterson's wife desert him for another man.'

'You know, when you look at it like that, it's so simple.'

'To a crazy mind, you mean.'

Madison laughed. 'Maybe.'

Inspector Webb lapsed into deep thought. 'You know, I would have sworn she took Peterson's daughter.'

'She confessed to everything else, why not that?'

'God knows. All I know is we still haven't found her. It's as if she's vanished from the face of the earth.'

'Peterson hasn't come out of this unscathed either. He's let his business go, and he wanders about like a soul in torment. Locals say he's down the valley every day, calling for her.' Madison shook his head. 'He's got nothing now except the roof over his head and a weekly cheque from the social.' His voice softened with regret. 'In a way I'm sorry I hounded him now.'

'You've changed your tune, haven't you? *After all, we don't know for sure that he didn't murder that little girl, do we?*'

CHAPTER SEVENTEEN

The following summer, Rosie went looking for Mike in the valley where she knew he spent most of his time. He was seated on an upturned log at the foot of the valley.

'Hello, Mike,' she said. 'How are you?'

He nodded. 'I'm fine.' But he wasn't fine. He was a broken man. Nothing would ever be the same again.

'Do you mind if I sit here?'

He shook his head. 'No.'

They got talking, about when they were young, and life was fun, and they didn't give a sod for anything. 'You were always a wild thing, but I did love you,' Mike said. Admitting it after all this time was like coming alive. 'I should never have left you,' he confessed ashamedly. 'It was the thought of being a father. I was too young for that . . . we both were.'

'It's all in the past.' She nudged his arm. 'There's a lovely little café in Bridport. You can treat me to a sticky bun and a coffee if you like.'

'You always were one for sticky buns,' he remembered.

The café was packed. Bridport in summer was

a favourite spot for tourists. 'Two sticky buns, one pot of tea, and a coffee.' While the waitress wrote down her order, Rosie studied her features. 'I've seen you somewhere before, haven't I?' she asked. 'What's your name?'

'Alice Henshaw.' Slimmer and happier, she said, 'There was a time when it was Nurse Henshaw, but that was a long time ago' – before she realised there were more men on the horizon than Mike Peterson; young men, men of her own age. 'Hello, Mr Peterson,' she said, and went away with a smile on her face.

'I'll walk you back, shall I?' All these weeks she had watched him and bided her time. Now, she felt the time was right to make her claim.

'If you like.' He needed her. He knew that now.

They walked back together, talking as if they had never been apart. For the first time in ages, he smiled, and even laughed occasionally.

'My wife's left me, you know that, I suppose.' It seemed everyone knew his business.

'Yes.'

'She and Jack have gone to live abroad with her mother. From what I understand, they're running a high-class restaurant in Marbella.' When they arrived at the house, he told her, 'She left me this, if nothing else, signed her half over to me before she went.'

'What else could she do, Mike?' Rosie was angry. 'It was probably bought with your hard-earned money in the first place.'

'Do you want to come in?' he asked.

'You know I do.'

'I can't offer you much.'

As she followed, her face was filled with love. 'You've invited me into your home,' she said softly.

It was a start.

PART FOUR

July 1996

There Once Was a Girl

CHAPTER EIGHTEEN

For weeks now, the old woman had been ill. Only when the girl insisted did she let her call for an ambulance.

Now, after the doctors had examined her, it was plain the old woman would not see the night through. 'I'm sorry,' the nurse was kindness itself, 'we've done all we can, but she's very old. Is there someone you want me to call for you?'

The girl shook her head. 'No,' she murmured, her blue eyes swimming with tears. 'Mary is all I have.'

'She wants to see you now,' the nurse told her. 'Stay with her for as long as you like.'

The old woman had been sleeping, but somehow she seemed to know when the girl came to sit by her. 'Hello, my lovely,' she whispered. 'I wondered where you were.'

'I was talking to the nurse,' the girl answered. 'I'm here now. I promise I won't leave you again.'

The old woman smiled. 'I wish I could promise you the same,' she answered sadly, 'but I can't.'

'Please, don't say that.'

'I heard them talking and I know I don't have long.' She looked at the girl's sad blue eyes, and that wonderful mane of fair hair, and she thought of her own colouring, dark like a gypsy. 'Listen to me now,' she murmured. 'I have something to tell you. Something I should have told you a long time ago.'

'Ssh! Don't tire yourself.'

The old woman took the girl's hand in her own. 'I must go to my maker with a clear conscience,' she said. 'It was a long time ago, so long I've almost forgotten – eleven, twelve years. You were only five or six when she brought you to me. I was travelling the road then, free as a vagabond. I didn't know until afterwards what had happened. When I found out they were searching for you, I couldn't let you go, not then, not after I had come to love you so.'

Confused, the girl didn't want to hear any more. *But as the old woman went on, a memory of something long ago was triggered in the back of the girl's mind. Curious now, she listened intently.*

'She was evil, I know that now, and I should have told them. But they would have taken you away, and I didn't want that.' She smiled, taking a breath, drawing courage. 'She stole you from your father and brought you to me. All these years and I've never told you. I'm sorry, child.'

'The woman . . . why did she take me from my father?'

'Because she wanted to hurt him. She wanted them to put him back in the hospital where she could have him all to herself. I learned all this when she was . . . when she . . .' Even now, she couldn't bring herself to talk about the awful deeds committed by that woman. 'Your father was devastated when he lost you. His loss was my gain, and I couldn't let him have you back.' Tears ran down her face. 'I've been a wicked woman, I know. But, oh, you have been such a joy to me in my lonely life.'

As her mind opened up, the girl recalled something of what the old woman was saying. 'There was a storm . . .' Vaguely, she remembered. 'I called out for him, but he didn't come.'

'Echoes. Sometimes the valley plays tricks, you see.'

'My father, where is he now?'

'Oh, he's still there. He won't move from that place. They say he still wanders the valley, searching for you, calling your name.' She stroked that lovely face. 'Not the name I gave you,' she said. 'Your *real* name.'

'What is my real name?'

'Susie.' The old woman closed her eyes. 'Susie Peterson. In my bag you'll find everything you need to know.' She gazed at the girl, the light in her eyes dimming. 'Go to him,' she pleaded. 'He needs you. Tell him . . . I'm sorry.' Her eyes closed, and she was gone.

A short time later, the nurse came to comfort her. 'There's nothing more you can do,' she said. 'Come away, child. Go home now.'

* * *

309

Sometimes, Mike could hear her calling. He would sit here, listening to the wind blowing in the trees, and she would call him: 'Daddy! D . . . a . . . d . . . d . . . y.' It tore him apart.

'Mike?' Rosie was near. 'Someone's come to see you.'

When Mike turned, Rosie stepped aside, and there she stood, a tall, slim girl with long blonde hair and blue eyes. For a long time, Mike stared at her, hardly daring to believe. Then she called his name and he knew. 'Oh, dear God!' Like a child he sobbed, helplessly, unable to speak.

Tumbling into his arms, her tears mingled with his. 'I didn't know,' she whispered. 'Oh, Daddy . . . I didn't know.'

Behind them, Rosie cried too, her happiness complete. Softly, she crept away, leaving them together, letting them learn to know each other all over again.

Over the years, Mike watched his girl blossom into womanhood. He and Rosie stood proudly in the church when she married a boy from the next town. And, when his first grandchild was christened, Kerry came to see him. 'It's time we made our peace,' she said.

Mike and Rosie took her into their home, and while the christening party got underway, the sound of laughter emanating from that house was like sunshine after the storm.

CHAPTER NINETEEN

Dressed in jeans and carrying rucksacks, the couple trudged through the valley. 'Looks like a bad storm brewing.' The man peered up at the skies. 'I think we'd best find some shelter.'

Like him, the woman was in her thirties, unkempt and in need of a wash. 'There's a café about two miles away,' she remembered. 'We can stop there. I'm hungry. We've been walking since early light.'

Thoughtful, the man sighed, 'I think I've had enough of the wandering. We're getting too old for it . . . never knowing where we can lay our head, or if we'll get a farmer's pitchfork up the arse. And it's getting harder to earn a crust.' He hitched his load up over his shoulders. 'This bloody rucksack gets heavier every time I strap it on.'

'You could have a point,' she agreed. 'When the weather's fine, it's OK, but I'm getting so I can't stand the cold any more.' Glancing at him, she recalled, 'Last winter, when I got the flu, and we had to hole up in that derelict shed, I really thought I was a goner.'

He thought about that for a time, before softly

laughing, 'Remember that bad storm, the year we first set out?'

'Somewhere out Bridport way, wasn't it?' She smiled wistfully. 'We were just kids.'

'Jesus! I *really* thought we were goners then . . . *the way that wind whipped us up and carried us along.* I'll never forget that.'

'It was a long time ago.' She quickened her step.

'You're right!' Striding out to keep up with her, he licked his lips. 'I fancy you. How about it?'

Pushing him aside, she laughed, 'I'm hungry. You'll have to settle for a pint and a fat, juicy burger.'

He licked his lips. 'Lead on,' he said with a twinkle in his eye. 'There's always another time.'

Another day.
Another chance.

If you enjoyed this book here is a selection of other bestselling titles from Headline

FEAR NOTHING	Dean Koontz	£5.99 ☐
SCARLET	Jane Brindle	£5.99 ☐
CHANGELING	Frances Gordon	£5.99 ☐
PASIPHAE	William Smethurst	£5.99 ☐
AFTER MIDNIGHT	Richard Laymon	£5.99 ☐
NO HEAVEN, NO HELL	Jane Brindle	£5.99 ☐
BLACK RIVER	Melanie Tem	£5.99 ☐
THE RISE OF ENDYMION	Dan Simmons	£5.99 ☐
CADDORAN	Roger Taylor	£5.99 ☐
A DRY SPELL	Susie Moloney	£5.99 ☐
SACRAMENT OF NIGHT	Louise Cooper	£5.99 ☐
THE SILVER SCREAM	Ed Gorman	£5.99 ☐

Headline books are available at your local bookshop or newsagent. Alternatively, books can be ordered direct from the publisher. Just tick the titles you want and fill in the form below. Prices and availability subject to change without notice.

Buy four books from the selection above and get free postage and packaging and delivery within 48 hours. Just send a cheque or postal order made payable to Bookpoint Ltd to the value of the total cover price of the four books. Alternatively, if you wish to buy fewer than four books the following postage and packaging applies:

UK and BFPO £4.30 for one book; £6.30 for two books; £8.30 for three books.

Overseas and Eire: £4.80 for one book; £7.10 for 2 or 3 books (surface mail).

Please enclose a cheque or postal order made payable to *Bookpoint Limited*, and send to: Headline Publishing Ltd, 39 Milton Park, Abingdon, OXON OX14 4TD, UK.
Email Address: orders@bookpoint.co.uk

If you would prefer to pay by credit card, our call team would be delighted to take your order by telephone. Our direct line is 01235 400 414 (lines open 9.00 am–6.00 pm Monday to Saturday 24 hour message answering service). Alternatively you can send a fax on 01235 400 454.

Name ....

Address ....

....

....

If you would prefer to pay by credit card, please complete:
Please debit my Visa/Access/Diner's Card/American Express (delete as applicable) card number:

Signature .... Expiry Date ....